CHAPTER ONE

"Sweetheart, I've given this a lot of thought."

Ryan's eyes meet mine. There's such a coolness to his expression like nothing in the world could rattle him.

"I'd like to make you my wife." He pulls a soft, blue ring box from his slacks and slides it open.

Holy shit.

The ring is enormous. A princess-cut diamond, two carats at least, in a white gold setting.

It must have cost a fortune.

Ryan's gaze is still on me. He's waiting for my reaction. To see the joy register on my face. This is supposed to be the best day of my life.

I try to speak, but my mouth is too sticky. "I, uh..."

He doesn't blink. He doesn't falter for a second. He's sure I'll say yes. It wasn't even a question. More a statement of his desires.

I nod. "Of course."

He smiles, more of an *I'm glad we can do business* smile than anything, and slides the ring onto my fingers. It's heavy and cold and it catches every damn flicker of light in the room.

It's expensive. Ryan doesn't spend money on things unless they're important to him.

He runs his thumb over my hand, all his attention on the ring. "It's beautiful on you."

"It's breathtaking." My lungs are so tight I can barely get the words out. It only proves my point, proves how damn breathtaking the ring is.

"This is what you want, isn't it?"

I nod, of course. Ryan has been my best friend for a long time. And he's always looking out for me. If this is what he thinks is best...

I'm only 23. And he's only 26. But that's Ryan. He doesn't waste time when he wants something.

He smiles. It's a little sweeter, a little softer. There's something in my chest, a heaviness, but it must be nerves. Ryan isn't the best boyfriend in the world. He's not the sweetest guy. But he's always been there for me, even when other people would run for the hills.

"Should we order dessert?" I ask.

His jaw tightens. "Sweetheart, that isn't a good idea." He leans down and plants a kiss on my hand. "I'd hate to ruin the night by triggering you."

Part of the fun of being a recovered bulimic is all the trigger foods. Two bites of dessert, and I'm desperate to binge and purge. In theory. I haven't had two bites of dessert since I got out of inpatient treatment some eight months ago.

"It should be fine."

"Alyssa. It's not a good idea." His voice is stern, harsh. A warning not to go against his advice. He pulls his hands back to his lap and fishes for his wallet.

I nod, fine, and wait for him to pay the bill. There's a cool breeze on the patio. I pull my arms around my chest in an attempt to find warmth, but it doesn't help. It's still cold here.

Ryan helps me out of my seat. He slips out of his suit jacket and slings it around my shoulders.

His arms are on my back, his breath on my ear. "You're going to make a beautiful wife." He takes my hand and walks me through the restaurant, to the main entrance.

It's cooler out front. I shiver, pulling the jacket tighter around my shoulders. There's a flash—the bright light from someone's camera phone—and I squint to avoid it.

"What was that?" Ryan asks.

"Probably someone's birthday." It's not like anyone is all that interested in C-list actress Alyssa Summers. Not enough to snap a picture without asking first.

He shakes his head, cursing my tiny hint of fame yet again. But he drops the irritated look and slings his arm around my shoulder. It's the tiniest bit warmer. It's not much. But it's something.

We're halfway home when Ryan's phone rings.

"Sweetheart, can you check that?" His eyes are on the road, his fingers curled gently around the steering wheel of his luxury sedan.

I slide my fingers around the phone's slick glass back. "Incoming call from Luke Lawrence," I read from the screen.

Ryan lets out a heavy sigh. Luke is his business partner, the other divorce lawyer at their tiny firm. It's not clear why Luke is a constant source of annoyance, if he's incompetent, annoying, or simply unwilling to follow Ryan's *my way or the highway* mentality.

"He must have a stupid question," Ryan says.

"On a Sunday?"

"He has a court date in the morning."

"I thought this guy was all about getting out of the office by six p.m." Because he cares about whoever is waiting at home for him.

I bite my lip. That's not fair to Ryan, but it wouldn't kill him to get home a little earlier.

The call ends, and Ryan glances at the phone like he's debating calling back. The phone answers for him—lighting up with another incoming call from Luke Lawrence.

Ryan grabs the phone and answers the call. "What is it?"

There's noise on the other end. Nothing too frantic or desperate. But something direct and to the point. Ryan shakes his head, his grip on the steering wheel tightening. "I'll be there in twenty minutes."

I can barely make out the voice on the other end, but it sounds like "I can handle it."

Ryan is curt. "Then why did you call me? I'll be there in twenty minutes." He hangs up the phone, sighing again, and turns to me. "I'll drop you at home."

This night means so little to him that he'd rather drop me at home than allow his business partner to handle business.

I take a deep breath, willing away the tension in my chest. Ryan has never been romantic. He's not going to start now. It's possible this really is important.

"I'll come with you." I try to squeeze his hand, but he brings it back to the steering wheel.

"It might be a while."

"I have my Kindle."

"I can't imagine you want to stay in that dress." His eyes pass over me quickly. There's a hint of want on his face. Not enough to delay this meeting. Not even when I'm wearing an incredibly low-cut, incredibly clingy dress.

"It's more comfortable than it looks." Besides, I had a different vision of how I'd get out of this dress, and it didn't involve cuddling up with Netflix.

"It will be deadly dull."

But not as dull as going home with me, apparently.

CHAPTER TWO

Half the lights are off in the empty lobby. There's something strange about it, but Ryan rushes into the elevator before I can register much.

He leans against the mirrored wall inside, his eyes on the doors as they slide shut. He's already done processing his proposal. It's time to work. Again.

The elevator lifts off the ground. I squeeze the safety bar to stay upright. These shoes make it damn hard to balance.

"Do you think you'll stay long?" I ask.

Ryan offers me a halfway apologetic look. "Hopefully not."

He motions for me to come closer. I do, and he presses his lips into my forehead. I lean into him, wrapping my arms around his waist.

The elevator dings and the doors slide open. Ryan pulls away, his hand sliding to my wrist. He pulls me into the beige hallway, and I struggle to match his determined gait. These shoes aren't doing me any favors.

His office is around the corner. An oak door with a gold label. *Lawrence and Knight.*

It must kill Ryan that his name comes second.

He releases my hand to open the door, and he whisks me inside. The firm is a three-room suite. A lobby, Ryan's office, Luke's office, and a nook for their assistant. It looks just like a TV law firm—cream walls, maple floors, gold accents here and there.

Ryan points me to a chair in the lobby. "Why don't you sit down, sweetheart?"

"I'll sit in your office."

He shakes his head and points me to the chair. Again. "It's nothing personal. This is an emergency."

"It's always an emergency."

He rubs my shoulders and plants another kiss on my forehead. "I'll make it up to you."

I shake my head. Yeah, he'll make it up to me. He'll come home tomorrow at nine instead of ten.

An unfamiliar voice jars me. "Oh, shit. Did I ruin your date?"

That must be Luke.

I turn towards the sound. Luke is in the hallway, leaning against the wall.

He's handsome—dark hair, coffee-colored eyes, completely perfect lips—and tall. His white V-neck is clinging to every muscle in his broad shoulders. His jeans are slung low around his hips. Fuck. That's not exactly office attire.

He offers his hand to shake. "I'm Luke."

"Of course." I nod, offering my hand. I know I have met him, but I can't see how the memory isn't burned into my brain.

His eyes connect with mine. Jesus, his eyes are amazing—the darkest of browns, big and full of life. I nod. He's Luke. Ryan's partner. My fiancé's partner.

Luke brushes his fingers across my wrist, and a rush of electricity floods my body. I gulp. It's nice enough when Ryan touches me, but it's nothing like this. Nothing so intense.

Ryan coughs. "Yes. You two have met several times before. Luke, Alyssa. Alyssa, Luke." He turns to Luke. "Shall we get started?"

Luke nods, his eyes still on me. "It was nice to see you again."

They turn and make their way into Luke's office, closing the door behind them.

I suck a deep breath into my lungs. Jesus. How is it possible I don't recall meeting Luke? He's smoking hot.

I catch my breath for a moment, then sit and fiddle with my Kindle. I'm in the middle of reading *The Handmaid's Tale* for the fifth time. It's one of my favorites, but, tonight, the words aren't sticking.

I skim the page a dozen times, but I'm no closer to concentration. Forget it. I slip my heels off and shift into a cross-legged position. It's not the most graceful thing, but it's comfortable enough.

"I don't want to interrupt again." It's Luke, standing in that hallway again.

My heart pounds against my chest. "You scared me."

"Sorry. I'm quiet in these shoes." He points to his black Converse sneakers. "Can I get you something to drink?" He takes a step into the lobby. He's still a good ten feet away, but he seems so close.

"Aren't you needed?"

"Ryan is taking over for the moment." His eyes pass over me again, only briefly lingering at my chest. "What are you reading?"

"Margret Atwood."

He smirks. "Is that supposed to scare me off?"

"No. It's just...Ryan hates books. He especially hates 'literature.'"

"I'm not Ryan."

I close my Kindle and slip it into my purse. "*The Handmaid's Tale.*"

He nods like he's familiar. "That is quite literary."

"You've read it?"

He nods. "At an all-boys high school if you can believe it." He takes another step towards me. Until he's almost close enough to touch. "If you don't want something to drink—coffee or tea—I'll leave you to your literature."

He offers his hand, but I push myself off the chair.

Luke leads me to the mini kitchen. It's in the hallway, across from the office where Ryan is working. The office with an open door.

I swallow hard. Of course the door is open. I'm only accepting an offer of coffee. There's nothing Ryan shouldn't hear.

Luke shows me the many options for a drink from their single-cup machine. "I'm guessing decaf at this time of night."

I nod. Decaf is fine. It's not like I need the energy tonight.

He loads the machine, adding exactly the right amount of water. My heart beats faster and faster. I swear I start sweating. I shouldn't be alone with him. It's not appropriate.

Especially when he's so fucking handsome.

He brings his attention back to me. "You were amazing in that film, *Mahogany.* You stole every scene you were in."

"Thank you."

"You must hear it all the time."

"Only occasionally." I'm on an acting hiatus, and it's a bit of a sore subject.

His eyes are wide with enthusiasm. "I remember when it came out. I think you and Ryan had only been dating a little while. And he was bragging about how gorgeous and talented you were. But he hadn't seen it. So I told him, and—fuck, you probably got the short end of the stick on this one. I told him that you do a strip tease in it."

"Well, aren't you a fucking instigator?"

"Did he throw a fit?"

"He wasn't pleased." Ryan is, or was, never happy about me playing a character who was anything but a virginal good girl.

"Sorry, but the look on his face... God, he was so jealous. I thought he might punch me."

"Oh, please. You did it just to annoy him. You would have worn a black eye like a badge of honor."

"Maybe." He laughs. "Probably."

"That's why you came over here to make me coffee, isn't it?"

"Well..."

"Well?"

"I've been dying for a chance to have an actual conversation with the great Alyssa Summers."

"Are you saying that because he might overhear?"

Luke shakes his head. "I was hoping you'd be a bit more..."

"Vacuous?"

"Show off." He brushes his hand against mine for no particular reason, his eyes locked on mine, studying me for a reaction.

I bite my tongue to keep from blushing. He's touching me on purpose.

"It's not because you're gorgeous. And not because you played a slutty cheerleader on that TV show."

My heart beats faster. He thinks I'm gorgeous.

"And not because all actors are idiots." I offer.

He nods. "I couldn't imagine Ryan being with someone smarter than him."

"Than he is."

I brace for an eye roll, but he smiles, his big, brown eyes lighting up.

"I'm jealous. I've never been with someone who corrects my grammar."

"Ryan hates it."

"Fuck Ryan." He hands me the cup of coffee and points me to the packets of cream and sugar. His eyes pass over me again, stopping at my engagement ring. "Fuck Ryan." His jaw drops. "How long have you two been engaged?"

I grimace. "Not too long." An hour maybe. Perfect timing for him to go into the office.

"He didn't say anything." His eyes are on me like he's studying my expression.

"It's not a big deal."

Luke shakes his head, his messy hair falling over his eyes. "Finding someone you want to spend your life with is a pretty big deal."

"I guess."

He laughs. "Then what the hell is a big deal?"

I take a long sip of the coffee, trying to formulate some kind of coherent response. Nothing comes, so I take a step backwards. "Thanks for the drink."

"My pleasure."

His hand brushes against my back, only for a second, and my body surges with electricity.

"I'm sure you need to get back to work." I squeeze the paper cup, feeling its warmth against my fingertips.

He returns to the office. I move back to the lobby.

I don't bother with my Kindle. My head is buzzing with all sorts of thoughts I should shut down. His hands felt so damn good on my back. But on my bare skin... On my ass or my chest or between my legs...

CHAPTER THREE

I'm on my way to the elevator of Ryan's building, gripping my purse tightly. Ryan is still working, of course, and I've given up on waiting. I drag my heels to the elevator and press the button. I'll be home soon, able to wash this all out of my head.

But there's a voice behind me. "Alyssa." It's low and deep and damn familiar.

I turn to face it. Luke. He's standing there, in those snug jeans, that T-shirt with a criminally low V-neck.

"You forgot this." He hands me my Kindle.

How stupid. I'd never forget my Kindle. Not by accident.

The elevator doors slide open and I step inside. He follows me. I back into the wall. He steps closer. Closer. Until he's inches from me.

The doors slide closed behind us.

"Ryan is an asshole." His eyes are on me, glued to me.

I nod. Ryan is an asshole. But that doesn't mean...

He presses his hand against the wall, pinning me to it. I should be alarmed. This guy is practically a stranger. But I'm shaking. He's so close. His body is almost against mine.

"You don't deserve to go home alone tonight."

I nod. I don't deserve to go home alone tonight. But he can't mean... I can't...

Luke brings his hand to my cheek, brushing a hair from my eyes. His touch is so hot, so electric. I feel it all the way to my toes.

His hands slide down to my bare shoulders. He looks at me as if to ask, can I? I nod, yes.

He leans down, pressing his lips against mine. His lips are soft and sweet, and his hands are on my bare skin. There's no stopping this. There's no way I can resist.

I jerk out of bed, pushing the comforter off my chest. It's so damn hot in here, I'm drenched with sweat. My hair is a damp, knotted mess.

There's no way I just dreamed that. No way I dreamed about kissing some other guy the night after I got engaged.

Kissing. Right. It was obviously going to stop at kissing.

I exhale as deeply as I can. It's early. I'm tired. I need a shower and coffee and everything will be back to normal.

In the kitchen, Ryan is hunched over his laptop. He's got a sour expression on his face. His brow is furrowed and his lips are tight.

So much for making it up to me.

He looks at me, shaking his head with the utmost irritation. "You're not front-page news, but you made a few gossip blogs."

"BOA is a popular restaurant."

"It's supposed to be private." He shakes his head again, turning his attention back to his laptop.

It's like this is my fault. Like he didn't know, going in, that I am just famous enough to be interesting to people interested only in fame. Like our engagement is less special because people know about it.

Like it could even be less special than blowing it off for work.

"If you wanted it to be private, why didn't you do it here?" I ask.

"I'm not going to ask you to be my wife over takeout in the condo." He sinks into his bad mood, poring over the gossip sites.

I do my best to ignore his attitude. I pour myself a cup of coffee and add just the right amount of almond milk and honey.

It's sweet and creamy. Hell, coffee is my only real indulgence. Everything else I eat is clean and healthy and totally void of any hint of temptation.

Ryan looks up from his laptop. "I guess I underestimated how much everyone wants to talk about you."

I bite my lip. I'm not going to let his attitude upset me. It's his issue, not mine. "What do you want me to do about it?"

"There's nothing you can do." He slips his suit jacket over his shoulders and closes his briefcase. "In a few years, no one will remember who you are, and we'll never have to deal with this kind of thing."

"Only if I quit acting."

He looks at me like I'm an idiot, like quitting acting is the only logical decision.

"I'm not quitting," I say.

"Now isn't the time." He stands, curling his fingers around the briefcase.

"And when is the time?"

"Sweetheart, we agreed you'd take a one-year hiatus to focus on your health. It's only been eight months."

"Not if you count the time I was in treatment."

"I'm not fighting about this."

Yes. We're sure not to fight as long as he gets his way.

"Okay. Then when are we going to discuss this?"

"I've got to get to work." He takes a step towards the door. "I'll be home late tonight."

"Ryan." I hate how whiny my voice sounds. I take a deep breath, and fold my arms over my chest in my best *don't mess with me* pose. "Then I'll come to the office for dinner."

"Alyssa."

"Ryan."

He sighs, shaking his head. "Fine. Come at seven. I'll order takeout."

"Good."

I release my arms, sucking in a deep breath. So much for my air of confidence.

Ryan offers a small smile. He presses his lips against my forehead. "I'll see you tonight." And then he's out the door and the day is mine to fill.

It must have been seven years ago now, the first time Ryan saved me. We were at a party, a *big deal, only the cool kids are invited* kind of party. It was my first high school party and I was in heaven, sitting back and taking it all in.

All the better when Jacob, the coolest of all the cool guys at the party, started talking to me. I was on the couch, pressed up against the armrest. He sat next to me. Right next to me, so I had no room to breathe. He was polite at first. He asked all the usual questions—how are you tonight, I like your dress, how are you finding your way around school?

Then he moved closer. Too closer. He mentioned upstairs. I needed to start high school off right. With a guy like him. It would be fun. Easy. And what was I, a prude or something? I tried my most polite brush-off, but he persisted.

Then he kissed me. I pushed him off, and hard. He muttered something under his breath about me being a stupid whore and stared at me like he was going to hit me.

No one at the party noticed or cared. No one except Ryan.

Ryan, seventeen-year-old Ryan, stepped in between us. He put a hand on Jacob's shoulder and sent me a knowing nod. "Everything good?"

Jacob shrugged Ryan off. "It was until you got here."

"I think it's time for a break, huh?" Ryan pushed Jacob, ever so slightly, towards the backyard.

"What do you think you're doing?" Jacob asked. He scowled at Ryan like Ryan was ruining his good time.

Ryan stood his ground. "Leave her alone."

"You think this bitch is going to pay you back for your kindness?"

"I'm not asking again."

Jacob scoffed. "Get real. She's a stupid whore. Not worth the effort."

Ryan said nothing. He smiled, dug his hand harder into Jacob's shoulder, and he swung.

He hit Jacob so hard the asshole stumbled backwards. Then he smiled and nodded to the backyard. "Either you can leave or we can take this outside."

Jacob muttered some curse, but he stormed out the door.

Everyone at the party pretended as if this was no big deal, but Ryan looked me straight in the eye and asked if I was okay. I shook my head yes, but he still spent the evening by my side.

He drove me home that night. Yes, there was a bit of a lecture—be careful who you talk to—but he was sweet. He gave me his number and an offer to call anytime.

And, unlike everyone else in my life, Ryan stayed true to his word. He saved me from a dozen bad situations in high school alone. When I was stranded at the mall because my mom was too drunk to drive us home. When the girl I beat for the role of Juliet stole my backpack. When I was at a party, crying in the bathroom because another asshole wanted me to pay him back for his kindness.

He picked Harvard to stay close to me. Then USC Law after I moved to LA to pursue acting.

But none of it compared to when Ryan convinced me to go into treatment.

It was about a year ago. I was in the hospital for dehydration after a solid three days of purging, and I was counting down the hours until I'd be released.

Then, like some vision of strength, Ryan appeared. He crawled into my hospital bed and whispered that he loved me, that everything would be okay. It was the first time he'd ever said it like that, like we were more than friends. We'd been dating for a while, but it was casual. It was nothing.

He stayed up with me all night, holding me and stroking my hair while I cried. He let me talk, let me scream, waited until I got everything out. Then, as the sun was rising, he asked me to go to treatment. Not for me, for him. Because he couldn't bear to see me like this. Because he needed me to be healthy.

I agreed.

I fought him every step of the way, but he remained patient. He visited every day of inpatient treatment, and he moved me into his apartment when I was released. He made sure I went to therapy, that I did my weekly weigh-ins, that I ate everything on my recovery diet, no more, no less.

I never would have survived without him.

Maybe Ryan has become a workaholic asshole, but he's always been there when I needed him.

I expect my phone to flood with calls, or at least texts, of happy congratulations, but I don't get much. It's still early, and all the actors I know are either sleeping in or too busy to pay attention to gossip websites.

The only person desperate to reach me is Corine, my agent. I don't pick up until her fourth call. I'm not ready to hear her perky voice and make a statement on "official word from Alyssa Summers" vis-à-vis this engagement, or my sad, sordid past dabbling in bulimia—half the news blurbs felt the need to mention that unverified fact.

"Mazel tov, darling." She's bright and cheery. "I'm so happy for you."

"Thanks."

"I hate to cut the congratulations short, but I have an audition for you."

My stomach twists in knots. It's been so long since I've done any acting. Nearly a year. I've been sitting on my ass, "working on my health" for nearly a year.

I try to catch my breath. There's an audition. For me. That means there's a role. For me. If I get it, if I don't fuck it up, I might have a life again.

"What is it?" I ask.

"A friend's client is a showrunner." The head writer and producer of a TV show. "They're firing their lead actress. Or she's leaving. Rehab. Drugs. I forget. It doesn't matter. They're short one luscious blonde and you're available."

I cringe. My hair hasn't been blonde for a while and whatever luscious is supposed to mean, it does not accurately describe my size-eight body.

Corine continues. "Don't tell me you're insecure. Curvy is in. And you're what, a size six? Really, you should play up this bulimia thing. You'll be a role model."

"I make a terrible role model."

"Nonsense. It's a very inspirational story. You're a true artist. The stress of your craft led to an eating disorder. You were spiraling out of control, but you got help. You found love. Hell, all you need is the marriage and the two kids and you'll be the picture of happily ever after."

My stomach twists. It's not the most pleasant thought.

"The show is perfect for you. It's a cable comedy. Nice, easy, thirteen-episode season. Barely four months of work. And the lead is such a fun character. A former model."

"You're kidding, right?" I'm a long way from a former model. It's not like I was ever super thin. On *Together* I played the slutty cheerleader—Cindy Bleachers. She was supposed to be all tits and ass, busting out of her teeny uniform. But a former model?

No way in hell.

"She's post-rehab. She's not supposed to be a size zero anymore. I wouldn't try to put you through that. Do you know how bad I would look—putting my bulimic client up for a part that would require her to lose weight?" She says it so casually, like it's totally normal that everyone in the freaking world knows I spent the better part of three months in treatment for an eating disorder.

"I don't know."

"Auditions are tomorrow," she says. "If you want to get back into the game, you aren't going to find a better opportunity."

"Not as a model."

"They're desperate and you're perfect."

My heart pounds against my chest. It's screaming for me to say yes, to schedule the audition. Ryan won't like it, but I can figure out how to convince him it's a good idea. I need to be back on set, reading scripts twenty times, finding the nuance in every line. I need to slip into a role, so I can finally channel every awful thing in my head into the scene.

I need this so badly.

"I have to talk to Ryan," I say. I bite my lip. It's not what Corine wants to hear. Hell, it's not what I want to say.

But I do need to talk to Ryan. He may have a specific idea about how my recovery should go, but he is looking out for my best interests. My last acting gig nearly killed me.

"Do you remember when you first moved to Los Angeles and tried to audition for a role as Ophelia?" Corine's voice is rich with irritation, like it's oh so pathetic I'd even consider discussing an acting job with my fiancé.

"Yes."

"And I told you my girl is not going to play a role where she throws her life away over some brooding loser?"

"I seem to recall something more along the lines of 'Fuck Shakespeare, no one enjoys that thou and thee bullshit.'"

"Before you got *Together*, you would have killed someone for this kind of opportunity."

"I know." I try to think up excuses to convince myself. I'm not ready. I'm out of practice. I'm still on hiatus. But none of them matter. I want this. I need this. I need this so much, it will crush me to say no.

"Listen, darling, I know Ryan did a lot for you, helping you when you got sick, but you can't let him run your life." She pauses to take a long breath, her voice getting more serious. "You'll hate yourself if you ignore this opportunity."

I take a deep breath, willing my tight muscles to relax. She's right. I need to take this opportunity. "Okay. I'll audition."

I'll think of something to tell Ryan. Some way to convince him.

I have to.

CHAPTER FOUR

I let daydreams get the best of me. I am back on set, playing my role expertly, making jokes between takes. I'm back to real life, to something beyond reading my Kindle and watching reruns from the time Ryan leaves to the time he arrives home.

It's not as if I'm forbidden from leaving the apartment. There is temptation everywhere—bakeries and ice cream shops and fast-food restaurants—but I can manage a little bit at a time. A morning at a coffee shop. An afternoon walking around the bookstore. A sunset jog around the marina behind our building.

It's not much of a life, but it's better than eating disorder hell.

I walk to Ryan's office instead of driving. It's a little over a mile away, but it's a nice walk. Right along the water.

The setting sun casts a gentle glow over the concrete. There is something so warm about it, even as the wind picks up. I pull my sweater tighter around my shoulders. I'm not dressed as nicely as Ryan would like—jeans, a cardigan, and canvas sneakers—but it's late enough that it shouldn't matter.

I shake my head. I should have put on a dress and heels. Something that would put Ryan in a more accommodating mood.

I wipe my sweaty palms on my jeans as I enter the building. This should be easy. Ryan may be strict about my recovery rules, but he's only looking out for me. He's not going to keep me from the one thing that makes me happy.

There are signs of life tonight—people waiting for the elevator, cars pulling out of the underground lot, lights turned on upstairs.

In the office, the assistant, Janine, scowls at me like she's sure I don't belong in an upscale law office. "Mr. Knight is at an off-site meeting," she says, as if I am not on a first name basis with my own fiancé.

She looks me up and down, stopping to pay extra attention to the ring. She's clearly not happy about it.

She has a crush on Ryan. It's obvious, but he won't admit it.

"We're supposed to have dinner tonight," I say.

She glances at the computer. "I don't see that on his schedule."

"You can take my word for it."

She frowns but doesn't press it. "Take a seat, Ms. Summers." She nods to the uncomfortable chairs in the lobby. "Mr. Knight should arrive shortly."

One of the office doors opens and footsteps move down the hallway. If Ryan really isn't at the office, that's Luke.

My stomach twists again. It must be nerves about the audition, about working this out with Ryan. It certainly can't have anything to do with Luke being ungodly hot. Or anything to do with the dream I had this morning.

"Where is your hospitality, Janine? What if Miss Summers was a paying client?" Luke stands in the hallway, his hands in the pockets of his slacks.

He's in a sharp black suit and a royal blue tie. His jacket hangs off his shoulders perfectly. God, those shoulders are perfect.

Janine throws him her best *fuck you asshole, but you're my boss* smile. "Making coffee for Mr. Knight's girlfriend is not part of my job description." She reaches under her chair and collects her purse. "I'm about done for the day. I'm sure you can handle this."

He moves out of Janine's way and motions for me to come here. I do, and we walk to the tiny kitchenette.

"Pick your poison," he says, pointing to the coffee selection.

"Have any dark roast?"

He picks up two packets of coffee—a regular and a decaf. I point to the regular. I need all the energy I can get for dinner with Ryan.

Luke fills the machine with water and sets it to brew. He leans in close, his voice a low whisper. "Don't take it personally. Janine has a crush on Ryan."

"You think so too?"

He laughs. "I thought I was the only one."

His fingers brush my arm, and my body hums, like every part of me is turning on. I squeeze my legs together, pressing my fingers into my palm. It's no big deal. Just a crazy hot guy accidentally touching me.

He turns his attention to me. Those eyes are so big and wide and full of life. I've never seen anything like it.

"Did you manage to salvage the rest of your night?" he asks.

"That depends on your definition of salvage."

He shifts his hips and runs a hand through his hair. "I'm really sorry. If I knew you two were on a date, I wouldn't have called."

"It's not your fault."

His eyes connect with mine, and my heart pounds against my chest. It's hard to breathe.

"There has to be some way I can make it up to you." His fingers brush my hand. "Something I can do."

"It's not your fault," I say again.

"Can I at least keep you company until Ryan gets here?" His eyes are so big, so earnest. He really wants to wait with me. He really wants to talk to me.

"I get the feeling there's no way I can stop you."

He nods, turning his attention back to the coffee. He hands me the finished cup, his fingers brushing against mine with the most pleasant buzz. God, I hope he touches me again.

I dig my fingernail into my thumb until it hurts. There is something wrong with me. I shouldn't enjoy his touch this much.

Luke's eyes pass over me. "You okay?"

I nod. I'm fine. I'll be fine as soon as Ryan gets here and I'm away from the huge temptation in front of me.

No, I'm getting ahead of myself. Luke is a hot guy, but that's it. There's no way he's interested in more than a cordial relationship. There can't be.

He cleans out the machine and pops in a packet of Earl Grey. "This thing makes truly awful tea, but it's all we have." He turns his body towards mine, his eyes on me. "How is *The Handmaid's Tale*?"

"That was two books ago." I take a sip of the coffee. It's not great, but it's enough to wake me up.

"It's barely been twenty hours."

"When you have the whole day to yourself, you get through books pretty quickly."

He shakes his head like he's impressed. "What were the two books?"

"*Death of a Salesman* and *Doubt*."

"Those are plays. Anyone can read two plays in a day."

"How many plays did you read today?"

"Touché." He laughs. "Damn, those really are two depressing plays. Do you always read such horribly depressing stuff?"

"I don't mind depressing."

His eyes lock with mine and he stares like he's looking through me, like he's weighing every one of my words for meaning.

Finally, he nods like he accepts my sentiment and takes a long sip of his tea. "This is an abomination."

He opens a plastic tube of honey, squeezes a drop onto his fingertip, and brings it to his lips. Jesus. His lips look so soft, so perfect. They must taste like some delightful mix of honey and tea and Luke.

Luke shifts, leaning against the counter. "So I'm going to take a wild guess. You're here to surprise Ryan with a quickie."

I nearly spit out my coffee. "That would be right up his alley. You know how much Ryan loves to step away from work."

"He adores it." He squeezes a drop of honey into his tea, stirs it slowly, and takes another long sip.

"And this would be the outfit to do it. Nothing sexier than jeans and a sweater." I press my fingers into my coffee, trying to pry my gaze from Luke's lips or chest or shoulders.

He looks me over like he's assessing whether or not he'd fuck me. "It would work on me." He takes a sip of his tea and moves away from the counter. "Hypothetically speaking, of course."

I swallow hard. My body feels light. I swear I might float off the ground. He's only speaking hypothetically. He's not saying that he would sleep with me if I asked.

He leads me back to the lobby. "You saw me last night in my seduction outfit. It's only fair I see yours."

"Something tells me you don't have any trouble with that."

He smiles, his eyes lighting up. Jesus, his whole face lights up with the purest joy I've seen in ages.

"Miss Summers, you shouldn't inquire about people's sex lives."

"Oh really?"

"It's very rude." He nods cockily. "It's not like I started it or anything."

"Not like that at all."

I check the clock. Ryan is late. He might get the wrong idea about this friendly chat, but I can't bring myself to ask Luke to leave. It feels so damn good to talk to someone who is actually listening. Even if it's about nothing in particular.

We talk for forty-five minutes without mentioning Ryan once. It's the pulpy crime novel he's reading, the horrible lack of good tea in the office, how we both like living in the super-suburban Marina Del Rey. It reminds him of his parents' place in San Diego. It reminds me of all the assholes in high school who thought they were better than I was.

The door swings open, and Ryan takes in the scene. It's totally innocent. Luke and I are sitting with an entire chair between us, our hands firmly at our sides.

"Sorry I'm late, sweetheart," he says. He motions for me to follow him into his office, then turns to Luke. "Are you finished with the Jones contract?"

"Yes, but I'll take one more look before I leave." Luke glances at me. His eyes don't leave mine until I turn around and follow Ryan into his office.

It's sparse and clean. Impeccably organized, like everything in Ryan's life.

He takes a seat behind his desk, turning his attention to me. There's something on his face—exhaustion or irritation or impatience—but I can't figure out what.

"I hope Luke wasn't bothering you," he says. "He doesn't know how to turn it off."

"What's he supposed to turn off?"

Ryan rolls his eyes. "He flirts with all his female clients. These forty-year-old divorcées-to-be eat it up. A little attention from an attractive young man." Ryan sighs like he finds this oh so distasteful. "It's half the reason why I work with him."

I take a deep breath. This should be okay. Ryan is reasonable. I can convince him this is what's best for me. I fold my hands together. "I'm ready to start acting again."

"Would it be so bad to finish up the year?" He taps his fingers against the desk. "I'd feel better if you had four months of recovery under your belt."

"I know you're looking out for me, but I need this. I can't spend my whole life in the apartment."

"What about your books?" he asks.

I curl my fingers into fists. Don't get me wrong. I love books, but they're no substitute for having a life or a career. "It's been almost nine months and I've been doing well. I'm ready."

Ryan leans towards me and lowers his voice. "It's been five years. Don't you think it's time to move on?"

"I was a series regular for the last three years. And I killed myself trying to get those parts."

"Listen to yourself."

"I only meant I worked hard."

He takes my hand, but there's no warmth to it. "You did nearly kill yourself."

"You can't blame my eating disorder on acting."

"You didn't have any hint of an eating disorder before you started acting. What should I blame it on?"

"I went through treatment. I'll go back to meeting with a therapist every week. Please. I miss it so badly. Please." I sound so whiny and pathetic. So desperate for his approval.

"You're an adult. I can't force you to stay on hiatus. But I wish you'd put your health first. We agreed on those ground rules for a reason."

We did agree when I got out of treatment. A one-year hiatus to focus on my health, so I could properly learn how to deal with stress and constant pressure.

"Do you ever want me to go back to acting?"

"Of course not. It nearly killed you." He offers me a sympathetic look. "I know this is what you want, but you don't have the best history of wanting things that are good for you."

"This is different."

"Please, sweetheart. You don't remember how bad it was. How miserable you were."

I press my back against the chair. It was miserable, but this is miserable too. I clear my throat. If Ryan understood how much I missed this, maybe he'd let up. "Corine called."

"You mean the Corine that watched you run yourself into the ground?"

"You were there too. You can hardly blame her."

Ryan scowls. Still guilty he didn't notice my fun descent into bulimia. I'm not helping my case.

"What did Corine have to say?" he asks.

"There's a part for me. It's a great opportunity."

"What if you can't handle it?"

"I can."

"It's a lot of pressure on you, sweetheart. Everyone's eyes are on you. Everyone talks about how your body looks. Do you really want to see articles debating who is hotter—you or your costars—or, God forbid, articles about how you are too fat?"

"It will be different. They want me. They want my abilities. My fat ass."

"Your ass isn't fat."

"You know what I mean."

"Take it back," he says.

"Okay, my ass is normal."

"It's a joke today. Tomorrow, it's a diet plan or a personal trainer or a bottle of herbal metabolism boosters."

"I won't do any of that. I swear."

Ryan sighs. "Say no to this one. The year will be up before you know it."

I bite my lip.

"It's what your therapist would recommend."

"Ryan."

"I can't watch you destroy yourself again. I can't."

I nod. He's not going to budge today. I usually trust his judgment, but he's wrong here. He has no idea...

"Talk to me, sweetheart."

"I'm tired and I'm sure you have a lot of work." I hug my purse to my chest. "I should let you get to it."

"Have you eaten dinner?"

"I'll pick up something on the way home."

He nods okay, then gets up and kisses me good-bye. "Give it a few more months."

I nod. I can't stomach any more of this conversation. Better to end it now.

We say our good-byes and I let myself out of the office. In twenty minutes, I'll be home, and I'll be able to cry and scream about this as much as I want. I'll be able to figure out some way of convincing Ryan he's wrong.

I look for the elevator—this stupid building has such a confusing layout—and press the call button.

There are footsteps behind me. Fine. This is a large office building. There must be someone leaving work right now.

I turn around. The person behind me isn't a stranger. It's Luke.

CHAPTER FIVE

Luke takes a step towards me. He's six inches away, maybe less. Close enough that I could touch him, that I could wrap my arms around his waist and kiss him.

Jesus. I need to get ahold of myself.

He leans in, so close I can feel his breath. He smells like peppermint. Like he's been sucking on a peppermint candy.

"Are you okay?" His voice is so low and soft. Like he really cares.

"It's nothing. I'm fine." I turn back to the elevator. I need to get out of here ASAP. I can't be around him right now. He's too much temptation, especially when I'm in desperate need of a pleasant distraction.

Those lips, those arms, that touch... what a fucking distraction.

He takes another step towards me. "I can't let you go home miserable two nights in a row."

"It's not your fault. And I'm fine."

The elevator doors ding open. Fuck. This is not my dream. I am not dreaming. And he's not going to kiss me, then take me in the elevator.

I can handle this.

I turn back to Luke with my best everything-is-great smile. "Really, it's fine. I just want to go home and make a TV dinner."

"You're not filling me with confidence."

I step into the elevator and reach for the button to close the doors. "I'm fine."

He blocks the elevator door. "You don't look fine."

I take a deep breath. There must be some way to convince him to leave me alone without setting off any more of his you-don't-look-fine alarms. I try my best to exhale casually. "I'm only tired."

He stares at me like he doesn't buy this for a second. But he steps back, still blocking the elevator door with his arm. "I'm sure it's none of my business, but..." He releases my gaze but doesn't budge. "Look me in the eyes and tell me you're fine and I'll go."

"It is none of your business."

"Agreed."

"And there is no reason why I should humor you." But I don't move from my spot. I don't look away from him.

"You could do it because you think I'm hot."

My heart thuds against my chest. There's no way he just...

I look into his eyes, determined to convince him to leave me alone. But there's something in his expression—he actually cares how I feel.

I clear my throat. "What if I'm not fine and I'd rather not talk about it?"

"I'll respect your wishes. But I'd still like to do something to apologize for ruining your date last night."

"You're already forgiven."

"How about I buy you dinner?"

"Isn't that a date?"

He shakes his head. "More of an apology."

"That's not necessary. It wasn't your decision to bail on our date. It was Ryan's."

"Still. If I hadn't called, he wouldn't have left." He looks me straight in the eyes. "Come on, Alyssa. You have to let me do something to make it up to you."

Like rip off my clothes, press me against the wall, and touch me? That would be ridiculous.

"If you really want to make it up to me, why don't you let this go?" I take a deep breath. What a stupid thing to say. There's no way for him to touch me again if he leaves.

Luke takes a step towards me. "Is that really what you want?"

I nod. Absolutely.

"Can I at least buy you takeout? So you don't have to resort to a TV dinner."

"They aren't that bad."

He takes a step back, motioning for me to follow him. "I'll tell you what. I have, well, my seduction outfit, in my office. I'll change and ask Ryan if he minds."

I inhale slowly, attempting to put together a polite rejection. But when I open my mouth, I say, "Okay."

Luke smiles, his eyes lighting up. "Would you rather wait here or in the lobby?"

"Here."

He nods, and turns back towards the office.

This will be fine.

It's not like I have a terrible track record for giving in to temptation. Not at all.

It's way past sunset, and the dim lamps in the restaurant do little to supply light. It's a casual place across the street from Ryan's office.

We're sitting on a cushioned bench, looking over the takeout menu. It seems silly to order takeout when we could sit down to a meal, but Ryan would get the wrong idea. That this is a date and not a friendly... whatever.

Luke offers me the menu. He stretches his arms over his head, inhaling deeply. "If I were you, I'd order the most expensive thing on the menu as a big *fuck you*."

I shake my head. "I really don't blame you for last night."

"Then do it because I'm charging the meal to Lawrence and Knight."

"Is that legal?" I scan the menu, looking for whatever it is I usually order from this place. It has to be something light, something that won't set off any you-fucked-up-so-you-might-as-well-binge-and-purge alarms.

"If we discuss business." He takes my hand, tapping the enormous rock on my ring finger. "I see that you're engaged. Are you planning on a prenuptial agreement?"

He certainly doesn't look like a lawyer in his jeans and his V-neck. It's blue today, a bright sky blue that somehow brings out his dark eyes.

"Ryan can take care of that."

"Miss Summers, it's very unwise to allow your future husband to act as your counsel. In fact, it's unwise to share counsel for a prenup." He smiles.

He's joking. But there's something about it...

"Isn't it a conflict of interest for you to represent me?"

"Not necessarily."

"I'm okay, but thanks for the offer." I turn my attention back to the menu. There it is. Seared sea bass, baked yams, sautéed kale. No, that can't be right. I don't eat anything that's sautéed. Too much oil. Too much temptation.

I usually ask for light oil. No, Ryan asks for me. He orders all of my meals for me when we go out. Even when I ask him not to.

I bite my tongue. This isn't supposed to be so complicated. But it always is. A TV dinner would have been easier. It has a proper portion. Its calories and fat and sugar are clearly marked.

"There are a lot of choices here," he offers.

"Yeah. I just need a minute." It's fine. I'll ask for light oil. This is Los Angeles. People make all sorts of food modifications everywhere. It's not a big deal. I fold the menu and bring my gaze back to Luke. "Ready."

He stands and offers his hand. I shake my head and push myself off the bench. The takeout counter is about twenty feet away, and it's through an empty area of the restaurant.

He walks next to me, our hands a foot apart. So far apart.

The woman at the counter smiles at me. It's a normal smile, not a do-I-know-you-from-somewhere smile. We place our orders—he copies mine—and return to the waiting area. It should be about fifteen minutes. Maybe twenty.

Luke sits on the bench kitty-corner from mine. His knees are close, almost close enough to touch, and he's facing me. Looking right into my eyes, actually.

"I'm getting the sense you're in agony," he says.

"No, I'm just..."

"Tired?" He leans forward, his shirt slipping to reveal more of his defined chest. "Please don't stay to spare my feelings if you'd rather leave."

I shake my head. "I'd rather stay." I clear my throat. "For the sea bass."

He laughs, just a little. "It's amazing here."

"Do you eat here a lot?" Jeez, what a lame question. I might as well ask him how he feels about the constantly warm and sunny weather.

"On occasion. I try to get home in time for dinner."

"Your girlfriend must appreciate that."

He laughs, a hearty laugh this time, and his eyes light up. "That's subtle. I like it."

"I'm not... I don't care if you have a girlfriend or not." I really don't.

"Mhmm." He sits up straight and brings his gaze back to me. "I suppose I won't confirm or deny that. Since you don't care."

"Good."

He smirks, and I can't help but smile. It was an obvious line.

Luke stretches his arms above his head, his T-shirt sliding up his torso, revealing a sliver of skin above his jeans. His body is taut. Perfect abs. And those v-lines, those perfect v-lines, going from his hips to his... I try to pull my gaze away from his crotch, but I only manage to get as far as the soft, black hairs below his belly button.

Fuck. I shouldn't think about anything below his belly button. I shouldn't picture him slipping off his shirt over his head, revealing the rest of his strong, lean body. I certainly shouldn't picture him unzipping his jeans and sliding them off his hips.

He rouses my attention with a dramatic, "Ahem."

I finally pull my gaze back to his eyes. "Sorry," I say, my cheeks flushing.

"You can stare all you want. I work out for a reason."

"And what's that?"

"To look great naked."

I will not picture him naked. I will not picture him naked. I will not picture him naked.

I swear I won't.

"So, what's your favorite movie?" I ask, in a lame attempt to occupy my thoughts long enough they won't create an image of Luke naked.

"Is that really the best you can do?"

"What do you mean?"

His lips curl into a smile. "Let's just say I'm not convinced you're actually thinking about movies."

"I'm not..." I barely manage to get it out. I clear my throat. I pretend to check my phone. This has to be enough time to come up with some kind of articulate response. I can't let him think I want to see him naked. Even if I do.

"I suppose you won't let me get away with *Law and Order*," he says.

"TV show."

"Then *To Kill a Mockingbird*."

"Really? It's so..."

"The next word out of your mouth better be amazing."

"Cheesy."

"Alyssa Summers, how dare you. Atticus Finch is the paragon of—"

"A character who is too good to be true. He's the best dad in the world and he cares about justice, and he's incredibly competent. He's superhuman."

He shakes his head. "It's not a happy movie, you know. It has its depressing parts."

"I like things that aren't depressing."

"Uh-huh." He releases my gaze, smiling like he's teasing an old friend. "Like what?"

"*Casablanca.*"

"A movie based on a play."

"Now you have a problem with plays?"

"No." He scoots a little closer, until our knees are about two inches apart. "I'm just noticing a pattern in your interests."

And then he moves closer, and our knees are touching. A spark threads through me, and I dig my fingers into the bench to keep from gasping.

It's quick. Three seconds maybe and he moves his knee. It could be an accident. Or it could be on purpose.

His eyes are wide, his lips curled into a smile. "*Casablanca* has to be the most popular choice for 'favorite movie.'"

"I didn't say it was my favorite."

"Good." He leans closer. "Because it's total bullshit."

"Excuse me?"

"The whole thing is a parable about how duty is more important than love. Bullshit."

"It's World War Two. Defeating the Nazis is more important than true love."

"Nothing is more important than true love."

"What about World War Two?"

"Not any war ever." He shakes his head. "You can't really believe what Rick and Ilsa had was true love. They barely knew each other."

"Well..."

"And he treats her like a child." Luke leans towards me, his fingertips brushing against my arm. He's animated, excited. "He's a fucking asshole, actually. He chooses Ilsa's destiny for her, then scolds her for wanting to leave the husband she doesn't love like she's some amoral piece of shit."

"But he loves her enough to sacrifice his happiness for her."

"No. He decides what the right thing is and he forces her to do it. That isn't love. That isn't even respect."

He has a point. The supposedly beautiful thing about *Casablanca* is the way it ends, when Rick, Humphrey Bogart's character, tells his love interest, Ilsa, that she needs to stay with her husband because the "problems of three little people don't add up to a hill of beans." He's telling her that her problems are irrelevant, that what she wants isn't as important as what he thinks is right.

"So what is love?" I ask.

"Victor Laszlo letting her choose if she wants to be with him or with Rick."

"Ilsa does end up with Victor."

"Yes. But it's presented as this great tragedy. This bullshit about putting duty ahead of love." He holds my gaze. "But nothing is more important than love. Nothing."

The woman at the takeout counter waves at us, and Luke goes to collect the food. I take a deep breath, willing my body to calm down. He's being friendly. We're having a friendly conversation. It's no big deal.

Luke returns and hands me my half of the order. "Would it be obnoxious if I offered to walk you to your car?"

"I uh..." I dig my fingers into the paper bag. I could easily say yes and put an end to this conversation. "I walked here."

"Then if I offered to drive you home?"

"It would be slightly obnoxious."

He chuckles and bites his lip. It's such a sexy gesture, the kind of thing he'd do in between moans.

His lips still look so perfect, so soft...

"I'll take that as a yes." He leads me out the door.

It's a short walk to the car, and a very short drive back to the condo. Luke parks in an empty guest spot and gets out of the car to open the door for me. I insist it's not necessary, but, still, he walks me to the elevator.

His fingers brush against my lower back. That same gentle buzz moves through my body. He's so close, close enough to grab me and press me against the wall.

So I nod good-bye, and offer my hand and mumble some kind of thank you. He hugs me good-bye. It's a close hug, tight, the kind of hug you give your best friend. I can barely breathe, but I stay calm.

He doesn't press me for any more information or insist on walking me to my door.

The elevator doors slide closed, and I'm alone. I sigh, every tense muscle in my body relaxing. I'm out of the way of temptation. I'm good. No, I'm great.

There's a ding, and I'm at my floor. I walk down the hallway and slide my keys into the door. It's quiet and all the lights are off. Ryan is still at work, of course.

I drop my takeout on the counter and move to the bathroom. I'm a sweaty mess, and I need to clear my head before I even think about eating.

It's so bright and white in here, and the tile floor is so cold on my bare feet. I turn on the shower and dip my finger in the running water. Not warm enough.

I pull my sweater over my head and slide out of my jeans. My breath speeds. Luke's hands shouldn't have felt so fucking good on my back. His presence shouldn't have tied me up in knots.

I'm engaged, for Christ's sake.

So, I try not to imagine what it would feel like if it were Luke unhooking my bra or slipping my underwear to my knees. What he looks like stripping down to his boxers, then to nothing. I try not to imagine him, here, pulling me into the shower and pressing me against the wall.

The water of the shower pounds against my back, easing my tense muscles. It's so warm here, so comfortable. I slide my hand between my legs and try not to picture Luke naked. Try not to picture his hands roaming over my body, his sweet lips pressing into mine.

CHAPTER SIX

Ryan arrives after I've gone to bed, and he leaves for work while I'm still asleep. It's not like this most days. Most days, he wakes me up to kiss me good morning. Hell, most days, we have breakfast together.

I spend the morning sipping cup after cup of coffee and poring over the script for the audition. Ryan is still against the idea, but he'll warm up to it, once I convince him I'm healthy enough to handle acting.

It's a single-camera comedy. Which means it's shot like a feature film—each scene is done one shot at a time. Which means twelve- to fourteen-hour days, endless takes, and a ton of waiting around on set.

Still. The premise is funny. It's called *Model Citizen* and the lead character, my character if I nail this, Marie Jane, is an ex-model fresh out of rehab. She moves in with her stuffy sister and does everything she can to avoid reforming her ways.

I can play a woman like Marie Jane, and I can use my reputation as a practically has-been actress to my advantage. Not that I'm famous enough to have much of a reputation.

Corine set my audition for tomorrow afternoon, so I spend the entire day studying the scene. Marie Jane has just arrived at her sister's place, and she is dead set on ogling the hot seventeen-year-old boy across the street. She is dead set on convincing the hot seventeen-year-old boy he wants to fuck her. She could not care less that he is only seventeen. She could not care less that it will ruin her sister's reputation.

It's a scene about desire. And, if I want to impress the casting director, I need to find the desire, the thing I want more than anything. I try to think of Ryan, of our first night together, when I was desperate for him to think of me as more than a friend. But it doesn't work. That was a sweet, dull want born out of companionship. This Marie Jane is not a companionship kind of girl. No, she's a jump in headfirst, fuck-me-now-or-I'm-going-to-scream-fire, the-word-reckless-is-not-in-my-vocabulary kind of girl.

I try to channel my thirst for the part, but it's not enough. That's a strong need, but it's sensible, more or less. I need something that could consume me. Something that could destroy me.

Something like Luke. Not that I want him. But what if I did? He's my fiancé's business partner. Anything between us, even a kiss, would be bad news. It could destroy my life. It could destroy his business. He is handsome, yes, and something about him is so appealing. It would make sense if I wanted him, and it wouldn't be wrong. A want is just a want. It doesn't hurt anyone.

What did the call sheet say? Marie Jane is fresh out of rehab. So it's not so much that she wants this seventeen-year-old kid. She wants an escape, something to make her forget who and where and what she is for fifteen minutes. And there's no better, more self-destructive escape than fucking your boyfriend's business partner. There's no better way to ruin your life without resorting to drugs or alcohol or binging and purging.

All morning, I practice. I read my lines until I can recite them backwards and forwards. And I use Luke as a trigger every time. I shouldn't—I'm going to feel so tempted when I see him again— but I can't help it. No one else works, and the thought of him rouses something in me. I can't describe it. I can't even think about it. I just need to get through this audition and never think about him like that again.

There's no traffic on the road. I get to the production office an hour early and hide out in my car. My stomach is butterflies and it doesn't respond to deep breaths or slow sips of water.

This isn't a normal audition. It's a chance to get the fuck out of the doldrums of my boring, housewife-to-be life. It's the difference between long, lonely days doing nothing and a career.

I had a career once, and it was going well. I was on TV, a second lead on a cable show, but it was still TV. It paid well. And, better yet, I loved it. I was in movies, a bunch of tiny movies with limited releases, but still they were movies, and I had a few starring roles, and I totally killed it with my performances.

I take a deep breath. I can do this. I can do this. Can I do this? Fuck, can I actually do this?

I get out of my car and walk to the entrance. It's all so familiar. White walls, beige carpet, air conditioning on full blast.

An assistant sits at a desk in front. She looks up at me, only vaguely interested by my presence. "It will be a few minutes," she says.

It's an important enough audition that no one else is here. They're probably not seeing many people. My odds are good.

I wait at an empty desk, reading over the script, whispering the lines to myself. I'm so rusty. But I have to fake confidence. I have to get this part.

A door down the hall opens. I can hear some pleasant conversation, but I can't make out the details. It's probably some other actress, some other audition, some other meeting.

The assistant looks up at me. "Alyssa Summers, right?"

I nod.

"They're ready for you. It's the second door on the left."

I nod thank you, and walk down the short hallway. Deep breath. I try to slip into my best smile, my best attempt at Marie

Jane. She is fun, charismatic, fearless. She is an amazing train wreck, all instinct and need. I can play that. I can get this part.

The room is drab and gray, empty except for a long table and two women behind it. One looks like a casting director—a woman in her forties, in a sensible suit, serious look on her face. The other I recognize from her IMDB page—it's Laurie House, the showrunner. She's younger than I expected, in her late twenties maybe, black, with curly hair and big red glasses.

"Thanks for coming in," she says, incredibly cheerful. She makes small talk and asks a few basic interview questions. Where are you from, what inspires you, same old, same old.

The casting director nods to me. "Let's take it from the top of the scene. I'll read with you. Whenever you're ready."

I turn around and prepare. I try not to resort to my trigger. I try to picture the hot underage kid standing in front of the window, enticing me with his perfect body. There's a sexy, off-limits escape in front of me, and I need it. I need him. I've never needed anything more than I need him under me.

But it's too generic. I don't feel anything. If I really want to nail this, I need to think of Luke. I need to harness that feeling in my body when he touched me... The way I felt like a nervous schoolgirl. The way I wanted so, so badly to throw everything away just to feel those hands some place besides my back.

How the fuck can he do this to me? I barely know him.

Marie Jane barely knows this hot kid. All she knows is that she wants him. And all I need to know, all I need to feel, is how much I want Luke.

So I close my eyes, and I let the desire wash over me. When I open my eyes, I am not Alyssa Summers. I am Marie Jane and I want this hot kid. My only concern in life is convincing him to fuck me. Everything in my life will be perfect if I can kiss him and touch him and ride him until I come.

I recite my first line and lose myself in the scene. By the time I finish, my heart is thumping in my chest. My legs are weak. I haven't wanted anything this much in such a long time.

"Thank you, that was great," Laurie says. "We want you to hold your availability."

Fuck. They're considering me.

I have a chance. I have an actual fucking chance.

I nod. "I will. Thank you," and step towards the exit.

"I really loved you in *Mahogany*," Laurie says on my way out the door.

I hear the casting director scold her for such personable, unprofessional behavior, but I still take it as a good sign.

CHAPTER SEVEN

I try to spend my evening reading, but I'm full of nervous energy. I might get this part. I might have an actual life again.

Once upon a time, when I was worked up in a state like this, I would have eaten and thrown up two pints of ice cream. But I need to work on what my therapist called "healthy coping mechanisms." Doing something with my feelings besides stuffing them to the bottom of my stomach.

I change into a sports bra, shorts, and sneakers. Exercise falls under healthy coping mechanisms, even if my eating disorder-craving brain loves counting how many calories I'm burning.

I take the stairs to the ground floor, sliding my fingers over the railing in case I slip.

It's beautiful out. Just after sunset, with a view of the water for miles. It's a little cold to go without a shirt, but I'll live. I'll be hot as hell once I start running.

The marina is quiet, almost empty. I head for the concrete path that wraps around the water.

But then I see Luke, sitting in the grass, under the shade of a tree, a dog-eared paperback in his hands. He licks his fingers and turns the page. He's wearing a white V-neck and blue gym shorts. He's flushed and sweaty, like he just finished a run. Or a particularly vigorous fuck.

I pull my hair behind my head and secure it with the elastic band I keep on my wrist. So much for working off all my energy.

He looks up from his book, slowly scanning my body, his eyes wide with delight.

"What are you doing here?" I ask.

He points to his book. So, it was a stupid question.

"I live in the building," he says.

"Since when?"

"A few months."

"I haven't seen you around."

"I've been preoccupied."

I don't ask what's been preoccupying him. He already made a point of not mentioning his relationship status. Not that I care either way.

He pushes himself off the ground, slips his book into his pocket. "Can I join you?"

"You look like you've already exercised."

"I'm up for a second round," he says, his lips curling into a smile.

His hand grazes my arm, and I feel that electricity again, surging from my fingertips to my toes, filling me with nervous energy. My mouth is dry. My stomach is butterflies. My heart pounds so loudly, I can barely hear anything else.

"I don't own the sidewalk," I say.

"If you don't want me to come, just say so."

I will not think about him coming. I will not think about him coming. I will not think about him coming.

"No. You're welcome to come."

So I'm thinking about him coming. It's only a thought and a thought never hurt anyone. It's not as if I'll find out if he bites his lips or moans or digs his nails into my back. Not that it would ever be my back.

We break into a jog as soon as we're at the concrete path. He's fast. Really fast. But he slows down to match my speed.

The view is nothing but ocean and sky. It's such a beautiful night. A night for picnics on the grass, long walks on the beach, making out under the stars.

I run faster and faster, until I can concentrate on nothing but my breath. In. Out. In. Out. In. Out. Easy.

Then my foot hits something—a crack or a rock—and I stumble forward. My hands hit the pavement with a painful thud, and my ankle twists in an altogether unpleasant direction.

Luke stops short and sits next to me. "Are you okay?"

He's inches away. How could I possibly be okay with the electricity overwhelming my body?

"I'm fine."

I try to get up, but he holds my shoulders down.

"Let me check your ankle."

"Don't tell me you're also a doctor."

"I just know a little first aid."

His fingers glide over and around my ankle. He checks my wrists next, his hands lingering near mine. I make a motion to get up, but he holds my shoulders down.

"You need to wait a few minutes."

"I'm fine."

His hands slide down my shoulders, onto my arms. Fuck. I can barely breathe, barely feel anything in my body except the spots he's touching.

His eyes find mine. He's serious. "When you hurt yourself, your adrenaline surges. You don't always notice the pain."

"I know what a sprained ankle feels like."

"Is it really so bad sitting next to a hot, shirtless guy?"

"You're not shirtless... I mean." I clear my throat.

He smiles, his eyes lighting up. Fuck, his whole face lights up. I never see that kind of enthusiasm. Not anywhere.

"I'll take it off if it will keep you from trying to run on a sprained ankle," he says.

"It's not sprained."

I fold my arms, but he doesn't budge. I suppose he's right. It's not so bad sitting next to a hot guy, even if he's wearing a shirt.

Even if he's so close I can barely breathe.

I turn to Luke. "You're really fast."

"Only as fast as the person I'm with."

"You don't mean..."

"I mean running."

I swallow hard. I will not think about him coming. I will not thinking about him coming. I won't.

"Miss Summers, your mind is in the gutter."

My eyes narrow. He grins, that million-dollar smile lighting up his gorgeous brown eyes.

"Surely an engaged woman wouldn't think about the sexual prowess of someone other than her fiancé," he says.

"Don't flatter yourself," I say. I stand up and put my weight on my ankle. It hurts, but it isn't totally horrible.

"You look miserable."

"I'm fine."

He shakes his head. "Give it ten more minutes. You might not get another chance to stare at my shoulders."

I bite my lip. "I don't stare."

He raises his eyebrows and I can't help but smile.

"Okay, I stare a little."

I try to sit, but my ankle isn't cooperating. My leg slides out from under me, and I fall right onto Luke's lap.

My face flushes red. His skin is on mine. His breath is on my neck. He's so close. He could kiss me, slide his hands into my sports bra, push me onto the grass, and fuck me until...

There must be something wrong with me. I'm not usually this insatiable.

"I'm sorry." I shift off him, planting my ass on the ground. And not anywhere near his cock.

I swear I won't think about his cock.

"I can carry you back to the apartment. It's no problem," he says.

"No, that would be..." Too much to handle.

"Inappropriate?"

"Yeah." I lean back, onto the grass, turning my eye to the sky. It's too early for stars, but they'll be out soon. The few that show up with all the city lights in the way.

He follows my lead, lying on the grass next to me. He's so close I can hear his breath. His fingers are a few inches from mine. Almost like he's going to hold my hand.

His fingers brush against mine, and my body tingles with anticipation. I haven't wanted someone this much in such a long time.

"It would probably be inappropriate if I asked how the rest of your night went," he says.

"Oh, uh..." It definitely didn't end with me in the shower thinking about Luke as I... Fuck, I'm blushing.

"Damn, Alyssa. It must have been pretty good..."

"No, I..."

He laughs. "I won't tell Ryan."

"How do you know it wasn't Ryan?"

"He called at ten thirty with a work question." He scoots a little closer. "I wouldn't blame you if there was someone else."

My breath catches in my throat. "Who would you blame?"

"It's hard to be in a relationship with someone who is never around."

I shake my head like it doesn't bother me. It can't bother me. I can't allow any more of these thoughts into my brain.

We're quiet for a few moments. We watch the sun fade all the way behind the horizon. Luke is still close, but he's not touching me. Not at all.

He turns to me and offers his hands. "Why don't we try again?"

This time, I let him help me up. His grip on my hands is strong, protective even. If the circumstances were different, if I was single, and we were alone, and there weren't these stupid clothes in the way.

I suck a breath between my teeth. It's a crush, a little lust, nothing I can't get over.

Luke nods, a *go ahead* kind of nod, and I take a step forward. There's a slight bit of pain. But it doesn't feel like a sprain.

"I won't carry you, but there's no way you're running."

I make no objection. There's no way I'm running on this thing.

We walk for a few minutes, but my ankle is hurting more and more. Luke looks over at me, reading every hint of pain I'm trying to hide.

He shakes his head. "Here." He hunches down, offering his shoulder as some kind of human crutch.

"I'm fine."

"I can call Ryan if you'd prefer."

"And tell him what—I've been flirting with your girlfriend, but she won't let me carry her?"

His stops and runs a hand along the railing that surrounds the water. "Flirting, huh?"

"Yes."

"Miss Summers, that's an awfully serious allegation."

"Uh-huh."

"Besides, you're flirting back."

I try to come back with some reasonable excuse, a claim that I am not flirting, that I am not interested, that I would never, ever, ever do anything to hurt Ryan. But all I can do is sadly restate the facts: "I'm engaged."

"I'm well aware of that," he says, eyeing my bare ring finger. "We're only friends."

"Do you flirt with all your friends?" I ask.

"No," he says. "Only the friends who correct my grammar."

"You're not... we're not. We're only friends."

He nods. It's a simple affirmation. He's not mocking me for repeating his obvious statement. He's not questioning my intentions.

He's just agreeing.

"You wouldn't... you and Ryan are business partners. You wouldn't actually pursue his fiancée, would you?"

His eyes find mine. "You or some hypothetical fiancée?"

"Hypothetical."

"Well," he says, "I wouldn't really think of her as Ryan's fiancée. She's a person, not his property, and I'd respect her wishes."

"That's not an answer."

"Say this hypothetical fiancée was interested in me." He leans back, pressing his hand against the railing. "Say I enjoy my business relationship with Ryan, but I don't exactly respect the guy. He's a good enough lawyer, the best divorce lawyer I know, but he's a condescending prick."

"But that's your business."

"Alyssa, are you trying to talk me out of a hypothetical affair?" He smiles, some attempt to lighten the mood.

I exhale, rolling my shoulders to release some of the tension in my back. This is getting a little much. A little serious. "You're right. It's just a hypothetical."

"I wouldn't pursue something, but I would consider the possibility."

"Oh." I try to take another step. It's not so bad. I can manage it. "What would make you decide to go through with it?"

Luke follows me, offering his arm for support again. I refuse, again.

He looks at me, completely earnest. "I don't want to make you uncomfortable."

"Try me."

His mood shifts. It's playful. "Are you sure? You are engaged, after all."

I roll my eyes. "I can handle it."

His eyes connect with mine. "Mostly, it would depend on how much I wanted to make her come."

My eyes go wide. My heart pounds. My breathing stops. I try to formulate a response. Something to remind him I am engaged, that I am not the kind of girl who cheats on her fiancé.

But all I say is, "Oh."

I can't even convince myself.

CHAPTER EIGHT

Corine calls on Friday, at exactly 4:45. She skips the pleasantries. "Are you sitting down?"

"Yes." I'm in the apartment, on the couch, failing at paying attention to the TV. Waiting for this call, basically.

She takes a long breath. "They want you."

I close my eyes and open them, expecting to wake up from a daydream. But I'm still on the couch in the living room. It's still bright in here. It's still almost five on a Friday afternoon.

"You're their first choice for Marie Jane," she says.

"You better not be fucking with me." I dig my fingers into the couch. It's still here. I'm still here. This is really happening.

I might have a life again.

"The showrunner wants to meet you next week. They'll do a chemistry read, send over the contract. Everything will be official by the end of next week."

"When do they need an answer?"

"You can't tell me you're considering rejecting this offer. The per episode they're offering is practically unheard of for someone—"

"I get it. I'm not famous or important enough to demand a high salary."

"It's thirty thousand dollars an episode. You're not going to get that on cable anywhere else."

I take a deep breath. "I know, but I have to talk to Ryan."

"You can buy a new Ryan with the money you'll make. They have an order for a thirteen-episode season. That's almost four hundred thousand dollars. I won't take no for an answer. Even if it means driving to your place and throwing Ryan off the balcony."

"Give me a couple days."

"You're better than this." She sighs like she disapproves. "But fine. I'll say you're away for the weekend, on a retreat, and you'll give them an answer by end of day Monday."

"Thank you."

"I'm not kidding about the balcony."

"It won't be necessary."

I'll convince him this is a good idea. Convince him he was wrong before.

I pace around the apartment, trying to think of a strategy, trying to think of anything other than Luke being open to fucking me. I never should have used him as a trigger. I never should have allowed myself to entertain the idea of my hands on his body, however amazing his body is.

I run the shower until the bathroom floods with steam. It's hot, so hot it will scorch every part of my skin, especially the parts that tingled when Luke touched them.

Ryan means well. He only wants to protect me. I did spiral out of control the last time I was on TV. And, as usual, he was there to pick up the pieces.

He rescued me from so many bad situations when we were teenagers. When I was at a party and some aggressive guy was harassing me, Ryan was there. When I was stranded at school, no ride home after rehearsals for the play, Ryan was there. When I was locked in the bathroom at the mall, crying after a fight with my mom, Ryan was there.

He used to hold me and tell me everything was going to be okay. We were only friends. It wasn't even romantic. I tried to kiss him a few times, but he always said no, that he wouldn't do it when I was upset, that I didn't owe him anything for his kindness.

Don't get me wrong. He was an asshole sometimes, but he was sweet.

I squeeze shampoo into my hand and run it through my hair. It's fruity, oranges and honey, the kind of thing a teenage girl uses.

He still treats me like I'm a teenage girl. Like I need to be rescued and told what to do.

I tilt my head back, rinsing the shampoo.

I do love Ryan. I really do. He's an asshole sometimes, but he wants the best for me. He's looked out for me for such a long time.

We won't have the most passionate marriage in the world, but passion doesn't do me any good. Passion is what sent me into a bulimic spiral. Passion is what nearly destroyed my life.

There has to be some way I can make Ryan understand why I need this so much.

I squeeze conditioner into my hand and run it through my hair. The water is still so hot, and the room is full of steam. It would be so nice to have someone in here with me, someone to hold me, and stroke my hair, and tell me everything is going to be okay.

My eyes flutter closed and I bite my lip. Ryan and I don't even have sex anymore. He's too busy. Too tired. Too obsessed with his damn job.

I need to keep my head in the game. Going back to acting is what matters.

Luke is a needless distraction. A confident, funny, hot as hell distraction, but only a distraction.

The front door opens. Ryan must be home early. It's not like him to get home before eight o'clock. Without a plan, I have little choice. I'll have to admit I was less than honest about my interview.

I rinse my hair, turn the shower off, and pull my towel tight around my chest. Maybe Ryan will be easier to convince if I'm naked. It certainly can't hurt.

He knocks and steps into the unlocked bathroom. "You know, there's a sauna at the gym," he says.

He takes another step towards me, and I drop my towel. Finally, something to get these thoughts of Luke out of my head.

I move fast, pressing my lips into Ryan's. My hands are already on his belt. Yes, come on. Kiss me. Touch me. Give me a release for all this energy.

But he steps back. "What are you doing talking to Corine?"

Was he looking through my phone or is he psychic?

"How do you know that?"

"You left your email up on the tablet," he says. His eyes bore into me. A demand I answer him immediately and honestly.

I pull my towel back around my chest. "You remember the job I mentioned?"

"Yes." He grits his teeth.

"I went to the audition."

"We talked about that."

"I know." I try to give him my sweetest smile. "I thought I was okay letting this one go."

Ryan steps back, but his eyes stay on mine. "This is how it starts—all this lying."

"It's not like that."

He looks at me like I've betrayed him. "What is it like?"

"I need to go back to acting."

"And?" He adjusts his tie.

"And if you read the email, you already know."

He stares at me like he can wait all day, like he's willing to stand in the bathroom in his clothing in order to win this staring contest.

But I don't budge. I fold my arms, squeezing the towel around my chest.

Finally, Ryan releases his gaze. "And you got the part."

I move to the sink and wipe off the remnants of my running mascara. "You could be excited."

He stands behind me, staring at my reflection in the mirror. "Why would I be excited that my fiancée feels the need to lie to me?"

"I'm sorry I wasn't honest." I reach for a cotton swab, and my grip on the towel slips. Fuck it. I drop the towel.

Ryan turns his eyes down, glancing at my body briefly. There's no lust in it, no want, nothing.

It's not like I expect passion from him.

I offer my best smile. "I can do this. I'm getting better."

He pulls a towel off the rack and hands it to me. "And what if you can't? You barely got out of your contract for *Together*."

"I can. I promise." I drop the towel and turn to face him.

This time, he stares like he's interested. He looks at my breasts, my stomach, my legs. Like they're actually of interest to him.

But, still, he brings his gaze back to my eyes. He's serious, all business. "That world isn't good for you. It's too stressful."

"Please, Ryan, I need this." My voice cracks into a high-pitched whine. Ugh, it's so awful. How does he always make me into such a whiny, awful mess?

Ryan's phone rings. "Hold on." He moves out of the bathroom, shaking his head like he's disappointed. He answers the phone with a curt, "What is it?"

I move to the kitchen, still naked, and look for a TV dinner. There's nothing remotely appealing in the freezer. I should invest some of my free time into learning how to cook. That, Ryan would be happy about.

"You think everyone is an asshole... maybe he is, but he's high profile," Ryan says into the phone. He sits at the kitchen table. "She's done it before. She's very charming."

He turns his gaze to me, focusing on my chest. He taps his fingers on the table impatiently.

The phone call is annoying him. Maybe, if he ends it quickly, we can end this stupid fight with a proper make up.

I make a point of bending over to reach into the freezer. There. I pick out an appropriate, moderate-calorie TV dinner.

"Don't make one of those awful things." Ryan directs this to me. He sighs, loudly, turning his attention back to his phone. "No, I need to talk to Alyssa... it doesn't involve you."

He pushes me out of the kitchen and pulls ingredients from the fridge. "What else do we have to talk about?" he asks the caller turning on the countertop grill and coating it with oil.

Another night, another dinner of grilled fish, steamed vegetables, and brown rice.

"I can do it."

He looks at me like I'm crazy. Then he's back to the phone. "Fine. But you'll have to keep it quick." He hangs up the phone and turns to me. "Sweetheart, why don't you put on some clothes?"

"That's no fun."

"Yes, well." He reaches into the fridge and pulls out a bag of green beans. "Luke is going to stop by to talk about work for a minute. I'd prefer he not see you naked."

Fuck. Luke is going to be in our apartment. Luke is going to be here. He's going to be near me. He's going to be twenty feet from my bed.

He's never asked to stop by the apartment before, not when I was home, and I'm always home. It couldn't be because of me. It couldn't be because I indulged his flirting. It couldn't be because he wants to make me come, could it?

I turn back to Ryan. "I'll get dressed when we're finished talking." If I don't stand my ground, I won't convince Ryan.

"We are finished."

"I need to do this."

He presses the chef's knife through a broccoli stalk with a sigh. So maybe I am getting through to him. Maybe if I keep insisting...

"Fine, sweetheart, we'll talk about it more later. Now, go put on some clothing." He throws the sliced broccoli into the steamer.

"Something nice," he adds. "I don't want him to think he's welcome to hang out here."

And, of course, Ryan doesn't want Luke to think that I am anything less than a polite, demure trophy girlfriend.

CHAPTER NINE

Luke sits on our couch, stretched out like a cat—arms over his head, his shirt riding up his stomach, exposing inches of taut muscles. And those lines, those sexy v-lines.

It should be a crime to be so fucking attractive.

"Sit at the table at least," Ryan says. He takes a look at my chosen outfit—a tight, low-cut dress—with clear disapproval.

This is not what he meant by nice.

I shrug like it's no big deal, like this is the kind of thing I wear whenever I'm hanging out at home.

Luke looks me over from top to bottom. His eyes light up with interest. It's certainly more than I got from Ryan in the bathroom.

I nod. "Nice to see you again."

His lips curl into a smile, and he pushes himself off the couch. He's five feet away. Then four. Then three. Then I'm offering my hand to shake, and he's wrapping me in a hug.

Jesus. His body feels so good around mine. It's nothing, a friendly greeting, and it's over in ten seconds.

It's just a hug. A hug never hurt anyone.

I push Luke back, just a little bit. He tries to hold my gaze, but I look at the floor. His expression is too earnest. He's going to see right through me, to figure out how much I want him.

It's not something I can act on.

But Luke keeps his eyes on me, even as he addresses Ryan. "Don't you have a favor to ask Alyssa?"

I swallow hard, taking a step backwards. They're both looking at me like I'm a piece on a chess board. Like I may or may not be useful to them.

"Sweetheart." Ryan moves towards me, offering his hand. "Do you remember when you came to that dinner with me last month and charmed my client?"

"The old guy who stared at my chest the whole time?" I ask.

Ryan sighs. "Wasn't it fun?"

I stare laser beams at Ryan. "That depends on your definition of fun." Like if it includes a creepy old guy staring at your tits while you laugh at his bad jokes.

I offer a polite smile and take a seat at the table. This conversation isn't going to end well.

Luke turns his attention to Ryan. "What do we even want this asshole for a client? He's got an ironclad prenup. Even you can't wiggle out of it."

"There's no such thing as ironclad."

"You really want to whore your fiancée out to attract this asshole?" Luke turns to me. "No offense."

"You make it sound so dramatic. It's a friendly dinner. No different than what we're doing here," Ryan says.

Luke's eyes pass over me again. There's something in his eyes. It's almost like he's nervous. Or, at the very least, like he's imagining me without this dress in the way.

"Don't get me wrong," Luke says. "If I were this asshole, I'd be convinced. But it's still..." He clears his throat. "It's a cheap trick."

Ryan stares at Luke, assessing his intentions. "It's Alyssa's choice. All she has to do is be her gorgeous self." He looks at me like I'm supposed to agree.

I nod. This is part of my role. I'm the pretty girl on Ryan's arm. It's been this way since high school. School dances, graduation dinners, cocktail parties—it's always the same.

Ryan smiles. He got what he wanted. He scoops food onto ceramic plates and places them on the dining room table. He motions to Luke to sit, then takes a seat.

Luke sits on the other side of the table, next to me. There isn't much room between us. A few inches, maybe.

No big deal.

He pulls a bottle of tequila from his bag and offers it to Ryan. No way in hell. Ryan doesn't drink.

Luke offers the bottle to me. I nod.

He pours two glasses and hands one to me. His fingers brush against mine, and my body is buzzing again.

I take a deep breath. It's a tiny crush. It's nothing.

Ryan's hazel eyes bore into me. "Sweetheart, I'm meeting with this new client tomorrow night. I'd love if you'd join me, but I understand if you can't handle it."

So that's how he's going to play this. Either I do what he wants, or I can't handle a challenge.

Fine. I'll do what he wants if it will prove I can handle myself.

"I'll wear my shortest dress and my biggest smile," I say.

Luke's hand brushes against mine. My heart races. My eyes find his.

God, those fucking eyes, so dark and intense. And they're only the tip of the iceberg. Everything about him is amazing. His thick hair is begging for my hands. His soft lips are begging for my lips. His hard body is begging for my... Fuck. I suck on an ice cube in a hopeless attempt to cool down. It only fills my head with even more ideas of what I want to do to Luke.

"I'm surprised you're so gung ho to put in a bunch of overtime for this asshole," Luke says. "You already work eighty hours a week. Do you ever get a chance to spend time with your fiancée?"

Ryan scowls. "You're the last person I'd take relationship advice from."

Luke looks hurt, but he doesn't say anything. He just stabs his broccoli with his fork. What does it mean, that Ryan wouldn't take Luke's advice? It must be something. That girlfriend whose existence Luke won't confirm or deny.

Ryan looks at me. "We have to discuss a few legal details. Why don't you grab your Kindle or go watch TV?"

"It's okay. I'm used to boring conversations."

Luke laughs. "I think that's a dig at you."

"No, I didn't mean it like that."

His eyes catch mine and I can't help but smile. He looks so fucking sweet, so fucking cute.

I polish off my glass of tequila and Luke refills me. His hand brushes against mine again, for longer this time. His lips part into the tiniest of smiles. They look so soft. They look like they could do all sorts of things to me.

The boys talk shop, debating the figures on some piece of paper. Ryan wants to ask for more. Luke wants to compromise. It's dreadfully boring, so dreadfully boring I wish I had grabbed my Kindle when I had the chance.

I finish my second glass. Luke refills me again. He sits a little closer to me, a little further on the edge of his chair. His hand brushes against my thigh, just for a second, and my body floods with electricity. God, I want that hand on my body. Even if it was an accident.

Ryan cuts me off after my third glass, but I don't care. I am light and free and everything is so, so funny. I laugh as I crash on the couch, my dress riding up my legs, exposing my underwear. As Ryan suggested, I turn on the TV and flip around the channels, unable to find anything interesting.

"Stop," Luke says, moving next to me on the couch. "You just skipped past *Law and Order*."

"We're not finished," Ryan says.

"I'll rewrite the proposal tonight. We'll give his wife the vacation house. He won't even miss it." Instead of taking the remote, Luke holds his hand over mine, pressing my finger into the channel down button.

"Don't you have your own TV?" Ryan asks.

"I don't have cable in the apartment," Luke says.

"I think he's asking you to leave." I giggle and press my arm into Luke's.

We are so close, and his arm is so warm, and he doesn't even care that Ryan is watching us.

"Come here, Alyssa," Ryan says.

I pout, but I climb over Luke and scamper to Ryan.

"Get some water. You're drunk."

"Why can't I get drunk in my own apartment?" I ask.

"Let the girl have a little fun," Luke says. "It's probably the only fun she has in this apartment."

I burst into laughter. My knees buckle and I slide to the carpet. Ryan is glaring at me. He's glaring at Luke. He's pissed as all hell, but I can't stop laughing.

It is the only fun I have in this apartment. And Ryan had his chance. I practically threw myself at him.

When I finally catch my breath, I fetch my glass of water and drink the whole thing.

I move back to the couch and accidentally fall onto Luke's lap. Accidentally. I feel his hands on my sides as he lifts me and places me on the cushion next to him. I want to be closer to him, but Ryan won't like it. He doesn't like anything. I slide to the other side of the couch and hug the arm rest.

"Why don't you go home and get started on that report?" Ryan suggests.

"The episode is almost over. Don't you want to see if ADA Jack McCoy nails the murderer?"

"He was only asking to be polite," I say. "He wants you to leave."

"I know," Luke says.

"He'll get mad if you don't leave," I say.

"It's your place too, isn't it? Do you want me to leave?" Luke asks.

I try not to giggle, but I'm sure I do, and I'm also sure I twirl my hair around my fingers.

"Ryan doesn't watch TV. He thinks it's boring and pointless."

"Even your show?" Luke asks.

"He got too jealous," I say. "All my character did was make out with... well, with everyone."

"Come on, sweetheart," Ryan says. "Let's go to bed."

"It's early," I say.

"Yes, but you're making a drunken fool of yourself."

"I think she's a cute little drunk," Luke says.

"I'm not drunk! I'm only tipsy. And I agree. You should find it cute."

Ryan rolls his eyes. I know what this means. I push off the couch, again, and let Ryan escort me to the bedroom. It is early, but I am drunk, and I am much safer in here, with the door closed, with it impossible for Luke to touch me again. Or for me to touch him.

I hear Ryan turn off the TV and walk Luke out. He sighs, a heavy sigh, and returns to my room.

Ryan looks at me, a look of pity or disapproval or something like that. He shakes his head. "Alyssa, you're supposed to stop at two drinks."

"I'm fine." I roll over, pulling the covers over my head.

Ryan opens the dresser, pulls out my pajamas, and tosses them on the bed. I slide out of my dress, bra, and panties, but I don't bother with the pajamas.

It doesn't even faze Ryan.

"You need to be on your best behavior tomorrow."

"Have I ever been on anything less than my best behavior at one of these dinners?"

"You weren't tonight. You were practically flirting with Luke."

"Isn't flirting the point of these stupid dinners?"

He sits next to me on the bed and places his hands on my shoulders. "Alyssa..."

Ugh. It's the end of an argument whenever he says "Alyssa."

"How many drinks am I allowed to have?" I ask.

"You shouldn't have any."

"My therapist insists one or two is fine."

"Alyssa."

I don't respond.

Ryan kisses me on the forehead. "You'll feel better in the morning." He turns the lights off and leaves, closing the door behind him.

I stare out the window, at the rolling ocean, the black sky, the bright stars. I try to sleep, but I am too anxious, too wound up. I remind myself that Ryan has my best interests at heart.

I remind myself that I love Ryan, that we are engaged, and that I am not supposed to think about another man.

But, when Luke touched me, Jesus, I've never felt anything like that. And it was only his fingers brushing against my thigh. It was only his hands on my waist. It was only innocent.

Why did it have to be so innocent?

His hands could have been under my clothes. On my chest or my ass or between my thighs. He could be here, in this bed, with me. His body could be pressed against mine. His lips could be pressed against mine.

His cock...

I slip my hand between my thighs and finish my thought.

CHAPTER TEN

Two cups of coffee do nothing to ease my hangover. I should have listened to Ryan and limited myself to one drink, even if he was obnoxious.

I drink three glasses of water, but still, my head pounds. Ryan is spending this lovely Saturday at the office—shock of the century—and I can't bother to do more than lie on the couch, flipping through the channels. It's so bright and the TV is so loud, but there's something calming about the chatter of random channels.

Talk show. *Friends* rerun. Talk show. Cartoon funny to no one but fourteen-year-old boys.

Law and Order.

Jesus, this show is everywhere.

It ran for twenty seasons. And it's not like Luke is the only person in the world who likes it.

Watching the detectives question busy witnesses shouldn't make me think of Luke. It should make me think of New York City. It should make me think of all the times I auditioned for guest spots on police procedurals—I was almost cast as the kidnapped daughter once. It should make me think of something besides Luke watching with me on the couch, his body pressed against mine, his eyes wide with interest.

It's not like his big, brown eyes were wide and bright because of me. Like his breath was fast because of me. Like his cock...

Jesus, I'm going to tear my hair out if I stay in this apartment any longer.

I find my most oversized pair of sunglasses and slip into my flip-flops. It's a nice day outside. And I'm not that hung over. I can handle the flood of light outside. I can handle a walk around the marina.

I slip my essentials into my purse—phone, keys, wallet, water bottle, Kindle. It's early. I don't have to be back in this room, in my sluttiest cocktail dress, for another eight hours. The fresh air might help me think of a way to convince Ryan I can do this.

The elevator feels especially slow today. Its shiny silver doors feel especially oppressive. I avoid my reflection in the mirrored ceiling. I don't need the reminder I haven't slept.

A gentle breeze blows across my arms. It's late spring. Every day is like this—sunny, cloudless, warm but not hot. When I first moved to Los Angeles, I fell in love with the weather. Every sunny day was a love letter from the city to me, another sign I was right to get my GED and move the fuck out of Massachusetts. But, after eight months sitting in the condo, staring at the blue skies and sunshine from behind giant glass windows, the beautiful days seem more like a fuck you. Fuck you, Alyssa, you are stuck inside, trapped by your own pathetic inability to cope.

I round the corner, heading for the path that winds around the marina. But I stop in my tracks.

Luke is sitting under that same tree, the same dog-eared paperback in his hands. Pockets of sunshine fall through the leaves, casting a soft glow over his face and body. He looks even more fuckable than he did yesterday. He's not sweaty or flushed today. Not yet.

So, he's all kinds of sexy. That doesn't mean I need to have sex with him. It doesn't mean I need to imagine having sex with him. I am a fully grown woman. I have some self-control.

"I was hoping I'd run into you," he says.

He was hoping he'd run into me. He was thinking about me. He was...

I bite my lip. I need to snap out of this. "You're not at work?"

"It's Saturday."

"You say that like it's reasonable to expect someone not to work on a Saturday."

He pats the spot next to him and scoots over. "You want to talk about it?"

I shake my head.

His gaze is piercing, unrelenting. "Can I ask you a personal question?"

"Can I stop you?"

"It's terribly inappropriate."

My heart thuds against my chest. He's not going to ask to fuck me. It's not a big deal.

I nod. "Shoot."

"Are you in love with Ryan?"

I step backwards, almost losing my footing. "That's none of your business."

"Like I said, terribly inappropriate."

"It's not... I don't see how... I do love him." I press my fingers together. "What's the difference to you, anyway?"

He pushes himself up and takes a step towards me. "Remember that hypothetical?"

"About the engaged woman?"

He nods. "I thought about it a little more."

"Hypothetically?"

His shifts, rolling his shoulders back. Damn, those are some amazing shoulders.

Luke's eyes are on mine. "How do you feel about going to someplace private? Just to talk."

This conversation is heading into dangerous territory. I should say no, should tell him to fuck off and mind his own business.

But he's here, and he's listening to me, and it feels so damn good just to be around him.

"Okay."

He offers his hand, and I take it. Electricity again, but I bite my lip to temper it.

He leads me down the concrete path. The sun is bouncing off the pavement, right into my eyes. Even my sunglasses aren't enough to block it out.

We walk in silence for a few minutes, the only sound the *clip-clop* of my flip-flops. We cross a street, heading into a residential neighborhood. Where could we possibly be going?

"There would be a few factors in my decision with this hypothetical engaged woman," Luke breaks the silence. His gaze turns toward me. "How much I liked her, if I cared about her fiancé, if she adores depressing plays."

I take a deep breath and hold it in my lungs for as long as I can.

Luke looks right in my eyes. "But, mostly, I'd need to know if she really was in love with her fiancé."

"It's none of your business."

"I know. But I wouldn't want to get in the way of true love, real love, the kind of romantic, passionate love that leaves you breathless and keeps you together for eighty years."

"I'm not a romantic."

"Then you've never been in love," he says.

He stops in front of a two-story house. It's modest, but nice. White with blue trim. He leads me through the front yard, a mass of grass, and reaches over a blue gate to unhook it. Is this his house? It seems much too domestic and feminine for a guy like Luke.

"If you really love him, and you really want to be with him forever, I don't want to fuck that up. But I know, better than anyone, that women can't be stolen. They can only decide to stray. Or decide to leave."

"You talking about anyone in particular?"

"Come on, come in," he says. "Don't worry. It's a friend's place. I'm house-sitting."

I nod fine, and follow him into the backyard. It's suburban paradise. Rose bushes. Sleek patio furniture. Crystal blue pool.

Luke strips to his boxers. Jesus, his body is amazing. His arms and legs are sculpted. His back and shoulders are strong. His chest and abs are perfectly chiseled, right down to those amazing v-lines I keep staring at. His boxers hang around his hips. Just above his...

I am so fucked.

"You coming in?" Luke jumps into the pool.

He emerges, black hair sticking to his head, his body practically glistening in the sun.

"I'm not wearing a swimsuit," I say.

"And?"

"And my bra cost seventy dollars. I'm not going to ruin it with chlorine."

"No one is forcing you to wear a bra."

I fold my arms over my chest.

"Oh, come on," he continues. "I'm only kidding. There's a few swimsuits in the bedroom that she never... that have never been worn. You can have one. You can keep it here if you want."

What's he doing in some random house with some random woman's unworn swimsuits? It's weird, but it's better than nothing. If I get naked with him, I might not be able to put my clothes back on.

I nod fine, and he returns with a bag of unworn lingerie, tags still attached. There's a navy bikini. It's not my size, but I can make it work.

"Who did you buy the lingerie for?" I ask.

"You think you're the first girl I brought here?" He tries to say it with a smile, but his big, coffee-colored eyes betray him. He's still hurt over another woman.

It shouldn't bother me, but it does.

I ask him to turn around and I change on the concrete. He's a perfect gentleman, and he doesn't turn around to catch a glimpse.

I slide into the pool, and, finally, he looks at me.

"It looks good on you," he says.

"But it would look better on your floor?"

"Alyssa, I'm not going to spring some lame seduction attempt on you." He moves closer, his eyes on fire. "When I want to fuck you, I'll ask nicely."

Does he really think I'd fuck him standing up, in some pool at his friend's house? Does he think just because he's handsome and funny and interesting that I'll betray Ryan? Does he really think he has my attention?

Does that mean he doesn't want to fuck me?

"I like you," he says.

"Why?" I ask.

"Because you corrected my grammar."

"Is that all it takes?"

"It helps that you have great tits." He smirks. "And you get the cutest look when you're trying to pretend like you aren't nervous." He moves closer to me. "You seemed so lonely that night at the office. And I'm lonely all the time."

My heart thuds against my chest. "I'm engaged." It's the only thing I can think to say.

He slides his hands over his hips. Over the waist of his boxers. Is he waiting for my reaction? Is he waiting for me to untie my bikini and pull his boxers to his knees and wrap my legs around his hips like I'm some easy whore?

"I don't care. I like you, and I don't care about anything in the way."

My pulse races. My lungs empty. I can't remember the last time it was this hard to breathe.

"I'll be your friend," he says. "If that's all you want." He moves closer. "But I want a hell of a lot more."

I reach for his waist, my fingers sliding over his wet skin. Jesus, his body feels so good, and he shudders gently as my fingers slide around his waist.

The Lycra of my bikini bottom presses into his cotton boxers. We move closer, my crotch pressed into his, my stomach pressed into his, my chest pressed into his. He's taller than I am, and instead of making me rise onto my tiptoes, he slides his hands under my ass and brings me towards him. Why did I ask for this stupid bikini? His hands could be on my bare skin.

My lips press into his. They're soft and wet with a hint of chlorine. He sucks on my lower lip and opens his mouth, just a bit, waiting for my move. His hands press into my ass, pulling our bodies together, pressing my crotch into his. He's hard. We could...

I slip my tongue into his mouth and my hand... Oh, God, what is my hand doing?

I jump back and say, "I'm sorry."

"Don't be."

"But I can't. I'm engaged."

"You've said that a few times now."

"I'm sorry. I'm not a tease."

"Don't be silly." He smiles. "Teasing is half the fun."

"I have to go." If I don't get out of here, now, I'll be under him in five minutes flat.

I rush out of the pool, throw my clothes into my purse, and run across the concrete. I run so fast and everything is so blurry. I hear Luke call after me, *wait*, or *Alyssa*, or something like that, but I don't stop running until I am back in the condo, the door locked behind me.

CHAPTER ELEVEN

Ryan's hand tightens around my waist as we take our seats. He introduces me to Dave, no last name. No, they are already on a first-name basis. Dave is exactly as I imagined. A dirty old man squeezed into a designer suit that hasn't fit him in years. He doesn't even bother to bring his gaze from my chest to my face when he shakes my hand.

"Ryan, you undersold your fiancée's beauty. She's even lovelier in person," Dave says.

I struggle not to roll my eyes. It's obnoxious to play the ingénue, but this is the role that will convince Ryan I can handle acting.

"Smart, handsome, and good taste. That's everything I look for in a man." I smile. I bat my eyelashes. I play my part.

The waiter stops at our table and we order drinks. Tequila for me. Wine for the gentlemen.

I go to kiss Ryan's cheek. It's another part of our routine, but he presses his hands into my bare back and pulls me closer. Our lips collide, way too much of a PDA for a classy place like this.

It's not a sweet move. It's not a kiss that says I love you or even I want you. It doesn't even say you are mine. No, just like the flashy engagement ring, it says *she is mine, you better stay away from her.*

Ryan wasn't always this possessive. He used to be sweet. Caring.

He pulls away, and his gaze fixes on one spot: Luke, in black suit and navy tie, walking towards our table. Jesus. He looks amazing in that suit, his eyes as bright and wide as I've ever seen them. Did he see Ryan's obnoxious power play? Or did Ryan do it because he knew Luke was looking?

Luke shakes Dave's hand and kisses me on the cheek. I try to maintain my poker face, but it's a losing battle.

He's here to see me. He must be.

Ryan narrows his eyes. "I didn't think you were coming."

"And miss meeting David Taggart? No chance in hell." He offers his hand to shake. "It's Luke Lawrence. We spoke on the phone."

They shake and Luke slides into the seat next to Dave and across from me. He turns back to Dave. "I'm afraid you're stuck next to me and not next to Ryan's date."

I expect Ryan to scowl, but he smiles. Another reminder I'm a pretty trophy wife-to-be.

Dave looks at me. "It's Alyssa, right?"

Wow. He remembers my name. More than I expected from him. I nod yes. It's Alyssa. Not the girl next to Ryan with the great tits.

"I swear I've seen you somewhere before."

"She's an actor," Luke says. "Rather accomplished for her age too."

I press my fingers together under the table. I'd rather not talk about myself, and I'm certain Ryan would rather keep the focus on whatever boring legal shit this meeting is about.

"What have I seen you in?" Dave asks.

"I was on the teen soap, *Together*. I was the cheerleader."

"That's it," Dave says. "My soon-to-be ex-wife watched *Together*. You were very—"

"Naked. For cable at least."

Dave lacks the words to explain this. He stammers. "You were great."

Ryan steps in. "Alyssa would rather not talk about her career. She's on an indefinite hiatus."

I bite my tongue. I shouldn't bring it up now or here, but I can't let Ryan win this one. "That's not exactly true."

"Sweetheart, we'll talk about this later."

"When you're working tomorrow?"

"In the evening."

"I need to answer by Monday. You can't keep putting this off."

"Alyssa." Ryan raises his voice, his brow furrowing in irritation.

He never raises his voice.

"For whatever it's worth," Luke says, "it would be a shame if you didn't return to acting. You're wonderful in everything."

"Thank you." I shrink back in my seat, trying to put on my happiest face.

Ryan smiles. A perfect poker face, as usual. "We should get back to business."

Luke's eyes stay on mine. It's like he's waiting for my approval. I nod. It's fine. I appreciate the concern, but I don't need another overprotective man in my life.

I retreat to silence as the men talk business. It's all so dreadfully boring, I only tune in when I hear Luke's name. I make sure to finish my plate of salmon, to limit myself to two glasses of tequila, to stay at the table long enough to prove my food is staying in my stomach. Whatever it takes to convince Ryan I can handle having a life again.

The conversation shifts. It's not work anymore. It's small talk. The weather, the Lakers, how Dave likes his fancy Beverly Hills mansion.

Under the table, Luke's leg brushes against mine. I look into his eyes. That must have been an accident. But he's staring at me like he wants to consume me, like he's thinking about all the things he could do to me back at his place.

Deep breath. I'm getting ahead of myself. That's a lot for a casual look and the not-so-accidental brush of a leg.

"So, Alyssa," Luke says. "You're from the East Coast, right?"

"Massachusetts."

"How do you like living in L.A.?"

"I like it, mostly. The weather is gorgeous. And there are tons of excellent independent coffee shops. But Marina Del Rey isn't the most..."

"It's safe," Ryan says. "And it's nice."

It's nice and boring. Pretty, but boring.

"A lot like our hometown," I say.

Ryan motions to me like he's showing off a car. "We're high school sweethearts."

"Not exactly."

"What would you call it, sweetheart?" he asks. It sounds friendly, but there's a tenseness to it. A demand I answer the way he wants me to.

Honestly, I'd call it bullshit. We never even kissed back in high school. It was strictly platonic. But, fine, if he wants to sell us as high school sweethearts, we're high school sweethearts. Whatever Dave wants to hear.

I bat my eyelashes. "I never thought I had a chance with you. You were so popular, and so handsome. And a senior when I was a lowly freshman. All the girls in school wanted you."

Ryan's hazel eyes bore into me. So I've gone too far, played it up too much.

"It's true," I say. "There were so many rumors about Ryan. I'm sure he'd blush if he heard them."

"Do tell," Dave says.

"Well, one in particular was that Ryan was incredibly..."

"Alyssa, enough." Ryan frowns.

"That he had a massive cock."

Ryan's jaw drops, but only for a second. Then he's back to his poker face. He doesn't know whether to bask in the glory of his hypothetically massive cock or whether to politely tell me to shut the fuck up.

For the record, he's not massive. Not small, but certainly not massive.

He smiles. So he's basking in the glory.

Luke's eyes find mine. "Did you start acting back in high school?"

I nod. "That's where I fell in love."

"What was it specifically?"

"*The Crucible*, of course. A very uplifting play."

Luke's lips curl into a smile. His face lights up. I can't help but smile back.

"I was Abigail. I got to seduce John Proctor. It doesn't work quite as well when everyone is sixteen," I say. Ryan checks the time on his cell phone. "We should probably get going."

"Yes, you can have that conversation you keep putting off," Luke says.

Ryan offers Luke his best *fuck you* smile, and then he turns to Dave. "Why don't I walk you out?"

Dave nods. He takes one last look at my cleavage, then follows Ryan to the door.

It's just me and Luke at this table.

He leans towards me, his eyes on mine. "So what is it that you and Ryan have to talk about?"

"You're really not familiar with the concept of minding your own business."

"I'm a divorce attorney. Other people's business is my business."

"It's a role I might take. No big deal."

"Like how getting engaged isn't a big deal."

I nod, shifting back into my seat. Suddenly, the restaurant feels small. It feels like Luke is pressed up against me.

Luke's gaze doesn't falter. He's still staring right at me. "Is that why you were almost crying when you ran out of the office?"

I squeeze the armrests of my chair. "Yes." Deep breath. I look at the ground. At Ryan and Dave in the restaurant lobby. "But I shouldn't talk about it."

"That's what friends are for."

"You already made your intentions clear."

He sets his hands on the table, leaning towards me. "I would like to be your friend. If that's what you want."

"Ryan will get jealous if he sees us talking."

"I don't care."

"Yeah, but I do. I'm the one who has to deal with him."

Finally, Luke pulls his hands back to his lap. He leans back into his chair. "Hell, he works so many hours. I'm sure I see him more than you do."

"I don't expect you to understand, but I need him on my side."

"Why?"

His big, brown eyes are on mine. It's not harsh. It might even be sweet. But there's still something about it, something that demands a reaction.

I look to the restaurant lobby. Ryan is still talking with Dave. Smoothing all this over. Reminding him that he too could have a beautiful girlfriend with great tits. If only he'd go through with his divorce.

I take a deep breath. Now isn't the time. I don't have the energy. "Because I wouldn't survive without him."

"How do you know?"

"I know you think you're being helpful, but I don't need another man in my life who thinks he knows what's best for me."

I collect my purse and stand.

"I'm sorry. I don't mean to—"

"Yes, you do. You're no different than Ryan. You're just as happy to speak for me." I dig my fingers into the leather handle of my purse. "I'm not an idiot. I know he uses me as eye candy. I know he's a workaholic asshole. But I still get something out of this relationship."

"Enough to quit acting for him?"

My breath catches in the back of my throat. He might not realize what a cheap shot that is.

I take a step towards the lobby. "That's none of your business."

Luke follows me to the lobby. I suppose it's the only place to go. He also has to fetch his car.

Ryan goes through a formal good-bye with Dave. Then he turns to me and Luke. His brow is furrowed again, and he makes no effort to keep his voice down. "I don't know what you two are doing, if you're conspiring to make me look like a fool, but I'd appreciate it if neither of you would undermine me."

"Ryan, I'm only trying to talk to you," I say.

"This isn't the place."

"It never is."

He squeezes my wrist. "It's still not the place."

Luke shakes his head. He narrows his eyes at Ryan. "How you treat your girlfriend like this? You're acting like a possessive asshole."

Ryan shakes his head. He lets out a tiny laugh. "I wouldn't expect you to understand. Not after what happened with—"

"Keep her out of this."

"Then mind your own business." Ryan squeezes my wrist a little tighter. "Come on, sweetheart. We have a lot to talk about."

I follow him to the car, bracing for the worst.

We ride back to the apartment in silence. Ryan grips the steering wheel so tightly his knuckles turn white. He is mad. I can't stand when he's mad.

The walk to the apartment is silent. In the elevator, he shifts his weight between his legs. He watches our reflection in the mirrored walls. He is perfect in his suit, calm and composed. I'm a sweaty, heaving mess, dress stuck to my skin, makeup running.

The doors open, and he grabs my wrist again, practically dragging me down the hall. I'm in that same uncomfortable pair of heels, and I still can't walk for shit in them.

Ryan slips his key into the door and turns the lock. Fuck. We are almost inside and he looks like he's about to explode.

I try to stay in the hallway. "I'm sorry. I didn't mean to derail your meeting." I hate myself for how whiny and pathetic my voice sounds.

He stands there, in the doorway, like he could wait for me to enter the apartment forever. After a long breath, I do, and he slams the door behind me.

"How could you air our business in public?"

"You won't talk about it."

"Because you refuse to listen to reason." He takes a step towards the kitchen. "Do you even remember how bad things were this time last year?"

"I was there. I was the one miserable because of how much I hated myself."

"You were one bad purge away from dying of dehydration. Dying."

"I'm aware."

"You had no control over yourself. You begged me to do something to help you. You cried in my arms all night."

"Yeah, and when is the last time you offered to hold me all night? That you were willing to listen to me cry without telling me what to do?" I ask.

"Alyssa! You aren't listening. You almost died, and it was all because of the pressure of your acting career." He looks at me with sympathy. Or maybe pity. "You're not strong enough for that life."

"Fuck you."

"I know you're angry now, but you'll realize I'm right."

"You can't make me turn down the role."

His hazel eyes bore into me. He's sure he can make me. "You have a choice. You can live here with me or you can take the role."

"We're engaged, Ryan. We're supposed to be fucking partners!"

"And it's my job to look out for you."

"But..." I take a deep breath. What he's saying makes so much sense. I did almost die. I was miserable. Maybe he's right, and I'm not strong enough. Maybe he's right, and it's better to live this dull life of waiting. At least I'm alive.

"Sweetheart, you don't need to worry about your career. I'm always going to take care of you."

"But..." I try to look into Ryan's eyes, but his gaze is too strong. Too demanding. "I need this. I can't keep waiting around the house all day."

"No."

"Ryan!"

"I said no. I'm not changing my mind." His voice is strong, completely unwavering. "I'm not going to watch you spiral out of control again."

"You didn't watch the first time," I say.

"But I was the one who picked up the pieces. I was the one who made sure you ate your required meals, and went to weigh-ins, and saw your shrink twice a week. I was the one who kept you from yourself."

I press my back against the door, digging my fingers into my purse. "No. I was the one who pulled myself together. I was the one in therapy. I was the one eating those disgusting meals and pushing aside thoughts of how revolting and fat I felt. I was the one who gave up the only control I had in my life."

"I said no."

I look at the floor. "Don't you want me to be happy?"

"I'd rather you be miserable and alive," he says.

"Why should I bother trying so hard if I'm going to be trapped in the apartment?"

"Doesn't our life together mean something to you?" There's accusation in his voice.

I am ungrateful for the life he's given me. I am ungrateful for his love. I am ungrateful for his protection.

"What life together? I sit at home all day. You go to work. You get home. You talk about work. Why don't you go back to work if you adore it so much?"

"We're talking."

"No, you're talking. And I'm done listening. I'm done hearing that I can't handle my own fucking life."

"Because you can't, sweetheart. The whole time I've known you, you've never been able to handle your own life."

"Fuck you."

Ryan shakes his head. "Control yourself."

"Why? It sounds like that's your job."

He holds my glare, but it's clear he's not going to waver. It's clear there's no reasoning with Ryan.

He's made up his mind. I can do what he says or I can walk.

"You're such a fucking asshole."

"Because that's what you need me to be."

I shake my head. "Fuck you." A tear wells up in my eye, but I blink it away.

I turn around, open the door, and storm to the elevator. It comes so slowly, and it moves so slowly, but still, I wait until I am locked in the bathroom in the lobby to let that tear roll down my cheek.

I can't let Ryan see this. I can't let him know much this hurts me.

CHAPTER TWELVE

I half expect Ryan to follow me. I half expect him to come downstairs, to apologize, to beg for my forgiveness. But he doesn't. I should know better. He's never once admitted he was wrong. No, whenever I get emotional, he fails at calming me down, and he gets so frustrated by his failure—Ryan Knight could never fail at anything—that he offers me a dose of Ativan.

I'm not doing this again. I am not going to slink back to Ryan and apologize for standing up for myself. So what if he's looking out for my health? It's my health. It should be my decision.

It is my decision. I can take the part, but I'll have to face the consequences. Ryan will be angry. He might even go through with his threat to break up with me and kick me out of the apartment.

Fuck. Will I really be able to handle my health without Ryan? He was there. He did make sure I went to therapy and weigh-ins and that I ate all my required meals, no more, no less.

I bite my fingernails and check my phone, praying for an apology from Ryan. It's hopeless, but there might me something. "Please come back to the apartment" at the very least.

Instead, there's a message from Luke. At least, the contact is clearly labeled "Luke Lawrence." I vaguely remember something about Ryan programming his work numbers into my phone. Just in case.

"Are you okay?"

I take a deep breath. No. Not even close. But I can't say that, not exactly.

"I've been better," I reply.

Ding. "Do you need someone to talk to?"

There's no way he's after talking.

"Why? Do you know someone worth talking to?" I reply.

Ding. "This one guy. He can be an asshole, but he's good-looking."

I shouldn't be smiling over this. Luke may be funny and direct, but he's as arrogant as Ryan is.

He's reaching out to me. It's not an apology, but it's something.

"I have a no asshole policy," I reply.

Ding. "I can convince him to play nice. Maybe even to apologize for his acting like such an asshole."

"I'll consider it," I reply.

Ding. "If you ask nicely, he'll take off his shirt so you can gape at his abs again."

So I was obvious.

"Just talking?" I reply.

There's nothing for a minute, then he responds. "If that's what you want."

Ding. "The north tower, on the eleventh floor. Room 1113."

Does he really think I'll give it up in his apartment? No, Luke doesn't twist things like that. He's not a nice guy, not exactly, but he's straightforward. What was it he said? When he wants to fuck me, he'll ask nicely.

The elevator ride feels like an eternity. I check my reflection in the mirrored ceilings. I'm still a mess, but it hardly makes a difference at this point.

Deep breath. I walk to his apartment. There it is, the door marked 1113. I can't bring myself to knock. Not yet.

We're only going to talk, but...

I knock lightly and the door opens. Luke is standing there, leaning against the doorframe. He's wearing jeans and a V-neck and it's draped off his shoulders so fucking perfectly.

He grabs my wrists, gently, and whisks me inside. "I was hoping you'd come."

He shuts the door and presses me against it. But he doesn't kiss me. He doesn't even touch me. His body hovers over mine, a few inches of air between us. Not that I care.

"Are you okay?"

"I'm breathing," I say.

"That's a start." He moves a little closer. "I take it Ryan didn't apologize."

"You know him as well as I do."

He nods. "Yes, but I didn't agree to marry him."

Great. Another asshole doubting my judgment.

I clench my teeth. "You should watch what you say. You might offend someone by insulting her judgment."

He steps back, a smile on his face. "I'm sorry, but I can't bullshit a girl who uses such good grammar, even when she's mad at me."

He moves to the kitchen, opens a bottle of tequila, and pours two glasses. I look around the apartment. It's a little smaller than Ryan's. A one-bedroom probably. There's a long couch, a TV, a desk littered with papers and legal pads, enormous windows that let in the dark blue light of the ocean and the sky.

Luke cuts a lime into quarters and slides one between his soft lips. Goddammit, I can't drag my eyes away from those lips.

He smiles when he catches my gaze. Smug bastard.

"Can I ask you a personal question?" he asks, his dark eyes burning with intensity.

Please let it be something about kissing me or touching me or fucking me.

Jesus, I'm in over my head. Is it even possible I'll leave this apartment without fucking him?

It takes all my self-control, but I manage to maintain my composure. "I'm sure I can't stop you."

He hands me a drink, his fingers brushing against mine. "You'd think I'd be more grateful to have you in my apartment. Especially when that dress does such a great job driving me out of my fucking mind." His voice is soft and steady, sweet even. "But I have to know. You seem like such a smart woman. So confident and full of ideas." His eyes bore into mine. "You don't seem like someone who would let her boyfriend control her."

I am suddenly incredibly aware of how easy it would be to slide these straps off my shoulders. I am suddenly interested in nothing else but how Luke's fingertips would feel on my skin.

Deep breath. He's waiting for a response. I have to respond.

"That isn't a question," I say.

"Why do you let Ryan control you? Does he really make you happy?"

"There's more to life than being happy."

"Really? You'll have to illuminate me then."

I press my nails into my thumb. Do we really need to get into this?

"If you read the gossip blogs, you already know." I look into his eyes. At this point, I might as well tell him. It's not like it matters what he thinks of me.

"I have a hard time believing you need a controlling asshole for a boyfriend because you had a problem with disordered eating."

He makes it sound so quaint, so in the past. Like I had a problem and I got over it and now I'm fixed. I'm normal.

"It's not a problem with disordered eating," I say. "It's a fucking mental illness." I press my nails into my thumb. "If Ryan hadn't stepped in, if he hadn't convinced me to go to treatment... I probably wouldn't be here right now."

"Do you want to talk about it?" he asks.

"No."

He takes a step towards me, until he's close enough to touch. "Geez, Alyssa, I'm sorry. I didn't mean to get you riled up. It's just... I like you. I don't want to see you fade away under Ryan's control."

He could kiss me or touch me. But he doesn't.

"I need him," I say.

"How do you know?"

I bite my lip. "Because I got myself into this mess."

"The mess where you're engaged to a man you dislike or the mess where you're in my apartment, in that criminally sexy dress, ready to cheat on your fiancé?"

Well, I have to give him points for confidence.

I take a tiny step back. "I meant what I said at dinner. I don't need another asshole telling me what's best for me."

He nods. "I swear I didn't invite you here to antagonize you."

"Likely story."

"I'll make it up to you. I promise." He moves closer, his fingertips hovering over my skin.

God, I hope he means what I think he means.

"And how will you do that?"

"However you want."

I move a little closer to him. His eyes bore into mine, reading them for some kind of reaction. Then his hands make contact with my skin and my body surges with electricity.

"Listen, Alyssa, I can respect if you didn't come here to talk."

Now we're getting somewhere.

"And if this is some kind of 'fuck you' to Ryan, I get that. He deserves it and, quite frankly, if you're going to fuck someone to get revenge on your boyfriend... I'll make sure it's worth it. I'll make sure you have something you can remember for a long time."

He isn't reserved any longer. He turns towards me, his hand pressing against my bare back.

A heat spreads through my body, and I'm not sure if I can fight this desire any longer. It would feel so good to let his hands keep moving. It would feel so good to touch him and kiss him and fuck him. It might even be worth it.

"I like you, and I'd rather be something more than a revenge fuck." He runs his fingertips up and down my back. "But, well, you look so fucking sexy in that dress, and I am dying to make you come."

Jesus Christ.

Luke looks at me. "Now, if I completely misread the situation, and you're here to talk, then I'll shut up and listen."

His palm presses flat onto my back, pushing my body towards his.

"But?" I ask.

"But I'd much prefer to fuck you."

I gulp.

"I said I'd ask nicely. So, Alyssa, can I make you come or should we arrange for alternate entertainment?"

CHAPTER THIRTEEN

"I don't know," I say, "can you?"

He smiles. "Miss Summers, may I make you come?"

"You may."

And, like he can barely control himself, he pulls me onto his lap and presses his lips into mine. All the tension in my body releases, and I melt into him.

I straddle him, the fabric of his jeans rubbing against my thighs. He feels so good under me, so good touching me. Can I really do this? Can I really cheat on Ryan? Will I even be able to look myself in the eye tomorrow?

But I don't care how I'll feel tomorrow. My brain doesn't understand the concept of tomorrow. My brain is quickly passing the reins to my body, and my body does not know or want anything except Luke. I need him to touch me, and kiss me, and fuck me. I've never needed anything more than I need Luke inside me.

But if I'm going to do this, I'm going to relish it.

Luke sucks on my upper lip, gently at first, then harder and harder. Our lips part and his tongue slips inside my mouth, swirling around mine. My body surges with electricity again. Every inch of me wants every inch of him, and it wants it now.

I pull his shirt over his head and press my fingers into his hard muscles. God, his body feels as amazing as it looks. His back and chest are so strong, and when I slide my fingertips across them, he groans and bites my neck. His hands find my ass, pushing my crotch into his. He's hard.

He slides his hands around the curves of my hips and waist, then along the neckline of my dress. He traces my neckline with his fingers, down and up and down and up again. His touch is so light I can barely feel it. Then, his fingers inch forward, onto my skin, and he follows the pattern of the neckline. Down and up and down and up again. Jesus. I squeeze my thighs around him, but he doesn't change his pace.

Finally, when I think I will explode if he doesn't touch me properly, he pushes the fabric of my dress out of the way. He takes a long look, his hands on my hips, his hard cock straining against his jeans.

"God, you're beautiful," he says, and he strokes my breasts, his thumbs rubbing against my nipples. Pangs of pleasure shoot through my body, my sex screaming with desire. I'm already so achy. I'm already so ready. I press my mouth onto his, sucking hard on his lips. I grab his hand and bring it between my legs.

"Such impatience," he smiles. His fingertips brush against my thighs, his touch getting lighter the closer he gets to my sex. Then, he brushes his hand against my panties. I groan.

"Fuck me," I command, my voice weak and needy.

"We aren't even close to ready for that," he says. He pushes me onto my back and slides my dress to my feet. Then he kisses me, hard, his fingertips flirting with the edge of my panties. God, I want those hands on my skin, under my panties, inside me.

But Luke has other ideas. He presses his lips against my neck. A soft kiss. Then harder. His lips press into my shoulder. Harder. His lips press into my collarbone. Harder. His lips close around my nipple. Jesus. I groan and arch my body into his, my hands digging into his hair.

I feel his tongue, soft and wet, swirling around my nipple. Then his teeth. He bites gently at first. Then harder and harder, until I feel an equal mix of pain and pleasure. I dig my nails into his shoulders, but it only encourages his tease. He moves to my other nipple and sucks on it, the pressure of his mouth flooding my body with desire.

He slides his fingers up my thighs again. But this time, he strokes over my panties, pressing the smooth fabric into my sex. I am already wet for him. I am already desperate for him. But he is making me wait. He is cruel. He is evil. He is perfect.

He presses my panties into my clit and strokes softly. More. I need more. *Come on, give me more.* His fingers slip inside my panties, and, finally, I feel them against my bare skin.

"God, you're so wet," he says.

"Don't make me beg."

"Do you want me to stop?" he asks. He looks up at me, his big, brown eyes lit up with desire.

"I want you to fuck me."

"Soon," he says. He pins me to the couch and his lips trail down my body, kissing and sucking and nibbling. He lifts my ass, pulling my panties to my knees then off my feet. He pushes my legs apart, pinning my knees to the couch.

He nibbles on my thigh. Jesus. I need those lips on me. I need that tongue on me. He nibbles again, a little higher this time. Then higher. And higher. Until he's nearly there.

Then his tongue slides over my clit and my body screams with pleasure. I never want him to stop, but I want to fuck him now. He presses his lips around my clit, sucking gently. I feel his tongue, soft and warm, against my clit. I open my mouth to say something. *Stop, fuck me now, I can't wait anymore.* But, instead, I moan and tug on his hair. His eyes, those goddamn brown eyes, fiery and intense, lock with mine and he smiles. Then he's back to his task, lavishing my sex with attention. I'm so wet, and so close, and I do nothing but inhale the sensations—the pressure in my sex, the soft, wet feel of his tongue.

I moan and shudder and press my thighs into his chest. He pins my knees to the couch again. I feel his tongue, sliding around the edges of my sex, sucking on my lips. I feel his fingertips sliding up and down my thighs as his tongue makes its way around me, back to my clit, shooting pleasure through my body. The tension inside me builds, harder and deeper as I get closer and closer with every lap of his tongue. I start to shake. I am so close to the edge.

And then he pulls back, and I am certain I am going to collapse. I reach for him, my nails scratching his back, and then I feel his tongue on me.

The tension inside me builds to a crescendo. It is so hard and deep it almost hurts, and it builds and builds and builds, a little more, and then a little more, and then even more. And, finally, I can't hold off any longer, and I come, releasing everything, my entire body flooding with waves and waves of pleasure. I moan his name. Luke. And I relish the feel of it on my tongue. Luke. I could get used to saying that, to screaming that, to feeling like this.

My body relaxes as I come down. Jesus Christ. He wasn't kidding about making it worth my while.

He pulls me close, wrapping his arms around me. I sink into his body, my legs wrapping around his. He holds me as I catch my breath.

And when I finally find my breath, I kiss his lips and ears and neck. He groans, and I slide my hand down his stomach, reveling in the feeling of his hard muscles. I get to his jeans, and I unzip them, and slide my hand inside, feeling his hard cock against his boxers.

"Let me get something," he whispers. He shifts to his feet, and moves to the bathroom.

I could leave, put an end to this before it goes any further, but there's no way my body would allow it. I need him inside of me.

He returns from the bathroom, condom in hand. "You okay?" he asks.

"It's been a while."

"If you need a minute—"

"No, no, no," I say. "No more waiting. I want you inside of me now."

A groan escapes his lips. "Say that again."

"I want you inside of me."

He moves faster, shimmying out of his jeans and boxers. I finally get a look at all of him. Jesus. He's big. He sits up straight on the couch and pulls me towards him. I take the condom from his hands, unwrap it, and slide it over his cock.

I straddle him, my legs around his thighs, my crotch hovering over his.

I lower myself until I feel his cock against my sex. Jesus Christ. I abandon any thoughts of teasing him. I need him inside me now. I grab him and slide him inside me.

His eyes go wide as I take him in. He groans and presses his lips against mine, kissing me hard. God, he feels amazing inside me, but I want more. I want to make him come.

I bring my hands to his shoulders, using them for leverage as I move up and down. I start slowly, sliding my sex over his entire length, then back to his tip, just to feel him enter me again. He groans and digs his fingers into my skin, but I keep my pace. Up and down and up and down again and again.

He holds me, kissing my neck, and grabs my hips, pulling me towards him. I rock, riding him, my clit pressing against his pelvis, his cock further inside me with every thrust. Jesus. I groan. And I lose myself in the movements, my body flooding with pleasure.

He shudders. He's close. I can feel it.

"Jesus, Alyssa," he groans. He grabs my hips and pushes my body into his.

We are still, his cock filling my sex, and he kisses me, his lips sucking on my lips, his teeth scraping against them gently. He lifts me off him, bringing my chest to his mouth, and he sucks on my nipples until I scream his name again.

He wraps his arms around my back, lifts me off the couch, and lays me on the floor. I spread my legs as he lowers his body onto mine, his chest against mine, his arms at my sides. I gasp as he enters me again. He rocks his body into mine, thrusting deeper and deeper inside me.

I grab his ass and rock my hips towards him, pushing him deeper, savoring the feel of his cock inside me. I moan, "Harder," and he squeezes me tighter, thrusting into me again, and again, and again. I match my movements to his, my hips rocking to meet him, to push him deeper inside me, to hold it inside me for longer.

The tension builds, again, and it hits me quickly this time. I clench my sex as I get closer and closer to coming. My movements grow frenzied. I rock my pelvis into his. Harder. Faster. Luke matches my movements, his cock slamming into me. I squeeze my nails into his back. Almost. So close. I feel all his skin on mine, his chest on my chest, his arms around mine.

I squeeze my thighs around his back, bringing our bodies together, pushing him deeper inside me. And there it is. All the tension releases and I come, my nails digging so hard into his back I swear I feel blood. The pleasure is more intense this time, and I feel like it will never stop.

The look in Luke's eyes is magic. Some kind of lust and need I've never seen before. He groans and shudders and I breathe into his ear, "I want to see you come."

His teeth find my neck and he bites hard, so hard I am sure he will leave a mark, but I can't bring myself to care. He holds me tightly as he launches into a final thrust, hard and fast. He groans, "Jesus Christ," and he comes.

He stays on top of me for a moment, his arms around me, his breath on my neck. Then he shifts, moving away to discard the used condom.

Slowly, I become aware of my surroundings.

I am in Luke's apartment. It is dark outside. It is getting late. I can't stay here forever.

He collapses next to me, pulling my body into his. I slide my head into the crook of his neck and he kisses my cheek.

Finally, I snap all the way back to life. "Should we talk?" I ask.

"Yes, but it's late and I don't want to get you in trouble," he says. "Now, come on. Let's destroy the evidence."

He leads me into the shower, and we spend a long time in the steamy stall, lips locked, hands roaming each other's bodies.

CHAPTER FOURTEEN

I cross my fingers as I unlock the door. It's late. Maybe Ryan went to sleep.

Shit. The apartment is dark except for a light from his laptop screen. He's awake, but he's working. Maybe he doesn't realize—

The laptop clicks shut and Ryan moves towards me in the dark. "Where were you?" he asks.

"I went for a walk."

"It's one a.m."

"I lost track of time." I move towards the bedroom like everything is normal.

Ryan stops me. He grabs my wrists, looking at me like I'm a child. "You didn't pick up your phone."

"I didn't want to talk to you."

He stares at me for a moment, then releases my wrists, stepping back. "I really don't want to fight with you."

He rubs my arms, more softly than I expected.

"Me either."

His eyes find mine. It's sweeter this time, like he really does care how I feel. "I thought about it, and you were right. If you don't start working on your career, you'll have nothing to focus your attention on besides counting calories."

I feel sick. If Ryan understands, if he's about to apologize and tell me I should take the part... then what the hell did I just do?

He takes my hand. "I called Corine for you. I told her you'll take the part."

"Why would you do that?"

"Isn't that what you want?"

"Yes, but it's my decision." I move towards the bedroom. He's giving me what I want, but only because he's decided it's what's best for me.

"What difference does it make?"

I shrug like it doesn't matter. However we got here, I got what I wanted. I'll be an actress again and I'll have my life back.

Then maybe things between me and Ryan will go back to normal. He'll be sweet. He'll hang out with me on the weekends. He'll listen to what I want.

I check my phone. I've got half a dozen calls and three messages from Corine. I go to call her back but Ryan stops me.

"It's one a.m.," he says.

Right. I need to calm down. I can call tomorrow, first thing. I can get my life back on track. My life with Ryan. With no place for illicit affairs. With no place for Luke.

Corine makes use of my lonely Sunday—Ryan goes into work, as usual—by scheduling a meeting with Laurie House, the head writer and producer of *Model Citizen*.

I spend the morning poring over the script. It's better than the two-page scene I used to audition. It's funny and smart, and Marie Jane is more nuanced than the slutty cheerleader on *Together*. She lusts after alcohol. She lusts after fame. She lusts after the hot seventeen-year-old Catholic boy across the street.

I'm nervous on the drive to the café. I squeeze my steering wheel until my knuckles turn white. I circle the nearby streets half a dozen times despite passing three decent parking spots. Parking in Santa Monica is impossible. I need to take one of the spaces before they fill up. I need to calm down.

I take a deep breath and hold it as long as I can. This is supposed to relax me. Slow inhale. Slow exhale. Release the tension from every part of my body.

On my next trip around the block, I pull into one of the parking spots. I can do this. I can't fuck it up any worse than I fucked up my personal life.

Maybe I can pretend last night never happened. Like I don't want to go straight back to Luke's apartment and spend the rest of the day in his bed.

I get out of the car and walk to the café. It's bright, the middle of the afternoon. I still haven't had lunch. If Ryan were here, he'd lecture me on responsibility. I must eat lunch by 1 p.m. I must not skip meals. I must adhere to the rules, whatever they are.

The café is tucked away. It's part of a small string of stores along Montana, an expensive wannabe Main Street in the middle of residential Santa Monica.

I order a latte, with almond milk of course, and a small salad. I should eat lunch. Anything to make this all feel more normal.

My Kindle is at home, but the time passes quickly. Last night was so... I try not to think about Luke's naked body on top of mine, but my brain doesn't want to cooperate. I try not to think that last night must have been the best sex I've ever had, at least a hundred times better than any roll in the hay with Ryan...

"Alyssa, right?"

Laurie is standing in front of me, her arm extended for a handshake. She's taller than I figured. She's wearing the same bright red glasses, but today, her eyes are lined in metallic purple. Her hair is pulled into a high bun, and she's dressed exactly like I expect from a writer—hoodie, sneakers, jeans.

I nod. "Yeah. Laurie, right?" Everyone in Hollywood is on a first-name basis.

"Gosh, you're so pretty in person." She takes a seat at my table.

"You don't have to say that."

"Well, your agent sent over your package. Scenes from that show you were on—"

"*Together.*"

"What a piece of shit. No offense. It's not like I haven't written on shit shows." She laughs and takes a long sip of her drink. An iced coffee of some kind.

"It was a little... It was shit," I say.

"But you were great on it. Way better than the writing deserved." She shifts, resting her head on her hand. "The point I was going to make is that they put you in so much makeup. You looked like a totally different person. Not bad, just—"

"Like a slutty cheerleader?"

"Exactly. We'll probably do the same thing. Tons of makeup and a platinum wig. Get that superficial party girl thing going."

I nod. This is all so familiar but so strange at the same time. A week ago, I wouldn't have guessed I'd be having a work lunch. That I'd be poised to star in a cable sitcom.

I take a long sip of my latte. It's warm, creamy, sweet from the excess of honey I stirred into it. It tastes like every other latte I've had. It's normal.

"The pilot is great," I say.

"Oh, thanks. I think so." She adjusts her glasses. "The network loves it, which is just bizarre for me. I expected to fight them every step of the way. I mean, at my last staff job, I was working on this stupid family sitcom. I was constantly getting into fights with the head writer because he didn't believe women like sex."

"He's probably just terrible in bed."

"Yeah, I bet. He was so ugly too." She shakes her head and sticks her tongue out. "I can't believe the support we're getting for a show about such a totally slutty bitch. It's amazing."

"Amazing."

"I'm sure you're sick of reading scripts where you're either the supportive girlfriend or the evil temptress."

I haven't been reading scripts for a while, but they did tend to fall along those lines. I could either be the boring, sweet girlfriend or the heinous bitch of an ex-girlfriend.

I nod. "Sometimes the role is for the wife, but she dies tragically to motivate the male protagonist."

Laurie laughs. "Tell me about it." She takes a long sip of her drink. So long she finishes a third of it. "So, this brings me to the awkward point of our original star quitting."

"Pretty awkward."

"It wasn't professional. It was personal. She had, um... a health problem."

"Rehab?"

Laurie nods. "And I'm not bitter at all. I'm glad she's getting help, even if it's court-ordered help. But, we do need someone who is going to pick up the slack fast. We have to reshoot the pilot and you'll have to jump right in. Minimal rehearsal time. The rest of the cast has already done it once. They've had a lot of time to prepare."

"Okay."

"We need someone who can bring it."

"So you're totally desperate."

She laughs. "Yeah, but you would have made my top three if you auditioned before we picked our previous Marie Jane. You deserve it."

"Right."

She sets her drink down and looks me square in the eyes. "I'm not going to take that attitude."

I bite my tongue.

"You know, my first job was a diversity hire. I'm sure you noticed that I'm a black woman. It's a whole thing. But I only got the job to fill a quota."

"Yeah?"

"Yeah, and who the fuck cares? My writing was great, better than anyone else's, and I killed it. Then, I killed the next job, and the one after, and eventually I got here." She adjusts her glasses and makes eye contact. "So who cares if I got a lucky break to start? I still earned everything I got. And you're going to do the same thing."

"No pressure."

She nods and lets out a tiny laugh. "Exactly. I need you to be amazing yesterday, but no pressure."

Cause I'm totally cool with pressure. It doesn't crush me into a million little pieces.

"I'll be honest, Alyssa. I get a good feeling from you. You seem like someone who isn't going to bullshit me. Someone who shows up off book and on time. That's ninety percent of what matters."

"That, I can promise."

"Good. I'm not going to bullshit you. A lot of people in this town will. Not that I have to tell you. People pretend they love you, praise your abilities, then never call you again."

I nod. I used to deal with that kind of thing, when I went on more auditions and met with more producers for possible roles. "A bunch of phony assholes."

"Yeah, like I need someone to pat me on the back. I'm sure you don't give a fuck if I liked you in *Mahogany*... Which was how I so rudely ended your audition, wasn't it?"

"I forgive you. You did give me the job."

"Right. That's all that matters. You don't want my praise. You want your paycheck."

God, it feels like it's been a million years since I've had a paycheck, since I've even had the chance to think about money.

I take a long sip. The caffeine is hitting my brain, waking me up to a pleasant state of alertness. This, talking about acting, is something I can do. It's terrifying, but I can do it.

"I don't mind a little praise," I say.

She bursts into laughter. "I promise to deliver." She shakes her empty cup. "The pace for this is fast. You'll do a chemistry read next week. Then we'll make everything official with a contract.

But you're definitely getting the job. We go into production in a week and a half. There's no time to find another star."

"Lucky me."

"No, none of that I-don't-deserve-it bullshit. I need you confident. I need you to walk in the room, flash that winning smile, and make everyone else believe you deserve it. Can you do that?"

"Of course," I say. Easy. No problem. Totally.

"Trust me. I don't care what the suits thought, you were my first choice. You killed it in your audition, and you're totally Marie Jane."

"Is that a compliment or an insult?"

"What do you think of her?" Laurie asks.

"She is a slutty bitch, but there's more to it than that. She's desperate for any kind of escape. Anything or anyone that can preoccupy her mind for fifteen minutes."

"That sounds good. I'm using that if I have to pitch it again."

I nod. This is happening quickly, and it's good, but I need to feel in control. Like I know what I'm doing. "Enough talk. How about we read some lines?"

She nods, hell yeah, and pulls out a paper copy of the script. Laurie loves it. Laughs at all the jokes. She even makes excuses for laughing at jokes she wrote.

We hug goodbye—she's a hugger—and she sends me off with an auspicious warning. "There's a lot riding on you. You are going to be the heart and soul of this show. It lives and dies by your performance. Get all your life shit out of the way now. I need you at your peak for this."

No pressure.

I return to my car and check my phone. Nothing.

Deep breath. I can do this show. I am an actor, a good actor, and I understand this character. I can play her well enough.

Maybe I need to talk to Ryan. I need to hear his steady voice, find the cold comfort in his arms around me.

But I don't call Ryan.
I call Luke.

CHAPTER FIFTEEN

"I didn't expect to hear from you today." Luke's voice flows through my speakers.

"I'm sorry," I say. "I should go. I don't know why I called."

"Maybe you like the sound of my voice."

I filter through sarcastic response after sarcastic response, but I can't bring myself to deflect the truth. I like almost everything about him.

"Are you okay?" he asks.

"I don't want to interrupt whatever it is you're doing."

"It's my pleasure."

"Can we meet somewhere and talk?" Please let him suggest we skip the talking and meet at his place. It would be the perfect distraction from all this pressure.

"I'm not sure how you want to handle this."

I swallow. He makes it sound so official, so adult, so much like we're sneaking around.

"Ryan is working."

"His loss."

I take a deep breath, and some of the tension in my chest eases. This is going to be a conversation and only a conversation.

"How about the bookstore on Maxella?" I ask.

"You sure? That's close to the office."

"Yeah, but Ryan wouldn't be caught dead in a bookstore."

Luke laughs, and I can practically see his eyes light up.

"I'll see you soon," he says and hangs up.

I feel my phone slip out of my hands, onto my lap. My palms are so sweaty and my heart is beating so quickly. I need to start the car, to pull out of this parking spot, to take the streets back to Marina Del Rey.

The bookstore is close to Luke's apartment building. But it's my apartment building too. It's not as if I suggested the location because it would be easy to slip in a quickie at Luke's place. I only want to talk.

Luke sits on the curb, reading his dog-eared paperback. He's wearing jeans and a T-shirt, and there's something so effortlessly sexy about it.

His eyes light up when he spots me. He slips his paperback into his pocket, pushes himself up, and greets me with his hug.

He's so close. His cheek is pressed against mine. His arms are on the small of my back. I can smell him, feel his breath on my neck.

My heart beats faster. There's something so intoxicating about him and it's drowning my judgment.

He releases me and leads me into the bookstore. "Are you okay?"

"It's nothing I can't handle on my own."

"Part of having friends means you don't have to handle things on your own."

"Is that what the kids are calling it?"

I expect him to laugh, but instead he looks at me, his coffee-colored eyes full of concern. His fingertips are on my forearms. My breath is so damn loud. And we're in a quiet store. It's not a place where I can touch him or kiss him or scream that I have no clue what I'm doing.

"I'm not saying we're going to be best friends, or that you'll decide to leave Ryan and we'll end up getting married. But I like you, and I'm going to be around if you need me."

I run my thumb over my ring finger. I'm not wearing my engagement ring. I took it off this morning. "I'm sorry. This isn't something I'm used to."

"Me either." He takes a step towards me, his hands sliding around my waist. "I'm not trying to fuck up your life. If you realized you're madly in love with Ryan, I'll get out of the way."

"I'm not."

"Good. I want to spend more time with you." His eyes find mine. "A lot more time."

"Naked or clothed?"

"Miss Summers, you have a very dirty mind."

"No, I..."

"Like seeing me naked?"

My cheeks flush. "I don't mind."

"Well, who wouldn't? I mean, look at me." He grins, and leans closer to me. "And I'm humble too."

He brushes his lips against mine. It's soft, and there's such a tenderness to it.

My head is swimming, but my body knows exactly what it wants. I pull him closer, sliding my hands around his back, over the waistband of his jeans.

Luke pulls back. He brings his mouth to my ear. "I've never been kicked out of a bookstore before, but I am willing to try."

I shake my head. "I'm not sure if I can do this. I barely know anything about you."

"What do you want to know?" he asks.

"What's your favorite book?"

"Guess."

"*To Kill a Mockingbird.*"

He laughs. "Perfect."

"What do you eat for breakfast?"

"Earl Grey tea. Usually cereal and a banana."

"Why Earl Grey?"

He slides his hand around my waist. "I have so much to teach you about tea."

His fingertips slide under my tank top. Damn. My body buzzes with electricity. This conversation is so silly when we could be getting horizontal.

I look up at Luke, into his big, brown eyes. "What were you like in high school?"

"Easy questions, huh?"

I nod.

He takes my hand and leads me down an aisle. "I was a normal teenager. Studied, went out with friends, spent my afternoons watching classic films with my mom on the couch."

"Normal?"

"It's very normal for fourteen-year-olds to watch French new wave with their mothers."

"Right."

He smiles, his attention on me. "My mom died when I was seventeen. I wouldn't talk to anyone. I just sat at home and worked through her movie collection. It was a bunch of art house stuff I didn't understand."

There's a weight on my chest. "Jesus, I'm sorry. What happened?"

"Car accident." There's a sadness in his eyes, but he pushes past it. "When my dad got tired of my attitude, he sent me to a fancy all boys private school. I rebelled by wearing eyeliner."

"What color?"

"My lips are sealed." He stops at the end of the aisle and turns to face me. "What about you? What's your favorite book. No, I'll guess." His eyes are glued to mine. "*Catcher in the Rye.*"

"You sure? It's not that depressing."

He laughs. "It's all about Holden Caulfield having a mental breakdown."

"But no one dies."

He scratches his chin like he's really thinking. "Okay, okay. How about *The Bell Jar.*"

"You think I'm crazy."

"Maybe a little." He moves closer. He's only a few inches away. Close enough to kiss. Then he lowers his voice. "I can't shake the sense I'm turning your life upside down."

"You are."

He brushes a hair from my face, his fingers sliding over my cheek. "I hope it needs it."

I nod. He leans into me. His lips press against mine. It's so much, so sweet and needy all at once. I can't bear to let go, to do anything besides kiss him.

He slides his fingers between mine, squeezing our palms together. It's such a simple, obvious display of affection. Everyone here probably thinks we're dating.

We wander around the aisles downstairs. I try to steer the conversation into neutral territory, but I can't think of much to say. My nerves over the show seem irrelevant now. I know how to act. I know where to go and what to do every day. I'm rusty, but I'll remember, and I'll get back into the swing of things.

I scour the classics table, trying get Luke interested in *Emma*, but he is unmoved. Not enough action, not enough feeling. *Pride and Prejudice* is better, he claims, taking delight when I am surprised he's read it.

He reads from a Sherlock Holmes novel, but it's too detached and impersonal.

We go through aisle after aisle, trying to find common ground. He's read a lot, but I've read more. I never went to college, but I didn't want to miss out on a proper English education. So I read two books a week for four years straight.

Up until I went into treatment.

Luke stops when we finish with the selection downstairs. "There's something I have to tell you," he says.

"Is it important?"

"Probably." His eyes lock with mine. His hands slide down my shoulders. "No, forget it. We can deal with that later. You have enough on your mind."

"I can decide how much I want on my mind."

"I'll tell you what. We can talk about it next week if you still want anything to do with me." He takes my hand and leads me up the stairs. "Now, tell me what happened with your acting job. You don't seem to have left Ryan yet, so he must have changed his mind."

"I would have taken the role even if Ryan asked me not to."

"I believe you."

"I would."

"I still believe you." We pass the children's section, heading for the never, ever popular non-fiction section in the back. It's quieter there, but it's not quite secluded enough for any funny business.

"Is that what's bothering you?" he asks.

"There's a lot riding on my shoulders. And, historically, I don't have a great track record for dealing with stress."

"That's not a life sentence."

"But Ryan... he's pretty much expecting me to fail. Any misstep, and it will be proof I couldn't handle it, that I'm not strong enough, all that bullshit."

Luke stops dead in his tracks. He turns to me, staring at me with a serious expression. "Fuck, Alyssa. Do you have any idea how messed up that is?"

"It's not like that."

"Yes, it is. He's rooting for you to fail. Is that the kind of behavior you want in a husband?"

"I'd rather not talk about Ryan."

"I don't want to talk about him either, but you really can't put up with that kind of stuff. You don't deserve it. My ex... Well, whatever I should call her, that whole thing is royally fucked up, but I was always, always happy for her, even when she was outshining me."

"Your ex-what?"

"A guy who really loves you is happy for you. I'm not saying I'm that guy, and I'm sure Ryan does have one or two good qualities that do something to make up for his God-awful personality... but if he doesn't support you, it doesn't matter how funny, or smart, or sweet, or rich—and mind you, these are just examples, Ryan isn't any of those things."

"He's smart."

"Okay, he's smart." Luke squeezes my hands. "But you deserve someone who supports you. Someone who cares about what you want. Someone who actually wants you to be happy."

"I get your point."

"Am I that much of a broken record?"

"A little," I say.

"And to think I came here to charm you." He runs his hand through his hair, his teeth sinking into his lower lip. "Are you as sick of talking about Ryan as I am?" he asks.

I nod.

"Good," he says, and motions to the marquee of a movie theater next door. "There's a show starting in five minutes."

"I've already seen that one."

"Me too."

Oh.

CHAPTER SIXTEEN

The glass doors do little to shut out the sun. With every step we take towards the door of our theater, the light grows more fluorescent.

Luke pulls an usher aside, whispers a few words in his ear and nods to me. He slips the usher a flattened bill. I suppose the poor usher only makes ten dollars an hour. Why not take a bribe?

I reach for Luke's hand reflexively and squeeze it tight. I need to calm down. It's three in the afternoon. No one is here. No one can see me.

He kisses my cheek. I release his hand and nod to the bathroom. The bathroom is perfect. Quiet. Bright. Fluorescent.

I catch my reflection in the mirror above the sinks. I used to stare at myself for hours, looking for fat to pinch, for excuses to proclaim myself disgusting. Today, I only glimpse. Something is different about me. Confidence or maybe recklessness.

My head is still swimming. I splash water on my face, but it does nothing to clear my head. I've already crossed the line. What does it matter if I do it again?

I splash my face with water again. I don't have to figure this out now. I can have another afternoon with Luke. I can enjoy this time without dwelling on its meaning.

I pat my face dry with a paper towel and straighten my skirt. I can do this. No, I need to do this.

The lobby is empty except for the usher and he flashes me a knowing look. No big deal. I pull the door—Theater 1—and step inside.

It's dark, but it's empty. Except for Luke, in the back row, spread out in a seat like he's waiting to be mounted.

Previews flash on-screen. Some romantic thriller, sappy and cheesy. Two pretty blonde teenagers, lean bodies, linen-and-blue skies.

I sit next to Luke. "I never took you for an exhibitionist."

"We can go back to my place if you want."

Luke takes my hand. It's shaking. I'm not usually such a nervous wreck.

I feel Luke's breath on my ear. "Or we could just watch the movie."

I open my mouth to agree. To ask Luke to go easy on me, to leave this cool, dark room and go someplace safe and bright, where his body will not be pressed against mine, where I will not be close enough to feel the heat of his breath.

But I can't do it.

"I'd think about it," I say. "But this movie wasn't very good."

Luke grins, that million-dollar smile of his. And his eyes, those fucking brown eyes, sparkle with electricity. No, lust, need, passion. Because of me. He is filled with lust because of me. Because he wants me. Because he needs me.

The lights dim as the last preview ends. We're watching some indie drama, quiet and subdued and easy to ignore. Luke laces his fingers with mine. Somehow, I'm sweaty and shivering at the same time.

I turn towards Luke and press my lips into his. And with every motion of his lips and tongue, my doubts are pushed further and further away. Every part of my body wakes up, and every part wants his touch.

But it's only his lips on my lips. I slip my tongue into his mouth and swirl it gently. He's responsive. He kisses me harder, dragging his fingertips up and down my arms and shoulders. The straps on my dressare so flimsy they fall off my shoulders with a single shrug.

I sneak my hand under his shirt and explore the muscles of his hard body. He shifts and groans as I touch him, his kiss getting harder and harder. Finally, he pushes my dress to my waist and cups my breasts over my bra. God, keep touching me. More. I need more.

And then Luke's fingers find their way inside my bra, and all conscious thought flees my body. I am not in a public movie theater. I am not Ryan's fiancée. I am not in the middle of stepping back into the spotlight. I am not anything but here, right now, with Luke. All I know is how much I want him, how much I need him to touch me and to touch him in return.

I arch my back and shift onto him, my back against his chest. His lips hover over my ear, the soft rush of his breath sending shivers through my body. His teeth scrape against my earlobe, gentle nibbles all the way down. I unzip my dress and push it past my feet.

His lips move to my neck. Hard kisses, then it's teeth. Soft at first. Then harder. And harder. Until it hurts just enough to feel amazing. I groan. "Fuck me."

"Not until I'm finished with you."

Hard to object when he puts it like that.

He pulls me close, my back flat against his chest, his hard cock pressed against my ass. He traces the outline of my bra, from my back to my front and back again, his fingers never slipping beneath it. Finally, he unhooks my bra and peels it off my skin. His hands slide over my sides, around my ribs, to my chest. He cups my breasts, rubbing his thumbs over my nipples in slow, easy circles.

He pulls his hands away from my breasts and returns with his fingertips. One at a time, each fingertip slides over me, around my nipples, softer and softer until I am shaking with desire. Then, his hand plants on my knee. It slides up my thigh, lighter and softer, until I can barely feel it. He brushes his hands against my inner thighs, getting closer to my sex, then retreating. Closer. Closer. Closer.

Finally, I grab his wrist, and press his hand over my panties. He grins and kisses me, so hard and deep I lose track of where I am. I moan. I dig my nails into his skin as he pulls my panties past my knees.

"Jesus, Alyssa," he says. "You're so sexy. It's driving me crazy."

"Then fuck me," I say, and I rub my ass against him.

His hands slide up my thighs, closer and closer, until his fingers slide over my clit. Jesus. I groan. I shake. I reach behind my back, rubbing his cock over his jeans. He groans and I know I've got him. I know he'll finally fuck me.

I lift my ass. He kisses my neck, pulling a condom from his pocket and sliding out of his jeans. Then, his teeth are on my ear, and his boxers are at his knees, and the condom is on.

I shift back onto his lap, my back pressed into his chest, my sex hovering over his cock. The tip strains against me, teasing me, sending waves of pleasure to my fingertips. I lower myself slowly, his cock slipping inside me until it fills me.

He touches me everywhere, stroking my breasts and stomach and thighs. His hands settle on my hips and he rocks me backwards and forwards. I arch my back to meet him, fuller with every motion of my hips. I feel his teeth on my neck, sinking hard as he groans.

I close my eyes, aware of nothing but the sensation of him inside me, rocking against me, filling me, sending pleasure through my body. I blink my eyes open, no idea what the images on the screen mean, and grab the seat in front of me. I need more of him. I need to be fuller. I use the seat for leverage, grinding into him, pushing him deeper.

My body shakes with need. Every second of his touch is pure electricity, and I get closer and closer, the tension inside me building. He glides his fingers over my nipples, his breath heavy in my ear. I have to bite my tongue to keep from screaming. It feels so fucking good. He feels so fucking good inside me.

I am so close to coming, and I can't stop myself from moaning. He whispers in my ear, "Don't stop yourself. I want to hear you come." He strokes my nipples, his touch even softer, every brush of his fingertips sending sparks shooting through my body. I do as I'm told, panting and groaning as he thrusts into me. His lips are on my ear, sucking and nibbling gently. Then they move to my neck, biting harder and harder.

Then his hands are on my hips, rocking me faster, and he is going harder and deeper. I shake. Almost there. I feel the tension inside me. More and more and more, until I can't take it anymore, and I come, my body shaking, my moan so loud I am sure someone hears us.

But Luke does nothing to quiet me. He pulls my body into his, kissing my neck, squeezing me tight. His fingers dig into my hips and he rocks me, up and down, faster and faster. He groans, a soft whisper in my ear.

"Fuck," he groans again. He digs his nails into my skin. He sinks his teeth into my neck. And he comes.

We don't bother to finish the movie.

CHAPTER SEVENTEEN

Ryan arrives home at seven on the dot. He's all smiles today, his shoulders thrown back, his eyes bright. It's almost like the Ryan I knew in high school, before he adopted a constant scowl.

He tosses a bag of takeout on the kitchen table and wraps his arms around me. There's a sweetness to it. Nothing like when we were younger, but enough.

"Dave wants me to represent him." He grins and presses his lips into my cheek.

And I almost thought he was happy to see me.

"I'm glad."

He sets up dinner. Plates, silverware, coasters for our drinks. "I know I've been working long hours, sweetheart, but the firm needs it."

I fight a sigh. There's no apology, no promise the long hours will cease, no offer to spend time with me. It's a statement of facts—Ryan is going to continue working every night and weekends. He's going to continue ignoring me.

But now isn't the time to discuss it. Not when my head is swimming with possibilities of Luke.

So I nod and offer my best demure fiancée smile. "It's fine." Deep breath. "I was busy all day with meetings for my show."

Ryan nods, but he doesn't say anything. There's nothing on his face. He's not excited for me, not happy, not even concerned.

If this is all that's left of our relationship, there's no reason to stay.

But I know the old Ryan is there somewhere. The one who drove an hour to the middle of nowhere, because my drunk mom ditched me at the mall and I had no way home. The guy who held me all night before I went into treatment. I was so scared, I couldn't stop crying, and he never lost patience. He just pressed his arms around me and told me I'd be okay. He'd make sure of it.

Even the guy who spent afternoons with me without ever making me feel like I was taking up his precious time.

There must be some way to bring him back, at least enough of him that we can make this work.

"How was it?" Ryan asks.

I offer my best everything-is-okay smile. "Good. The showrunner is a little weird, but she's nice."

"A lot of nice people suggested you should lose weight."

"Ryan, I have it under control."

He arranges the food. It's the same thing as always—grilled fish, steamed vegetables, brown rice.

"You had it under control before," he says.

"You're not helping."

He shakes his head. "I'm concerned."

"If they ask me to lose weight, I'll let you know. Okay?"

Apparently, this is okay, because he finishes setting up dinner and tosses the empty containers in the trash.

I take a seat, and try to think up something we can talk about besides Ryan being a poor imitation of his former self. Everything about him is different. Even today, when he's in a good mood. His eyes are the same hazel color, but there's a dullness to them. A cruelness. Those are the same eyes that stared at me with concern, the same eyes that filled with so much resolve I was sure everything would be okay.

Those eyes turn towards me. There's something in them. It's not love, or even concern. It's not the way a guy looks at his fiancée. More like the way a guy looks at the puppy that keeps pissing on the carpet.

But I can't stomach this right now.

So I go back to that everything-is-okay smile, and I make eye contact with Ryan. "How was work?"

That gets him started. Ryan goes on and on about work, until I'm finished with all these little bites. I try to listen, but my mind keeps drifting back to Luke.

He said something about an ex-girlfriend. She means a lot to him or she meant a lot to him. It's a fucked up situation, but he did say ex.

Ryan would know.

I wait until a break in his endless story. "I'm sorry about last night. I didn't want to cause a scene, but Luke..."

"It's not your fault. He has a complex."

"Oh yeah?"

"Yes." Ryan rolls his eyes. Shifts back into his seat. "I hate to admit it, but it's useful. His female clients eat it up."

I nod like this means nothing to me.

"Was he bothering you?"

"No, we barely spoke."

"Not even when I walked Dave out?" Ryan's eyes are on me, but there's no suspicion there.

He probably doesn't think highly enough of Luke.

"Why do you work with him?" I ask.

"He's handsome and charming and women eat his shit up."

"Is that really it?" It certainly doesn't sound like Ryan.

Ryan turns his eyes to me. "I wanted to help him. He was an excellent student, but he seemed more interested in his girlfriend than in law school."

"Oh really?" Now we're getting somewhere.

Ryan sighs. "If I'd known how obnoxious he was, I never would have approached him about Lawrence and Knight." Ryan folds his arms, deep down in memory lane. "But, I have to admit, he's the perfect partner. He attracts sensitive women like honey attracts flies."

"Still, you don't like him."

"Jobs aren't always about what you like, sweetheart."

As if Ryan doesn't love his job enough to do it all day, everyday.

"I'm aware of that," I say. I arrange my silverware on my plate. "What happened with his girlfriend?"

"She took a job at another firm." Ryan scoots forward, his eyes narrowing. "Why?"

"It's just a question."

He looks at me funny. So he knows I'm getting at something.

But he doesn't say anything.

"Sweetheart, don't worry about it. You have a lot on your plate. You can't deal with the train wreck that is Luke's social life."

I take a deep breath. "You can't call it a train wreck and hold out on details."

"Since when do you care about gossip?"

"Since always," I say.

Ryan shakes his head. Fine. I collect the plates and move to the sink. I hate doing dishes, but it's better than sitting here with Ryan staring at me like I'm crazy.

"I'll do those," he says.

"It's fine." I turn on the water and rinse a plate.

Ryan shifts out of his seat and moves towards me. "I don't want you worrying about anything but getting healthy."

I squeeze soap onto the sponge and scrub the plate. There's barely any food on it, but I need to rinse off every speck of this dinner.

I need to drop this or Ryan is going to get suspicious. "I'm only curious." I shrug my shoulders like it's no big deal.

He shifts behind me until his back is against my chest. "It's too pathetic to be interesting." Ryan slides his hands around my waist.

He leans closer, squeezing me. It feels off, too tight, like I can't breathe. This is not how it should be, how it used to be. It used to be that Ryan's arms felt like home.

"You looked so beautiful at dinner. I'm sure every man at the restaurant was thinking about getting between your legs."

Why does he say it like it's a weapon or a liability? Or a tool he can use.

You're beautiful, Alyssa, we can use that to make other people jealous.

You're beautiful, Alyssa, we can use that as a status symbol.

You're beautiful, Alyssa, and that is the only reason why I keep you around.

Ryan offers to watch a movie with me. Some kind of consolation prize I earned by putting up with him never being around. I put on *Sunset Boulevard*, a Billy Wilder film about a screenwriter forced to work with a delusional has-been actress. Ryan pretends to pay attention for the first twenty minutes.

But he tires of the film and scoots closer on the couch. He presses his lips against my neck, slides his hand under my top. It's been weeks since he's tried to touch me. He's usually too tired or too busy with work.

His hands feel like nothing. This used to be different. He was never an amazing lover, but he was competent enough, and I wanted him enough. Hell, the last year or so, I've been desperate for any chance to feel close to him.

But tonight I can't stomach the thought. I shift to the other side of the couch and press my lips against his cheek. "I'm exhausted."

He scowls for a moment, but shakes it off. "I'll get home early tomorrow."

I nod, giving my best I-can't-wait smile. I know there's something horribly wrong when I'm cringing over my fiancé touching me, but I can't bring myself to add it to my growing list of concerns.

Corine was right. I can't keep allowing men to stand in the way of what I want. I am going back to acting, and I have no room for anything that might get in the way.

Ryan excuses himself and sets up shop at the kitchen table. He's back to work on his laptop, glaring at the TV with irritation every time its volume increases.

When the movie ends, I kiss him goodnight and get ready for bed.

The room is dark. It's quiet. It's calm. But there's something so suffocating about it, like it's a sick prison for my thoughts. There is too much swirling around my brain. I should have taken Ryan up on his offer if only for the fifteen-minute distraction.

Luke had a girlfriend. She was important to him. Or she still is. It shouldn't matter. I am resolved to focus on my career. I am resolved not to let any more men get in my way.

But I need to know.

I creep to the other side of the room, where my phone is plugged into the wall, and I text him:

Can I see you tomorrow?

He replies quickly. *I'll be in my apartment until 9:30. I'll leave a key under the mat.*

My stomach is tied up in knots again, but this will be the last time. I'm going to figure out what the hell I'm doing.

I'm going to find out exactly who this woman is and what she means to him.

CHAPTER EIGHTEEN

I wake with Ryan's 6 a.m. alarm and watch him dress. This early, there's a hint of something in his eyes. A warmth that's been missing forever. He looks me over as he buttons his shirt, his eyes filled with a strange mix of concern and something I can't put my finger on.

"Why don't you go back to bed, sweetheart." His voice is warm, but there's something else to it. "I don't want you exhausted tonight."

He kisses me on the forehead and moves to the kitchen. I can hear him fixing coffee and breakfast. I'm sure he's checking email on his phone. He'll drink his coffee and eat his food and then he'll leave. It shouldn't be any longer than thirty minutes.

Thirty minutes and I'll be alone.

Thirty minutes and I'll be able to sneak to Luke's apartment to demand an explanation.

Thirty minutes.

Unless...

I brush my teeth, wash my face, and change into my gym clothes. It's a believable excuse, and I am supposed to get regular exercise.

Ryan raises an eyebrow when I step into the main room, but he leaves it at that.

"I'll see you tonight," I say. I go to fill my water bottle, lace up my shoes, catch my damn breath.

"Be careful, sweetheart."

Then he's buried in his laptop.

I slide my keys into my pocket and step into the hallway. It's a short walk to the elevator, and there's already a car waiting. I step inside and stare at the buttons. The gym is on the second floor. I could probably use the distraction.

But there's no use in pretending. I hit the button for the eleventh floor, Luke's floor, and squeeze my eyes shut. It's possible I'm still dreaming, that all of this has been a nightmare. It's possible I'm still eighteen, and I'm still doing okay. I haven't fallen into a spiral of bulimia. I haven't become completely dependent on Ryan. I haven't fucked up my life yet.

The elevator stops and I blink my eyes open. I'm still here. This is still my life.

But I'm going to take it back.

The hallway is quiet, but it's bright already. The sky is already a brilliant blue, and the windows are flooded with light.

I stop at Luke's apartment and press my foot against the mat. It's a soft, black thing that reads "Hey, don't treat me like a doormat."

Bingo. I press the key between my palms. There's a lightness in my body. I can't let myself crumble. I need to go in and demand information. No excuses, no giving in to temptation.

I slide my key into the lock and push the door open. It's still early. Luke might be asleep. But it's quiet here, really quiet. Light streams through the windows, but there are no other signs of life.

He isn't here. I should leave. I should respect his privacy. But I'm already here. I'm already dressed. I look around his desk. An iPad. A laptop. A bunch of disorganized papers printed with legal language. His apartment is otherwise clean and bare.

I move into the bedroom. His bed is messy and there are clothes in a messy pile on the floor. He must be at the gym or on a run. He could be back any minute.

The bedside table is empty. There are a few suit pieces in the closet. An empty suitcase. A stack of faded paperbacks. But nothing interesting.

The dresser is similar. T-shirts, jeans, sweaters, boxers. I bite my lip to avoid imaging Luke without boxers.

My hand hits something hard. It's a silver keepsake box. Unlocked. I press my fingers into the cold metal of the box. It's none of my business. But, then again...

I pry it open and dump it on the bed. A dozen pictures fall out. Pictures of Luke with another woman. There's a note on the back. "Luke and Samantha."

Samantha. Her name is Samantha. She is one of those girl-next-door types. Long, brown hair. Perfect figure. Plain features, but still pretty. And she and Luke look so happy. In every picture, they smile and hug each other. Celebration pictures. Vacation pictures. Pictures around the house—Luke's house. And, in the last picture, a ring on her finger and an excited grin on her face. Engaged. They are engaged.

Luke is engaged to Samantha.

Or he was. But he has these pictures. He has them in a special fucking box like they're a sacred treasure.

There are notes on the bed. Handwritten notes. They must be love notes. I don't want to know what some other woman said to Luke. She was his, and he was hers. Reading them can't help things.

But my hands have a mind of their own. I unwrap a note and scan as quickly as I can. Love, passion, desire, blah, blah, blah. There's something about law school. So it's an old note. It might mean nothing. It might be a memento from the past.

I read another letter. It's the same thing. Talk about their life together. I want to hate this woman who has Luke's heart, but she's a damn good writer for someone so mushy in love.

The last note is different—a copy of a handwritten letter.

"Luke, I want you to know this isn't your fault. This is too hard, and I'm not strong enough to get through it. It hurts too much. I hope you understand. I hope you can forgive me for my cowardice. Love, Samantha."

Luke loved a woman and she left him. She left him. It happens to everyone. It doesn't mean he can't love me. It doesn't mean he's still in love with her. So he kept old pictures. So he kept old letters. Who wouldn't?

But there's a weight on my chest, an uneasiness in my stomach. I try to take a deep breath, but it's short and choppy.

My hands are so shaky I can barely return the letters and photos to their box. I mean to take the stairs back to the apartment, but I find myself in the parking lot, a sweaty, tired mess. Ryan's car is gone. He must be at work.

There's no one around. No one to see me fall apart.

Luke loved another woman. It shouldn't matter. It doesn't matter. I am not letting any more men get in the way of my life, no matter how much I want to spend time with them.

I need something to make this hurt less. I try to remember my recovery techniques. Deep breathing is supposed to help. I have to count out ten breaths, slow and steady.

I close my eyes. One. Two. Three. The only thing I can feel is the heaviness in my chest.

Four. Five. Six. I can't go home and sit with this feeling. I'm supposed to deal with this, to work through these awful feelings instead of stuffing myself until I burst.

Seven. Eight. But I can't. It's too much. It's too heavy. I can't stand it, even for another minute.

I open my eyes. There must be another way. I can watch TV. I can down three shots of tequila. I can look for those little white pills Ryan sometimes gives me. Anti-anxiety medication. A last resort to help me calm down.

But it's no good. They're locked in his desk somewhere. And I can't ask him about it. He'll demand an explanation. I'll break and confess and he'll leave me and I'll fall apart without him. I fell apart last time I was alone.

I can't do it again.

I get in my car and resolve to drive far away, to a place with no temptation. No food. But nothing comes to mind. It doesn't matter where I go. There will be something there to tempt me, something I can use to binge and purge.

So I stay in my car. I try another round of deep breaths. One. I'll clear my mind. I'll get through this. Two. It's nothing. I like a guy I can't have. I have a guy I used to like. Three. I used to love Ryan, but I don't anymore. There's no doubt in my mind.

Four. If I can get through this, if I can fight off this urge, then maybe I don't need Ryan. Maybe I'm strong enough to take life on my own.

Five. I'll get this job. I'll find a new apartment. I'll get back in touch with my old friends.

Enough. This isn't helping.

I get out of my car and walk towards the elevator. No, the stairs. I can't risk running into anyone.

It's a long climb back to Ryan's apartment, but it's quiet inside. And it's safe. There are no temptations here. Ryan made sure of it a long time ago.

I sit on the couch and squeeze the remote. My body is so heavy, I'm sure I'll sink into the cushions. It takes all the energy I have to stand, to move to the kitchen. Coffee should help. It certainly can't hurt.

I pour a cup and add almond milk. I reach for the honey.

Fuck.

It's right there, on the top shelf—the chocolate that is supposed to serve as my daily treat. It's good stuff, seventy percent dark, and there must be four or five bars.

It's supposed to be a daily exercise in self-control. I eat one square and stop. Enjoy a tiny taste and feel satisfied with only that.

The air leaves my lungs. If I have the self-control to stop at one square, I'm okay. I'm better enough that I don't need Ryan.

If I don't...

This hurts. Knowing Luke will never be mine hurts, but I can still eat one square of chocolate without losing control.

I reach for the candy, but it's too high. Fine. I pull a chair over, climb on it, and move the chocolate to the counter. It's wrapped in silver foil and white paper.

One square. I can eat one square.

I fall into the chair and pick up one of the chocolate bars. It smells so good, so familiar. It smells like everything I've denied myself for so long.

I peel the paper off it. Then the foil. It's soft against my fingers, already melting ever so slightly.

And it smells so damn good.

I break off one square and pop it into my mouth. It's so good, sweet and creamy, and it's been so long.

I eat another square.

A sense of calm floods my body. Why did I deny it? This is what I have to do. This is the only thing that's going to make me feel better. It's the only thing that ever has made me feel better.

I keep going, until I am done with the bar. Then I move on to the next one. It's so good, so rich, and I can't stop myself. I finish the bar. And the next one. And the next one. Until I'm stuffed. Until there is nothing left of the chocolate but the wrappers on the counter.

There's no sense in playing coy now. I move to the bathroom. It's fluorescent and bright and blindingly white. I'll feel better soon. This will all be better soon.

I take my position in front of the toilet. How did this go again? Yeah, lift the lid. Lift the seat. I find a tie on the corner of the sink and pull my hair into a ponytail. I brace myself for the awful feeling, the awful gagging, but it comes easily, like second nature.

I push my pointer and middle fingers into the back of my throat. I keep pushing them farther and farther. I hurl into the toilet. I do it again, and again, until my eyes burn, until my throat burns, until my stomach rids itself completely.

CHAPTER NINETEEN

"What the hell is this?"

Ryan stands in the bedroom door with his brow furrowed. He's holding the wrappers from the chocolate bars, the wrappers I hid in the bathroom trash can in an empty box of tampons.

"It's nothing."

What the hell was he doing looking in the bathroom trash can? I should have been more thorough. I should have gone all the way to the chute in the hallway.

"Don't fuck with me, Alyssa. I want an explanation right now."

I pull the blanket around me. I've been in this bed all day, mostly trying and failing to read. I'm in the middle of *Slaughterhouse Five*. Another one of my favorites. But it's not holding my attention.

"Alyssa. I mean now." His voice is loud. Angry.

This is the angriest I've seen him in a very, very long time.

I shake my head. I got through this pain alone. I'll continue to get through it alone.

"It's nothing."

He crushes the wrappers between his palms and takes a step towards me. "I checked the cabinet. There were eight chocolate bars there."

"It's nothing."

"You know our deal." He takes another step towards me. He lowers his voice until it's only raised and not screaming. "You tell me when something is going on."

"It's—"

"Tell me the truth." He holds the wrappers in front of my face. "Because this looks like evidence you tried to destroy."

I take a deep breath. There is no point in denying it. Ryan sees through my bullshit. "It just happened."

"Don't fuck with me."

"I'm sorry," I say. I pull my knees into my chest. "I was stressed, and I didn't know how else to deal with it."

"You've been doing so much better. Why are you throwing that away?" His voice is lower, softer. There's something in his eyes too. Real concern.

"I won't do it again."

"How am I supposed to trust that?" He sits on the bed next to me. Places his hand on my shoulder. His voice is low now, sweet even. "You know you're supposed to call me if you're tempted."

So he can yell at me and call me a failure. No thanks.

I shake my head. "I knew you were busy."

Ryan frowns. It's a real frown, like he really believes he fucked up. He leans into me, wrapping his arms around me.

"I'm sorry, sweetheart."

What? Ryan Knight does not apologize. I bite my lip, taking a slow breath to calm my racing heart.

Ryan squeezes me a little tighter. "I haven't been around lately. It must be difficult."

I nod. "It is."

"I'm sure you feel lonely sometimes, but I need you to tell me the truth. Why did this happen?"

He pulls back and looks into my eyes. I turn my gaze to the bedspread. It's so dull, so plain. The most awful shade of gray.

"We've been fighting. I... it's stressful."

He turns my head until our eyes connect. He's staring at me like he's determining if I'm full of shit.

"Tell me the truth," he says.

"That is the truth."

Ryan sighs and shakes his head. "I wish you would respect me enough not to lie to me." He shifts off the bed and moves towards the door. "Are you up for dinner?"

I shake my head.

"I'll give you a few hours to rest." He turns back toward me. "I hope you'll be ready to tell me the truth then."

Again, I shake my head. He sighs and closes the door behind him.

I bury myself under the covers and try to sleep. But it's too early, barely seven, and nothing comes.

I find my phone in the bedside table and I turn it off airplane mode. I have a few emails from Corine and half a dozen texts from Luke.

I know you were here. Give me a chance to explain.

Or at least call me and tell me to fuck off so I know you're okay.

After a few hours, Ryan knocks on the door. He looks tired, like this is weighing him down. There's something about his expression, something I haven't seen in a very long time. It's almost like the old Ryan is breaking through.

He nods and motions for me to come here. I do. There's dinner set up on the table. Not the usual grilled fish and steamed vegetables. It's some kind of soup.

I take a seat silently. He sits across from me, and stares at me until I dip my spoon in the soup. It's some kind of puree, carrots and butternut squash, and I eat without protest. My stomach is still tied up in knots, acid tearing at its walls, but it's nothing compared to how much this morning hurt.

After a few minutes of this, Ryan moves closer. He offers his hand and I take it. There's something so warm about it, so real. Like before he loved work more than anything else.

"You need to get this under control," he says. "I can't bear to watch you break down again."

It's sweet, sincere. He really can't bear to watch this. It really does hurt him. That part of him that loves me is still there. It's still buried in him somewhere.

"I will. I promise I will."

He nods, and he sits with me until I finish my soup.

Ryan dotes on me all night. We watch TV for a while, then he insists I go to bed early. Watches while I brush my teeth and change into pajamas.

I almost hope he'll kiss me, touch me, distract me for the next fifteen minutes, but I'm relieved when he doesn't.

He sleeps in the spare room. Supposedly, I need to be alone with my thoughts. I know better. It's not the thoughts that matter. It's the alone. He wants me to remember how it feels to be without him.

Outside my window, the ocean rolls for miles. I watch waves rock from the horizon to the sand. I spend so much time in this room, in this apartment. But is it a sanctuary or a prison?

Ryan wakes me at 7 a.m. and reminds me of my plans for the day. My chemistry read is this afternoon, as is an emergency session with my therapist. Ryan took the liberty of scheduling it for me.

I don't bother to complain about him trying to run my life.

He's in his workout gear. I don't want to be alone in the apartment, so I invite myself to join him.

"Only if you take it easy," he says. "Nothing more than a walk on the treadmill."

I nod, and change while he goes to check his email. Of course. He's so caught up in it that he urges me to go alone.

I take the stairs, squeezing the railing all the way. I have the slightest bit of dizziness, but it's nothing I can't handle.

The gym is small. A few treadmills, a few weight machines, a few exercise mats. And Luke, on the floor, sweat dripping off his chiseled abs. What is he doing lying on the floor, looking sexy as fuck, practically begging me to mount him?

"I was hoping I'd see you here," he says.

"Lucky coincidence," I reply and step onto the treadmill. Four miles per hour. Nothing faster than a brisk walk.

"I'm sure you'd rather discuss this somewhere private."

"Ryan should be here in five minutes."

He steps onto the treadmill next to mine and matches my speed. "Ryan has no say over what I do."

Lucky him.

"There's nothing to talk about," I say. I want more of an explanation. I want him to tell me this woman means nothing to him, that I mean everything to him, that us fucking is more than filling the void of our mutual loneliness.

But I'm done lying to myself about men.

"Fine," he says. He looks directly in my eyes. "Tell me you're in love with Ryan and I'll never bother you again."

"That's not fair."

"Then tell me you don't want to see me again."

I will myself to say the words, but I can't. I want to see him and badly.

He leans a little closer and lowers his voice to just above a whisper. "Are you okay?"

"Why?"

"You look like hell."

I squeeze the handles of the treadmill and focus on the display.

"If you ask me to back off, I will. But I like you too much to give up on this." His hand brushes against mine. "Whatever happened, you can tell me. Whatever you saw in my room—"

"That isn't necessary."

"Was it... did you have a... I know you used to have a problem—"

"It's called bulimia." I struggle not to roll my eyes.

He steps onto the sides of the treadmill and leans in towards me. "Call me next time you're feeling overwhelmed."

"Why? I barely know you."

"Because you want to." He steps off the treadmill. "And because I want you to."

I try to come up with a sarcastic response, but I can't bring myself to reject his offer. I do want to call him next time I'm overwhelmed.

"I want to explain whatever it is you saw about Samantha. I want you to understand."

"I'll consider it."

The door behind him opens. I turn. It's Ryan, and he has an irritated look. Or maybe it's suspicion.

Luke pats Ryan on the shoulder. "I'll see you later, buddy." He makes for the exit.

I wait until Luke is out of the gym to exhale. Steady now. One foot in front of the other. It's just walking.

I put on my headphones and shut out my thoughts. I want to run, I want to sweat out all these feelings, but I will get dizzy and I can't risk fainting.

We return to the apartment and eat our usual breakfasts. The war zone in my stomach has calmed, but it still doesn't feel quite right.

"Are you ready to tell me what happened yesterday?" Ryan asks.

"Nothing happened."

He shakes his head. "Alyssa, you don't know how much I worry about keeping you healthy. I couldn't sleep last night. I'll be a worried wreck all day today."

"You've never been a worried wreck in your life."

"I was every day you were in treatment."

He certainly knows how to shut me up.

"I'll be home late," he says. "But I'll call before dinnertime."

I nod. Fine. A call is something. It's not like the old Ryan, the one who truly cared about my health, but it's something.

Ryan showers and leaves for work. I sit at the table for a long time, sipping cup after cup of black coffee, psyching myself up for therapy.

I'm not ready to work through my thoughts. I want to stuff them into the back of my brain, to someplace where no one will ever find them. I don't care about the collateral damage. I don't care if I get depressed for weeks, if I have to binge and purge a hundred more times. I have to rid myself of any thoughts of Luke Lawrence. By any means necessary.

CHAPTER TWENTY

I sit in a casting room on a plush orange couch. Laurie sits across from me, next to a suit of some kind. An executive at the network or the production company. Something like that. Some business person who will decide if I am marketable, if I am fuckable enough for the 18-35 male demo.

If only she could ask Ryan. He would assure her that I am beautiful, and she can use that.

The suit—and her suit is a glorious slate gray—leaves to take a call on her smartphone. She speaks in low, hushed tones with the kind of seriousness usually reserved for the war room. I remember working with these kinds of people. The "TV is serious business, more important than curing cancer and you better take it as seriously as I do" people.

They excel at sucking the fun out of everything.

Laurie moves to the couch. She spreads out, her feet on the armrest, her head on my shoulder, her curly hair falling over my arm.

"Alyssa, I tell you. These suits are incompetent. Have you ever been in a meeting about meetings?"

I shake my head.

"I think it gets them off, seeing 'meeting' on their iCal." She rolls off the couch and stretches. "Or maybe they hate their families and would rather spend the day in pointless meetings." She sighs. "It's awful." She shakes her head and returns her glasses to their rightful place. "But don't worry about it. You probably remember what it's like. Everyone assumes the actors are idiots. They won't ask much of you unless you're on camera. Okay?"

"Okay."

"As long as you remember your lines, you take direction, and you don't act like a diva, they'll love you... God, listen to me. I'm so obnoxious. You were on that show for three years. You know the routine."

"It's fine," I say. "Really, I appreciate the concern."

Relief floods her face. Laurie is weird, but I get it. She's trapped in TV world. That kind of thing makes it hard to engage with normal life.

"You're reading with Danny and Naomi today, you know, the hot kid and the sister. And, girl, he is damn hot. I know you're engaged or something, but damn. I wonder if he really is into older women."

"Want me to remove his clothing?"

"Yeah... I mean, your character would do that. Wouldn't she?"

I throw her an *uh-huh* look. "So it's only about the character?"

Laurie clears her throat, blushing. "Do whatever feels natural. I trust you."

"Right..." I say.

The door opens.

"Oh, shit, the suit is back. On your best behavior now," Laurie says and gets back in her executive chair.

The suit enters with a young actor, eighteen or nineteen maybe. He must be Danny. Laurie was right. He's hot— handsome, tall, and muscular with gorgeous olive skin. He looks like a Spanish-American pop star. It's not hard to imagine why Marie Jane is interested in him, and it won't be hard to play scenes where he is the object of my character's lust.

I might not even need to use Luke as a trigger.

Laurie sets up a video camera, directing us to get within the frame. "Whenever you're ready."

Danny starts the scene—his character is working out in the yard. Much to Laurie's delight, I'm sure, he takes off his shirt to count out a round of push-ups. I don't have much to play, mostly watching him with my tongue hanging out of my mouth.

Even though it's only a chemistry read, we get into character. I look at him like he's the only thing I'll ever need. He looks at me with the kind of curiosity only a seventeen-year-old boy could have. It's fun and silly and, for a minute, I am Alyssa Summers, hardworking actress, instead of Alyssa Summers, Ryan Knight's fiancée.

When Laurie calls scene, I am desperate to get back into the flow of acting.

"Can we read the next scene?" I ask.

"We have time before Naomi, don't we?" Laurie asks the suit.

The suit nods and Laurie claps. Jeez, the girl is enthusiastic.

"Whenever you're ready," she says.

I sink into the role. I am Marie Jane, ex-model, desperate attention seeker. I need nothing more than a distraction. I need nothing more than this kid, under me, or on top of me, or behind me.

My character brain takes over and my actor brain recedes. It is just Marie Jane, trying to seduce this kid. And, when it comes time for the in-script kiss, when I have to play the deepest, hardest, most intense attraction I've ever felt, I close my eyes and picture Luke.

If it was Luke next to me, what kind of things would I do to him? I grab Danny's waist. I press my body into his. I do not go beyond a stage kiss—my lips are closed, pressed against his in a very technical, unsexy way—but I play the position of my body and hands big and loud, the way I would if it were Luke.

Laurie calls scene and we separate.

I apologize to Danny. "That wasn't too much, was it?"

He shakes his head, a smug little smile on his face. This is probably his first time playing the hot dude.

"Geez, Alyssa, I'm not going to get your fiancé coming after me am I?" Laurie asks. "I think we can consider that ample chemistry."

But this does not satisfy the suit. She is not amused by Laurie's jokes. She goes into details of the scene, the lines, the chemistry. They watch the scene again on their little camera.

We chat for a few minutes. Danny leaves and Naomi arrives. She offers the world's fakest smile and greets everyone with a "nice to meet you."

Then she shakes my hand. Her grip is weak like she can't be bothered to recognize my existence.

She sits on the couch. No script. She's off book. We go through our lines.

It's awful. Total shit. She's not trying. She keeps her eyes on her fingernails as she recites. There's no enthusiasm in her voice, no feeling.

Nothing.

Laurie doesn't like it. The suit doesn't like it. They leave the room to talk about us. They claim it's for a phone call, but it's obviously to talk about us.

Once they're safely out of earshot, Naomi turns to me. Her eyes narrow.

"You quit your last show," she says.

"I had to. Health reasons," I say.

"Which health reasons—Adderall or Percocet?"

"Different health reasons."

"Yeah, right." She mimes snorting coke.

I roll my eyes. Some people are impossible.

But she's signed a contract. I haven't. If I want to secure my role one hundred percent, I have to get her on my side.

"I know this is frustrating for you," I say. "You've done it before. But the only way we're going to get through it, is if you work with me. We both want this show to make it. We both want it to go for a hundred episodes and make us rich. So, can you help me convince these suits we're both right for these parts?"

"Yeah, whatever," she says.

But when Laurie and the suit return, and we read our next scene, Naomi gets into character. She tries. The sisters come to life, sparring and arguing to much more comedic effect. They like this version better. Hopefully they like it enough they'll keep me on.

My last chemistry read is easy. My character's ex-boyfriend. A sweet guy, but far too dull for Marie Jane. The actor, Brett, is gregarious and fun, but I can see why Marie Jane would leave a guy like him. She needs someone with more to offer. Someone more interesting. Someone who loves life and seeks out knowledge. Someone who cares about more than working to the bone. Someone who would fuck her in a movie theater.

There's a text message on my phone from Luke.

I'll be home this afternoon. I know you want an explanation.

I reply instantly. *I can be there in thirty minutes.*

CHAPTER TWENTY-ONE

I go straight to Luke's apartment. The door is open, but still, I knock. There are footsteps, then he pulls the door open and whisks me inside.

He wraps his arms around me. My body floods with the most pleasant warmth, like I've finally come in from the cold.

I never want to leave. I never want to feel anything except his arms around me.

"Are you okay?" he asks. His eyes are big and sincere. "Okay, stupid question. Can I get you anything?"

"Just water."

He nods, moves to the kitchen, and pours a glass. I take a few more steps into the apartment. The windows are open and there's a gentle breeze. I can smell the salt from the ocean, feel the warmth of the sun.

He looks back to me. "You sure you don't want something else? Tea? Coffee?"

"You have coffee?"

He checks his cabinets. They're almost entirely bare, except for a few boxes of cereal and a few metal tins. "Tea," he offers again. "Do you like Earl Grey or English breakfast?"

"I'd prefer an explanation," I say.

"Unfortunately for you, I already know that you're patient when it comes to getting what you want."

I swallow hard. My stomach fills with butterflies. Is that what I want—to be spread-eagle on top of him again? I can't say I'd mind even if now it's not the most opportune time.

"You'll like Earl Grey," he says. "It's strong but sweet."

There's a wounded look in his big, brown eyes. I want to wrap my arms around him again, but I'm afraid to make any movements at all.

"You could give me the Cliff Notes now and spare me a lot of agony," I say.

He turns his gaze towards mine. "And how would we put that extra time to use?"

"Uh... I... we..." I take a deep breath. "I'm sure you know a way."

He nods. "I'll keep that in mind."

He fills a fancy electric water heater. It's the only appliance in his empty kitchen.

"Did you see the pictures of me and Samantha?"

"Yes."

"The letters too?"

"Some of them."

"Then I'll start at the beginning."

"So you have no interest in sparing me agony?"

He shakes his head. "I'll make it up to you later."

A shiver runs down my spine, and I squeeze my legs together. This isn't the time to get distracted by promises of amazing sex.

The little red light on the water heater switches off. Luke grabs a tin of tea and scoops it into some kind of plastic tea maker. He pours hot water into the tea maker and sets a timer. Five minutes.

He turns to me, holding my gaze. "Samantha was my girlfriend. We met about three years ago, at USC Law. It wasn't a perfect relationship, but I was smitten with her."

I bite my lip. It's not as if I expected Luke to come with absolutely no baggage, but it still stings thinking of him loving some other woman.

"We drifted apart after school, but I wasn't willing to let her go," he continues. "So, after we both passed the bar, I asked her to marry me. She said yes. I have no idea why she said yes. In hindsight, it was obvious she was done with our relationship. She worked late, spent her weekends with friends, even made excuses for why she didn't want to screw."

There's a deep sadness in his eyes, and I want so badly to hug him and tell him everything will be okay. But it would be an empty promise. I don't even know if I'll be okay.

His gaze shifts towards the windows, to the miles and miles of ocean outside, then it's back to me. "Now is where it really gets good."

"Yeah?"

He nods. "Oh yeah. One day, maybe a year after we got engaged, I asked about the wedding. She insisted it was too soon to even set a date. I demanded something, even a year, and she broke down. She started crying. She was having an affair."

"Jesus."

"It gets better," he says. "It was with my father. She was fucking my father. Had been for years. And she loved him in a way she'd never loved me."

He tries to hide the pained look on his face, but I can see it. Is that what I'm going to do to Ryan if I confess? Am I any better than this woman who broke Luke's heart?

"And, even though she wasn't sure he'd have her, she had to leave me and take that chance. Poor girl had no idea what an asshole he is. She meant so little to him. He wasn't willing to risk his reputation. It wouldn't look good, a senior partner with an associate."

The tea timer dings and Luke takes the excuse to pour us two cups. He spoons honey into each. "Then the asshole had a heart attack and died suddenly."

He hands me a cup of tea, his fingers brushing against mine. I want to grab his hand and squeeze it tight and beg him to forget about this awful woman. To kiss him and promise to take this pain away from him.

But I only nod and sip my tea. "I'm sorry."

"She was miserable. I wanted to help her, but every bit of her sadness was a knife in my gut. We hadn't broken up yet but we weren't together. Not really. My dad, the fucking asshole, was dead and all I could think was that he stole my girlfriend."

He runs a hand through his hair, his eyes turning towards the sunny day outside. "I worked all the time. I couldn't sleep. I got this prescription for heavy-duty sleeping pills, and they worked, but they gave me nightmares, so I stopped taking them."

"Luke. What happened?" There's something haunting him, and it's more than his ex cheating on him.

"I fucked up."

I press my fingers into the cup. It's warm. It's still warm. "She's the one who hurt you."

He shakes his head, his eyes on the floor. "I left my prescription on the bedside table. It's not like I did it on purpose, not exactly."

He brings his gaze back to me. "But I knew she might see it. I knew there was a chance. I hoped she wouldn't take them, but I knew there was a chance."

My stomach drops. That wasn't a love letter at all. It was a suicide note.

"Is she okay?" I ask.

He nods. "She had a change of heart. Called 9-1-1. They pumped her stomach and put her in an involuntary hold."

I feel my heart in my throat.

"That was three months ago."

All the air leaves my lungs. I try to move my fingers, but I can't feel any part of my body. I can't feel anything. Luke's fiancée tried to kill herself. He left out his bottle of sleeping pills. He left them there for her. He must have known...

How is this possible?

"And you're still together?"

He shakes his head. "It's been over for a long time. We both know it's over. We weren't even living together."

"But she has your ring?"

"I don't want it back," he says.

I take a deep breath, but it feels like a knife in my lungs. "You should have told me."

"I know. I'm sorry."

I take a step backwards. This is too much, too complicated. "So what, you didn't want to ruin your chance of getting in my pants?"

"I didn't think it would go any further than that."

"What's further than that?" I ask.

He sets his cup on the counter and takes a step towards me. "Conversations like this."

"And you still love her?" I ask.

He shakes his head. "Not like that."

The room is spinning. I can barely feel my hands. "Do you still love her?"

"I thought I did. But when I met you." He looks me in the eyes. "I felt alive for the first time in months. Years even. It was like there was color in my life again."

"You barely know me."

I sit on his couch and sip my ignored tea. It's sweet, as sweet as my usual coffee, and it saves me from the need to form a coherent response.

"Were you ever going to tell me?" I ask.

"Eventually."

My head is swimming again. This is supposed to be an easy distraction. It's getting awfully complicated.

"What are you thinking?" he asks.

"That I should go back home."

"Please don't."

He grabs my wrist, harder than he has before.

"Stop it," I say.

"Please, Alyssa, I won't fail you, too. You need someone and it shouldn't be Ryan."

"You can't fail me, because we aren't anything. I'm not with you." Why does my chest hurt? Why does it feel hard to breathe?

"Do you even like him?"

"It's none of your business." My chest is still heavy. My stomach is still empty. I turn to Luke, holding his gaze. "I'm not your pity project. I can take care of myself."

"Do you even believe that?"

I squeeze the porcelain cup. "What the hell are you talking about?"

"Aren't you with him because you don't believe you can take care of yourself?"

"Fuck off." It's so bright outside. It's such a beautiful day outside.

"That's not what you want."

"I don't need anyone else telling me what I want."

He sits next to me, close, really. So close that I can hear his breath.

"Then tell me," he says.

"I'm sorry about your ex-girlfriend. I wish you never had to feel that pain. But it has nothing to do with me."

"Alyssa—"

"If you want a pity project, find someone else."

"Okay," he says. His hands are on my shoulders. It's firm, but it's not demanding. "If you tell me why you're with Ryan."

I try to push off the couch, but I've got one hand on this damn cup of tea. Luke grabs my wrist as if to stop me. But when I shake him off he lets go.

"He treats you like a pet," he says.

Slowly, I shift of the couch. "Don't lecture me about healthy relationships. I'm not the one who gave my fiancée the pills she used to attempt suicide."

The color drains from his face. I went too far. He loved her. He didn't do it on purpose. But still...

I'm not his fucking pity project.

I set my cup on the counter and move to the door.

This time Luke doesn't try to stop me.

I try to ignore the heavy feeling in my chest. I barely know Luke. He won't make me hurt. He won't make me lose control. Not again.

CHAPTER TWENTY-TWO

My body aches and a cup of coffee does nothing to ease the hurt. That look of pain on Luke's face shouldn't affect me. The thought of him sitting in his sad little apartment, by himself, shouldn't affect me. We had a fling. It's over. The end.

I try to talk myself into falling back in love with Ryan. We had something once. It wasn't romantic or passionate, but it was something. We did love each other. And he cared enough about me not to work eighty hours a week. He listened, and he didn't berate me. There was warmth in his eyes and in his arms when he held me.

The bottom of my coffee cup provides no answers. Would I want Ryan if he transformed back into his old self? He doesn't make my body hum. He doesn't make my heart pound. And his laugh doesn't put me at ease.

He doesn't laugh, actually.

I stare out my windows. It's a brilliant day outside. Blue sky, bright sun, puffy, white clouds. It's so beautiful, I feel sick. But I can't stay in the condo a minute longer, or I'll be in the kitchen, finding every single drop of junk in the cabinets.

If there is anything.

I change into my swimsuit and cover-up. I need the freezing cold water of the Pacific surrounding me, numbing me, allowing me to feel anything except this.

I take the elevator downstairs, trying to avoid my reflection in the mirrored ceiling. But still, I see it, and I am not sure I recognize myself. It's the same physically. There's something off about me, something I've lost.

The concrete path is blindingly white. It's warm against my feet, even through my flimsy flip-flops. It's so bright I squint. Why didn't I bring my sunglasses? I close my eyes for a minute and soak in the warmth of the sun.

And when I open my eyes, I see Luke, on the grass, under the shade of that same tree. He's sweaty and flushed. No shirt, blue running shorts. He looks at me as if I am some minor irritation, a bug flying in his face. Then he looks back to the grass in front of him as if I am even less than a bug. At least he'd try to shoo a bug.

"I'm sorry," I say. "I don't want to disturb you."

"I don't own the place." His voice is low and steady. He's hurting.

I turn toward the marina.

"Don't," he says. "I like your company."

"Even when I say awful things?"

"Your company, not the stupid things you say." He motions for me to come closer.

I sit next to him on the grass. The cool blades scrape against my legs. It's cool here, in the shade, but there's still something so warm about being near him.

"I'm sorry," I say again. "I don't think it was your fault."

"It was. I knew better. I could have done more to save her," he says. He moves a little closer. "I wasn't fair to you. I didn't think of how hard it must have been, to fall apart with no one to help but Ryan."

I nod.

"Of course you stay with him. He was the only person who helped you when things were hard. He was the only person who kept you from destroying yourself."

"Yes." I blink back tears. I barely survived with Ryan, but without him...

"Does it still hurt?"

"It's different now," I say. "Easier. But I still don't handle stress well. I'm still tempted. If I go off my recovery diet, I get this horrible feeling of dread in my gut, like nothing will ever be okay again."

"That sounds miserable."

"It is, but I can handle it."

"On your own?"

"I'm not on my own. I have Ryan."

"You can't stay with him. You'll never be happy," he says.

"But I'll be alive."

I move closer to Luke, until I can hear his breath. Until I can feel the warmth of his body.

"What if I could be the one to keep you from destroying yourself?"

"You can't," I say.

"How do you know?"

He doesn't force me to remind him that he failed Samantha. He doesn't force me to remind myself that he is trying to help me because of how royally he fucked up helping her.

"This is all so miserably fucked," I say.

"Maybe not. I like you and you like me. And you certainly like having sex with me."

I laugh, the tiniest laugh, but it's still warm. Luke looks into my eyes. He brushes a hair behind my ear. I barely know him, but there's something in his eyes. He really does care. He really does want to be with me.

"But I'm... I'm engaged."

He smirks. "You know that's not a life sentence."

I lean into him. "What the hell are we going to do?"

"Whatever we want."

He presses his warm, sweaty body against me. Then his lips. Then his hands. His expert hands, so gentle and strong, slip under my cover-up and untie my bikini. And his hands are on my body, touching me everywhere, so soft I purr.

And then they are gone, back at his sides. His body is not pressed against mine. He is only inches away, but the distance between us feels so vast and unconquerable.

"Leave him," Luke says. "Be with me. Stay with me. Love me." His hand brushes against mine. "Think about it. Take the day. Take the week. Figure out if there's any chance I could be the person to hold you together."

It's a sweet thought, but it would never work. I can barely handle breakfast, let alone my entire life. By the time Luke learns, I will already be halfway down the rabbit hole. I will already be flitting between purging and restricting, ten pounds below my healthy weight, throwing up catered lunches in my dressing room. I've been through this hell before and I'm not strong enough to drag myself out of it again.

He looks into my eyes. "I'll love you in a way he never has."

Luke insists on walking me back to the apartment. Maybe he senses it, that this needs to be the end. He grips my hand tightly. He kisses my forehead. He rides with me in the elevator.

The doors close. We kiss, long and hard, and my body floods with electricity. My body wants nothing but more of Luke, but I know better. The elevator stops at my floor and I have to leave. I have to walk back to my room and pretend this never happened.

I lock the door behind me. The apartment is empty. Of course, it should be empty. It's the middle of the day, a weekday. Ryan isn't due home for hours. I press my back against the door, my cover-up sliding over my skin. Every shift of the fabric is a jolt against my body. I close my eyes and pretend it is Luke touching me.

My hand slides between my legs. Maybe this will satisfy my craving. Maybe this will shake my desire. Maybe this will be enough.

Just one more time. I can think of Luke one more time. Get it out of my system. One more time, and then I will belong only to Ryan, think only of Ryan, be only with Ryan.

I slide my fingers over my clit and feel my sex clench. I am already so keyed up from kissing Luke. I have to slow down. I have to savor this.

Deep breath. I squeeze my eyes shut and drag my fingertips over my thighs. I have to do it slowly, the way he would. It's not the same, but it still feels damn good.

A few moments pass, and there's a knock on the door. I open my eyes, and pull up my bikini bottoms. Deep breath, composed expression. I open the door. It's Luke. Thank God. I feel my cheeks flush. Does he know what I was doing? Does he care?

"I have an answer to your question," Luke says.

"What?"

"I know what we should do." He pulls something from his pocket. A condom.

I nod hell yes, and he presses the door closed behind him.

"Ryan could come home any minute," I say.

"Do you really care if he catches us?"

"No," I say. And I really don't.

"God, how did I ever think I'd be able to resist you?" he asks and his lips find mine.

We kiss, long and deep, as Luke presses me against the front door. I feel his cock through his shorts, pressing against my clit. I kick off my bikini bottoms and push Luke's shorts to his knees. There is less between us now, but it is still far too much.

I pull my cover-up over my head and undo my bikini top. Luke pushes it aside. His hands slide up my stomach and around my breasts, teasing my nipples, sending pangs of need through my sex.

I groan and dig my nails into his back. "I swear you're trying to kill me," I say.

He smiles and sinks his teeth into my neck. My nails dig harder. His teeth sink deeper. It hurts, but I want more. I need more from him. So much more.

I grab the condom from his hand. He presses his lips against my neck again, a litter harder and deeper. I push his boxers to his knees, unwrap the condom, and slide it over his cock. Even through the rubber he feels damn good in my hands.

He grabs my hips, lifting them, pressing them against the wall, rearranging them so my sex hovers over his cock. But he doesn't enter, not yet. Instead he presses his lips to mine. His lips are warm and soft and sweet. They slide over my lower lip, sucking gently. Then harder. I feel the scrape of his teeth over my lips.

And I grab his ass, thrusting his cock into my sex. Jesus. My nails dig into his skin. I tear off his shirt. I need to feel his skin on mine. I need to feel our bodies become one.

I wrap my legs around his hips. He presses me against the wall, his hands on my ass. My back slams into the wall as he thrusts into me. I wrap my arms around him, pulling him closer, savoring the feeling of him inside me. He thrusts into me, harder and harder, and I shake with pleasure.

The pressure inside me builds—I am already so close—and I look into Luke's eyes and kiss him. Every part of him is mine. Every part of me is his. There is nothing else, except us, in the moment. Luke fucking me, his lips on mine, his tongue in my mouth, his cock inside me. I kiss him and I press my body against his and I do not stop when I feel the tension in my sex build and build and release. I do not stop when I hear the jingle of keys— someone in the hallway, going to some other apartment, thank God. I do not stop until Luke moans and sinks his teeth into my neck and slams me against the wall one last time. I do not stop until Luke comes.

I collapse into Luke's arms, my head resting on his shoulders. I feel his hands on my back, his strong arms around me. He carries me to the bathroom.

"I have to clean up," I say.

He nods and kisses me again, his hands lingering against my hips.

I sigh into him. "I wish you could stay."

"I can."

"That wouldn't go over well."

"I don't care how it goes over."

I turn on the shower. Luke kisses me again. And this time it is my hands that remain on his body.

We shower together, lingering in the room for much too long. Until there's the tiniest chance Ryan might come home early and catch us.

After, Luke kisses me goodbye and leaves without my asking.

I wipe the floor clean. And the front door. I can't be too careful.

CHAPTER TWENTY-THREE

Ryan, I have to tell you something.

Ryan, I'm sorry.

Ryan, I don't know what this means, but I can't lie to you anymore.

Ryan, I still love you.

I put down my pen. None of it is right. None of it is close to what I want to say.

This isn't something I can wing. I need to know what I'm going to tell him.

Ryan, there's no easy way to say this, so here it is. I fucked someone else. I still...

But I don't know if I still love Ryan or if I still want to be with him. I can't drop the I-fucked-someone-else bomb without a request of some kind. I need to beg for forgiveness or tell him it's over.

I press my fingers against the pen. Maybe I can do it in a letter. Say everything and beg not for forgiveness, but for mercy. To see if there's even a chance I can salvage things.

Ryan, I'm sorry, but I fucked Luke. The night of the dinner. It was my decision, not his. I can't blame anything for it. I wasn't drunk or coerced or anything but angry. And I wanted him, I wanted him so badly. I know I shouldn't go on about it, but it was the kind of passion I don't feel for anything but acting.

It was wrong. I should have told you earlier. I should have stopped, but I did it again and again. The truth is, I don't want to stop. I like him. I really, really like him. And I really, really like fucking him. We both know our sex life is nothing to write home about. You're not even trying.

I tear the paper in half. I can't tell Ryan any of this. It will hurt him too much. It would be easier for him if I lied. At the very least, I should keep the details to myself.

I tear the paper into tiny, tiny pieces. Until no one could read a thing on it. Then I gather it and flush it down the toilet.

A letter is no good. I need to do this in person. And soon. Not soon, tonight. I'll be honest, but I won't go into detail. I'll tell him the truth, but only as much of it as he needs.

My phone buzzes with a text message. It's from Luke.

I want to see you tomorrow.

My breath catches in my throat. I want to reply yes, to beg him to come over here and fuck me again. But that isn't helping me.

I turn off my phone. It's still early. I should have a few hours until Ryan gets home. But I can do this. I can figure this out.

I wake up to the sound of the front door opening. It's dark except for the light from the TV. The stars are shining outside the window.

It's late. Really late.

I push myself off the couch. I still remember the speech I rehearsed. Keep it short and sweet. The truth, no extra details.

Ryan sets his briefcase on the table. He moves to the couch and kneels next to me. I open my mouth to speak, but nothing comes out.

"Come on, sweetheart." He offers his hand and pulls me off the couch.

"Ryan, we need to talk."

"In the morning." He presses his lips against my cheek, leads me to the bedroom, and drops me on the bed.

"It's important."

He looks at me like I'm a kid who just doesn't understand the big, bad adult world. "You're tired and I have work."

"It's important."

"Then we'll discuss it in the morning."

I bite the skin on my knuckle.

"I promise we'll discuss it in the morning. Okay?"

I nod. The morning. We will discuss this in the morning. I will be done with this in the morning.

I can live with that.

Ryan leans over and kisses me on the forehead. "Goodnight sweetheart."

Once again, I wake to the door opening. But, this time, it is Ryan leaving.

I push my covers off and shift out of bed. I could run for him. I could grab him at the elevator and drag him back to the apartment. But there doesn't seem to be any reason to bother.

The alarm clock reads seven a.m. An hour before he usually leaves for work. I move to the main room in the hopes I'll see his briefcase and dress shoes—some sign he's headed for the gym and not the office—but it's no good. They're gone and his sneakers are next to the door.

This relationship means nothing to him. Is it really worth saving?

CHAPTER TWENTY-FOUR

"Damn. You aren't going to fit into any of Brittany's clothes." The head of wardrobe pulls a tape measure around my chest. "Not even close."

Her voice is neutral, like this is a simple fact. The sky is blue. Water is wet. Alyssa Summers cannot fit into her costume.

I nod. I'm too big to wear any of the clothes made for Brittany, the previous Marie Jane. She was probably on cocaine or Adderal or some other drug that kept her appetite and weight down.

But still, I am too big to fit into Brittany's clothes.

She pulls the tape measure around my waist. Until it's tight. Really tight.

"Maybe if we throw you in Spanx." She brings her gaze back to my chest. "You could squeeze into a few things. Your chest will be busting out, but that fits Marie Jane."

"No problem." I am anything but a temperamental actor. I still don't have my contract, not officially.

She motions for me to step out of my jeans. "You do have a nice figure," she says. "I don't work with many curvy actresses."

Curvy. Right. Not fat, curvy. It's a shape, not a size. It's a compliment. She sounded sincere.

I close my eyes. Ten deep breaths. Something to ease this tension. But all I can see is blog posts with the headline "Is Alyssa Summers Fat?"

"Here, try this." She hands me a skirt.

It's the world's smallest skirt. But I do my part. I nod okay, and I attempt to pull it on.

No good. It only comes to midthigh.

She smiles. "Excuse me." She pulls the tape measure around my ass and writes the measurement on a tiny piece of paper.

I slip off the skirt and check the size. It's a two. It's only a two. There's no reason why I need to fit into a size-two skirt.

I try my deep breaths again, but my stomach is still in knots. My chest is still heavy.

The head of wardrobe peers into the closet. "Oh, I know. I have a few choices for you." She pulls out a drawer of matching bra and panty sets.

Bra and thong sets. Teeny, tiny thongs with teeny, tiny strings.

"Which do you think best fits your character?" she asks.

I scan the underwear. It's underwear I'm going to wear on TV. Cable TV, but still, TV. I'm going to be on TV in one of these teeny, tiny thongs.

My breath catches in my throat. I try my best to think of Marie Jane. Which of these sets would she wear? One is black, silk. Too classy. One is white. A high-waisted vintage imitation. Not sexy enough for Marie Jane. One is hot pink, but it's tiny. Smaller than the others.

I bite my lip. It's not about what I want. It's about the character, and this hot pink bra and thong set is perfect.

"This one." I point to the hot pink underwear.

She nods and makes a note. "Try it on. Make sure it fits."

My head is swimming. Will I try on the tiny underwear, the tiny underwear I'll wear on TV? It's not like I usually mind tiny underwear. I certainly wouldn't mind wearing it for Luke...

But on TV?

I take a step back. "Sure, but I'm going to use the bathroom first."

"It's down the hall."

I nod, grab my purse, and walk down the hall as calmly as possible.

The bathroom is empty. No one else is in the building. I run the water and splash it on my face.

I can do this. I've done it before.

But my heart is still pounding. I dig into my purse and find my phone. I don't feel right calling Luke, but I need his voice in my ear.

I dial and hold the phone to my ear.

"Hey," he says. It's sweet. He's happy to hear from me.

"You said to call if I get overwhelmed," I say.

"I did."

"Well, I'm overwhelmed."

"You want to talk about it?"

I press my fingers into the counter. It's cool and smooth. I can do this. "I'd rather not talk about it."

A tiny groan escapes his lips. "I can be at my apartment at five thirty."

It's barely two now. That feels like an eternity, but it's worth it. "I can wait."

"You sure?"

"Yes."

"Meet me there."

My heart thuds against my chest. "Don't make me start without you."

"Go ahead. I'd love to watch."

Fuck. I take a deep breath. "I'll see you later." I hang up my phone and slip it back into my purse.

I arrive at Luke's fifteen minutes early. It's quiet, and I still feel like I'm doing something wrong, like I shouldn't be here alone.

I lie on the bed and will myself to calm down, but my head is still buzzing. I need more—his hands, his lips, his cock.

It's hot in here. I slide off the bed to open the window, but the breeze isn't enough to cool me down. Of course it's hot in here. I'm waiting for Luke to arrive and fuck me senselessly.

I strip down to my bra and panties. They aren't hot pink, and they don't match perfectly, but they're sexy enough.

Not that I have much interest in keeping them on.

I do my best to take deep breaths, to relax, to splay myself over the bed so there's no way he can resist.

Luke arrives a few minutes later, wearing a sleek, black suit. I watch as he removes his coat and tie, undoing the top two buttons of his shirt. He's going to torture me with the time it takes to remove that shirt.

His gaze moves over the bed, focusing on me. "You're trying to kill me, aren't you?" He bites his lip, his eyes filling with desire.

I shake my head and pull him onto the bed. He sits next to me, rubbing my shoulders as I press my lips into his.

He pulls back. "We need to talk first."

I brace myself for the worst. I made it clear I had no interest in talking. It must be something important.

"Is it about Samantha?"

"I called her last night and explained everything." He shifts away, but his eyes stay on me. "She understands."

My body relaxes. It can't be that bad if he explained everything to his ex-girlfriend.

He leans a little closer. "I don't want you having sex with Ryan."

I exhale every ounce of air. It's ridiculous, but...

"I haven't," I say. "I haven't touched him in months."

"Really?"

I nod.

His fingers graze my back. A soft stroke. "Has he tried?"

"Yes." A jolt of electricity runs down my spine. "Not hard, but, he has."

"What did you do?"

His hands reach my panties. He traces the waistline with the softest touch imaginable. My body is buzzing already. This conversation is going too long, but I have to explain.

"I said I was tired." I arch my back, melting into him. "I was."

His eyes connect with mine. He lowers his voice. "Did you want him?"

I shake my head. "He doesn't hold a candle to you."

He smiles, his face lighting up, and he moves closer. He drags his fingertips back up my spine, around the band of my bra.

"I know it's not fair to ask you not to fuck your fiancé, but I'm asking."

He looks at me with those big, brown eyes. No one has ever looked at me like that, like my response could break his heart.

"Okay," I say. "I won't."

"I don't even want you hugging him."

"He's going to get suspicious."

He unhooks my bra and peels it off my chest. I groan, my eyes fluttering closed. My body is humming from his touch. I should agree, anything to keep him from stopping.

But I can't lie to Luke.

"I'll try," I say.

He shakes his head. "You have to promise."

He cups my breasts, his thumbs rubbing against my nipples. Jesus. I try not to react, but a soft moan escapes my lips. He pulls his hands away for a moment. Then his fingertips are back on my skin, so soft and light I can barely feel them.

"You aren't playing fair," I say.

"I know." His voice is heavy.

He wants this too.

I groan and he lightens his touch again, hitting every nerve ending I have. His hand slides down my back and he pulls me towards him.

He's hard.

I grab his hips, pressing our bodies together.

This is a silly game of chicken. There's no way either of us could turn away now.

"Promise," he demands.

His teeth sink into my neck. He slides my panties to my knees, his fingertips trailing up my thighs ever so slowly. I grab his hand and press it against my sex.

"Jesus," he groans. "You're so wet."

"Fuck me," I say. "Make me come."

"Promise." He rubs me softly.

I gasp, my nails sinking into his skin. "I promise. No one but you."

And he makes good on his side of the bargain.

CHAPTER TWENTY-FIVE

I sign my contract Sunday. Everything is official. I'm committed to *Model Citizen*. Three seasons or whenever the network decides to ax the show. If the show is lucky enough to make it three seasons—most TV shows barely make it to the end of their first season without getting canceled—we'll enter contract negotiations.

My agent will ask for more money. They'll protest but give in. Bam, I'll be rolling in it.

At least, that's how it's supposed to go.

I text Ryan a picture of the signed contract, but his only reply is that he'll be home at nine. He's at the office, again.

I'm tempted to call Luke. He'd be happy for me. He'd celebrate with me. He would say more than "I'll be home at nine."

But I resist. There's something so intoxicating about him. It only makes this more confusing.

I spend the day with my Kindle, pouring over *Jane Eyre* and drinking as much coffee as my stomach will stand. My heart races. I shake. My mouth goes dry and my head aches. I'm filled with energy but I'm tied to this apartment.

I lie down and close my eyes, willing my body to fall asleep, but my head is racing. This is all too much, too fast. There must be something I can do to figure this out. There must be some way to know what I really want.

The couch is soft and warm, and it's finally dark outside. I don't remember eating dinner. I better make up something or I'll get an awful lecture from Ryan.

I lie on the couch for a while, willing my head to stop racing. It feels like an eternity passes, but eventually the door opens and Ryan steps inside.

I check the time on my phone. It's nine fifteen.

And I have three new texts from Luke. No big deal.

"Congratulations, sweetheart." Ryan sets his briefcase on the table. He's too far away to see my phone.

I go to the setting and add a password. I turn it to the most private setting, so the only way to see texts and calls is with a password.

No, that's not enough. Ryan will find a way around it. I delete the calls to Luke from my log. I delete our text history.

"How was work?" I ask.

"Busy." He sits next to me on the couch. "I'll have to work late all week." It's so calm and even, like working seven days a week is normal.

I nod okay. Next week is my last week of freedom. The last week before I start shooting *Model Citizen*. It's not like I want my boyfriend around to help me deal with this major life change.

"Let's go out Sunday," he says. "Someplace nice."

"Okay."

He kisses me on the cheek. Then on the neck. His hands find my hips. There's nothing soft about it, no attempt to seduce me, but his intentions are obvious. He wants more. He wants to relieve the stress of his eighty-hour work week. He wants his pretty trophy fiancée to make herself useful.

But I shake my head. It's not just that I promised Luke. I don't want it like this, like I'm a release from the difficulties of his day. Like I should be ready to lie back and take it the moment he gets home.

"I'm tired," I say.

He pulls his hands back to his sides. "You've been tired a lot lately."

"I drank too much coffee."

His eyes find mine. "Do you want to tell me what's really going on?"

"It's late. I'm tired. That's it."

He shakes his head like he doesn't believe me, but he doesn't push it.

The week passes slowly. The days are long, and I am too distracted by thoughts of *Model Citizen* to do much of anything. I rehearse my lines until I know them backwards and forwards. Until I'm sure I'll be able to hold my own against the rest of the cast.

When I run out of energy, I try to read, but the words feel like a jumble. I watch TV, but I find myself staring out the window instead of at the screen. Even my runs around the marina are useless. Luke is never waiting for me under that tree.

I run during the day, when he's sure to be at work. Of course he's not waiting for me. It's silly to get my hopes up.

Ryan arrives home late and leaves early. He texts to make sure I am doing well—eating my meals, following my routine—but there is no warmth or love to it.

But Luke, Luke is a different story. He texts to ask how I'm doing. He texts to ask if I'm excited about the show. He texts just to tell me about the movie he watched the night before. He couldn't sleep. He was thinking about me.

I try to keep my replies short and to the point, to avoid the temptation of long conversations. But my days are so slow, and I need something in my brain besides images of myself failing horribly at returning to TV acting.

So I reply. I reply with every single thing I can think of. It almost feels like we're in the same place together, talking for hours. It almost feels like everything will be okay, like I can handle my return to acting.

Saturday rolls around. Ryan is working again. He's working late. So he'll have time to take me out tomorrow. So he'll have two hours to spare for me.

It's a beautiful day—blue and brilliant—and I can't bear to spend it on the couch again.

I text Luke. "What are you doing?"

He replies a few minutes later. "I know what I'd like to do." There's an attached picture. It's Luke, from his chin to just below his bellybutton—his strong chest, his toned stomach, the jut of his hipbones, the soft trail of hair leading to his boxers.

God, he's hot.

I take a deep breath. I try to reason with myself. I need to figure this out, not to lose myself in another afternoon with Luke.

But then I look at the picture. Luke could be mine. He could be pressed up against me. I bite my lip. I start to shake, but it's not from too much caffeine.

I respond. "That could be arranged."

He texts back. "I'll pick you up in twenty minutes."

It's barely ten. That leaves a whole lot of time until I have to be back here. A whole lot of time for exactly what Luke would like to do.

Luke and I walk the path that curves around the marina. He holds my hand, even as we pass Ryan's office. We talk about little things—my week, the weather, that movie that we didn't watch at the theater.

He leads me into a residential neighborhood. There's something familiar about it, but I can't put my finger on it. I turn to him as if to ask for an explanation, and he nods as if to say soon. A few minutes later we're in front of that blue-and-white house, the place where we first kissed.

"I lied before," he says. "This isn't a friend's house. It's mine."

"So you're throwing away money on a mortgage you don't need?"

He laughs. "I wouldn't put it in those terms."

"How rich are you?"

He laughs, a hearty laugh, and shakes his head. "Miss Summers, you have no manners."

"I'm aware."

He squeezes my hand. "My father had a very generous life insurance police and a very generous savings account."

"So very rich?"

He raises his eyebrows. "I'm also partner in a law firm."

I swat him playfully. "Shut your bragging face."

He shakes his head and leads me into the house. We use a key to go through the front door this time. Like normal people.

It's quiet inside. Soft, white light streams through the windows, off the clean tile floor of the kitchen.

He presses the door closed and presses me against it. "It's not just mine. It's mine and Samantha's."

He has a fucking house with her?

I bite my lip. Deep breath. "What does that mean?"

"It's a legal technicality."

"You own a house with your ex."

His eyes connect with mine. "Technically." He slides his hands over my sides. "We haven't figured out who is buying who out."

"Who is buying whom."

His eyes are wide, filled with life. "Exactly."

I shift back, but the only thing behind me is the door. It feels damn good to have Luke's body so close to mine, but he has a house with his ex. A fucking house.

"You're freaking out, aren't you?" he asks.

"Owning a house is very grown up."

"So is getting engaged." He slides his hand around my waist. His eyes stay on mine. "My dad insisted on fronting the down payment when Samantha and I got engaged. Said no wife of mine was living in a shitty apartment in Mar Vista."

"And it was easier to let him get his way?"

He nods. "I thought it was a gesture of goodwill and not an 'I'm guilty I'm fucking your girlfriend' move." He steps back, his shoulders tensing. "But hey, that's the late Edward Lawrence for you."

"Do you want to talk about it?" I ask.

"How about some caffeine first?"

"Yes please."

He takes my hand and leads me into the kitchen. It's gorgeous, spotless, straight out of a magazine. There's a shiny coffee maker on the counter. A drip coffee maker that is likely to make only passable coffee.

But, still, it looks new. Like he bought it for me.

Luke opens a cabinet and pulls out a bag of coffee. Beans from a local shop. "The guy behind the counter at this place was wearing a fedora."

"So it must be amazing."

He nods and measures the coffee carefully. He seems a little lost, like he's never done it before. But he diligently pours water into a measure cup then into the machine.

"Why don't you stay here?" I ask.

He turns the machine on. "Too many memories." He turns back to me. "But that's all they are—memories."

His eyes are wide, honest. They're only memories. Somehow, I believe him.

The coffee maker sputters, then it's *drip, drip, drip.*

"It likes you," he says.

I laugh, shaking my head. "That's what all drip coffee makers do."

"Because they all like you." He smiles and takes a step towards me. Until his body is only a few inches from mine.

I move backwards, and my ass hits the kitchen island. Another giant expanse of counter.

Luke is so close, I can feel the heat of his body, hear his breath. My heart pounds against my chest. My skin tingles from anticipation. I need him touching me again.

He grabs my hips and presses me against the counter. "Will you forgive me if I don't wait until you've had your coffee?"

"I'll consider it."

His lips curl into a smile. "I'll take it."

He kisses my neck. It's soft, but there's such a hunger to it. A need. Like he can't wait another minute.

Hell, I don't want to wait another second.

I lean into his kiss. His lips are soft and warm, and every kiss sends sparks through my body. Then it's his teeth. He bites gently. He grabs my ass and lifts me onto the counter.

Drip, drip, drip. The smell of coffee fills the air. How did I ever think coffee was better than this?

Luke presses his lips against my shoulders, my collarbone, my chest. He pulls my dress out of the way, groaning as the fabric slides over my nipple.

He does the same with the other side of the dress. His eyes fill with delight. He arranges the fabric at my waist, his fingers sliding over my chest.

His eyes find mine. He watches me as he slides his fingers over my nipples, as I groan and bite my lip.

My breath is heavy. "Don't stop." Please don't stop.

He kisses me, hard, his tongue plunging into my mouth. And he rubs his thumbs over my nipples. Harder and harder and harder.

I dig my nails into his shoulders, anything to help me stay upright.

He drags his lips across my cheek, my neck, back to my chest. Then he brings his mouth to my nipple. He sucks, gently at first, then harder. Harder. Harder.

Then it's his teeth. A soft bite. Then harder. Harder. Until it hurts. Until want floods every inch of my body.

Until I need him inside me so badly I'm shaking.

He brings his mouth to my ear, his breath warm. "Spread your legs."

It's a request, but there's something possessive about it. Like I'm his. I close my eyes. I can be his, at least for a few hours.

I nod and spread my legs as far as they will go. My dress shifts up my thighs, until it's barely covering me.

He slides his hand up my thigh, closer and closer and closer. He grabs my dress and pushes it to my waist.

"Fuck, Alyssa." He groans. He's reveling in my lack of underwear.

I swallow hard. There's so much want in his eyes and his hands are so close. I'm so close to being his.

I lift my arms, and he pulls my dress off my shoulders. He takes a long look at me, like I'm his favorite thing in the world.

Then he presses his lips against mine. It's hard, intense, like he's marking me.

His hands return to my thighs, closer and closer and closer, until they're on my sex. He strokes me with the lightest of touches, and pleasure shoots through my body.

I'm his. Right now, I'm his.

He kisses me. I surrender to it, parting my lips to make way for my tongue.

I'm putty in his hands. I relax my body, lying against the counter. He pulls me closer to the end. His lips are on my breasts. Then my stomach. Then my hipbone. My thigh.

Then they're on me, sending pleasure all the way to my fingers and toes, making me feel so good I could scream.

He shifts to his knees and slides his tongue over my clit. Pleasure shoots through me. I groan, pressing my fingers against the slick counter.

He grabs my thighs, pushing my legs apart, and he licks me, over and over and over. He flicks his tongue against my clit. It's fast and hard, and my body responds quickly. I buzz with pleasure everywhere—my hands, my feet, my throat, my chest. And my sex, Jesus. I clench, sucking in a shallow breath.

I reach for him, but all I can get is the counter. He digs his fingers into my thighs, pulling me closer, holding me in place. His tongue is so soft and wet, and right now, I'm his.

All his. Only his.

The pressure inside me builds. It's so much. It feels so good I can barely stand it.

He licks me again and again and again. Soft then hard. Quickly then slowly. Then it's only his tongue against my clit, long, steady strokes.

My sex clenches again. There's no stopping it. Almost. I press my fingers against the counter, anything to make this last longer.

He licks me again. Again. Again.

The tension inside me builds.

I groan, I scream, I pant. He feels so fucking good.

Almost.

His tongue is soft and wet.

He licks me again.

There.

Everything inside me releases in a torrent of pleasure. I pant, slowly catching my breath.

Luke digs his teeth into my thigh. He shifts to a standing position, grabs my hands, and pulls me to my feet.

His hands find my hips and he presses me against the counter. Our chests, our stomachs, our thighs—every part of us is touching, and I can feel him through his jeans.

He's hard, and he's mine, and I need him inside of me, making me his.

I press my lips into Luke's, my tongue sliding into his mouth. He kisses back, aggressive, his hands tight around my hips.

I'm his. Right now, I'm his.

He pulls a condom from his jeans and places it on the counter. Then he turns his eyes toward me. He looks me over again, like he wants me so much he could scream.

I dig my hands into his back but his T-shirt is in the way. He's wearing too much clothing. I pull his shirt over his head. He groans, leaning into me so his bare chest is pressed against mine. His skin is on mine, his body against mine.

I unzip his jeans and rub him over his boxers. He sighs, sinking his teeth into my neck. I rub him harder and he catches a thin bit of skin between his teeth.

Pleasure shoots through my body. I gasp.

Enough waiting. I need him inside me and now.

I push his jeans to his knees. Then his boxers.

Fuck. That's all of him and it's all mine. He's ready for me.

I wrap my fingers around his bare cock and I stroke him. He groans, sinking his teeth into my ear. His eyes find mine. They're heavy with need, desire, lust. Whatever the hell I want to call it—he wants to fuck me, to make me his.

His mouth hovers over my ear. "Turn around."

I nod, pressing my body against his as I turn around. He grabs my hands and plants them on the counter. My legs shake, my skin tingling. He can do whatever he wants to me.

Then his lips are on my neck, soft and sweet. He kisses my shoulders, slides his fingertips over my thighs.

I suck in a shallow breath. "Luke..."

He sinks his teeth into my skin, grabs my thighs, and pushes them apart. I'm open wide for him, ready for him.

I dig my hands into the counter. We're almost there. We're so close to exactly where we need to be.

He unwraps the condom and slides it on. Then his hands are on my hips, his lips are on my neck.

I arch into him, tilting my neck so he can kiss me. He grabs my hair, tugging gently, and presses his lips into mine.

He moans into my mouth. Then he releases me. He turns me back around and spreads my legs a little wider.

I'm his and he can do whatever he wants with me.

His tip strains against my sex. Almost.

I press my hands into the counter and he slides inside me.

Fuck. I groan and take a deep breath. He feels so good inside me.

Luke holds my hips. He shifts into me with slow, deep thrusts. I can feel every inch of his cock against my sex. I can hear his heavy breath, his groans.

He presses his chest against my back and pulls me in for another kiss. I dig my fingers through his hair, exhaling as he thrusts into me again.

I'm his and he's mine.

He turns me back around, plants my hands on the counter again.

Fuck.

He runs his fingertips over my thighs, my stomach, my chest. He circles my nipples and sinks his teeth into my neck.

And he thrusts into me, harder and deeper. Again, and again, and again.

My body hums with pleasure. I never want this this end, never want anything but him inside of me.

He squeezes my nipples and my sex clenches.

"Luke," I groan.

He squeezes me again, kisses my neck. His breath is heavy. Strained. He groans and shifts into me. Harder, faster, deeper.

The pressure inside me builds. I'm close.

He kneads my breasts. He presses me hard against the counter.

And he thrusts into me. Deeper. Harder. Again and again and again.

My sex clenches. Almost. I reach back and scrape my nails against his thighs.

He groans. "Fuck, Alyssa."

I suck a breath between my teeth. "Harder."

I'm so damn close.

He thrusts into me, harder, deeper. His hands find my hips and he holds me steady.

"Harder."

He groans and I can feel it everywhere.

And he goes harder, deeper. He takes his time, filling me with every thrust.

My legs shake. Almost. There's such a deep tension inside me, so much I can barely take it.

His breath is hot against my ear. His groan is heavy, intense. Another thrust. It's deeper, harder.

My sex clenches. Almost.

Luke groans into my ear. He digs his fingers into my thigh and thrusts into me again, and again, and again.

Everything inside me builds and builds, until I can't take it another moment.

An orgasm rocks through me. I scream. I scream so loudly the neighbors are sure to hear.

He kisses my neck and holds me close.

I close my eyes, listening to his heavy breath, his low moans.

He's close. He's close and I need to feel him come, to make him feel as good as I do.

He thrusts into me again, his groans getting louder and louder.

"Alyssa." He squeezes my hips, his nails sharp against my skin.

One more groan, one more thrust, one more scrape of his nails against my skin.

And he comes, his breath releasing, his grip tight on my hips.

He sighs one last time and wraps his arms around me.

His lips find my neck, and he squeezes me tightly. "I better get you that coffee."

I nod, and I hold the counter to stay upright.

That was so much better than coffee.

CHAPTER TWENTY-SIX

We order lunch from a deli around the corner and eat it on the couch, our bodies pressed up against each other. We watch movies from Luke's collection. *The Philadelphia Story* then *Some Like it Hot.*

The sun rises in the sky, and he drags me to the backyard. "Have you ever gone skinny-dipping?" he asks.

I nod, even though I know it's not what he wants to hear.

"Oh, you're no fun."

"Like you don't get naked here all the time," I say.

He smirks and pulls his T-shirt over his head. It's only been a few hours, but it's still a damn good sight.

He slides his hands up my thighs, stopping when they're on my ass. My breath catches in my throat. I want him again. I want him everyday, all the time.

He pulls my dress to my waist, then my shoulders, then over my head. His eyes pass over my body briefly.

"You're amazing," he says.

My cheeks flush. I press my hands together.

"I've already gotten into your pants. I don't have anything to gain by saying it."

"I know."

He brings his hands to my hips and pulls me closer, until our bodies are pressed together. "I mean it. You're sexy as all hell."

I blush again. "You are too."

He brings his lips to mine. It's not like before. It's soft, romantic.

He pulls back, but I kiss him again, my lips soft against his.

When we break, he steps back and wiggles out of his jeans. He's wearing nothing but boxers.

He turns around, mock shy, slides his boxers to his knees, and jumps into the pool.

He comes up for air and his eyes find mine. "The water's perfect."

It does look perfect in there.

I close my eyes and dip my toe. It's warmer than the ocean, but it still feels cool against my skin. Fuck it. I jump into the pool.

It's a shock, but it's not too bad.

We swim all afternoon, splashing, chasing each other, floating calmly on top of the water. We swim until the sunset casts an orange light in the sky, until I'm certain I have to get back to Ryan's place.

I dry off and dress in the bathroom. When I emerge, Luke is splayed out on the couch like he's ready for round two.

He pats the spot next to him.

I bite my lip. It would be so nice, but I have to resist. "I should get going."

There's a sadness in his eyes, but he shakes it off like it's nothing. He shifts off the couch and motions to the door. "I probably shouldn't walk you home."

"Probably."

Still, he walks me to the door. He lingers there, his hands on my shoulders, his gaze on me. We stay like that for a while, until we both know it's time for me to leave.

The restaurant is quiet. Of course it's quiet. It's nearly nine on a Sunday. Later than Ryan promised. But it's something.

It's a restaurant I hate, actually. One with a strict dress code, snooty service, and all sorts of gentlemen diners who look at me like I'm a thing that can amuse them.

They only avert their eyes when Ryan squeezes my waist in his best *she's mine* gesture.

We take our seats on the patio. It's cool, especially when I'm wearing a tiny cocktail dress, and the heat lamps do little to warm me up. Ryan offers me his jacket, but I turn it down.

I need the cold, the reminder that this isn't comfortable.

"How was work?" I ask, like it is normal he was working all day Sunday.

Ryan goes on and on about the boring details of a divorce case. I nod and mumble something about how it's interesting.

A waitress arrives at our table. She looks at me like she recognizes me, but she doesn't mention it. "Good evening. What can I get for you?"

Ryan steps in. "We'll have two orders of the blackened salmon. No bread."

He folds his menu and hands it to her. Then he does the same with mine. He smiles at the waitress like he's the king of the world.

He turns his attention back to me. "I'm proud of you, sweetheart."

I nod and take a long sip of my water. "Thank you."

Ryan leans back in his chair. "Do you remember when you were in *The Crucible* your sophomore year?"

"Of course." I spent two months rehearsing for the damn play, and I totally killed it.

"Do you remember after? I brought you a bouquet backstage and what's her name—Ellie—started screaming how excited she was to see me."

I nod. Ryan was a much desired college boy when I was a sophomore. Not just a college boy, but a Harvard boy. He visited about every other weekend, and he still showed up whenever I needed him.

"And then she screamed about how lucky you were that Ryan Knight was your boyfriend."

"I remember."

Ryan leans in closer, his hazel eyes boring into me. "That's how I feel knowing I have you. Like I'm the luckiest guy in the world."

My stomach twists in knots. I nod. "Thank you."

I press my back into the chair, willing myself to take slow, deep breaths. I don't know if I believe a word he's saying or why he feels so lucky—if he really loves me or if he knows no one else would put up with his shit—but I can't listen to another word.

So I ask another question about work, and I nod along at his story.

I barely manage to make it through my salmon.

At home, Ryan presses me against the wall. He presses his lips against my neck, his hand sliding up my dress.

I close my eyes, shifting slightly to give him some idea. I can't. I promised Luke and my stomach is still in knots. I can barely breathe as it is.

But Ryan does not take the hint. He grabs my hips, pinching my skin, and he presses his lips against mine. He had a few drinks at dinner. It's unusual for him. It makes him aggressive.

I turn my neck, but he still doesn't take the hint. He kisses my ear, his hands finding their way to my ass.

I shake my head. "Not tonight."

"Don't you want to celebrate?" His voice is heavy. He doesn't want to turn back.

"I don't feel well."

Ryan snaps back to attention. He takes a step back and meets my gaze. "You haven't felt well for the last month."

"It was the salmon..."

"Don't lie to me." His hazel eyes bore into mine. This time, it's a demand for an explanation.

"I'm not in the mood."

He shakes his head. "You're always in the mood. Usually, you beg me."

My stomach drops. It's not far from the truth. He's usually too tired from work, and I'm usually desperate for some hint of intimacy.

I try to think up some excuse, but nothing comes.

"What's really going on?" he asks.

I shake my head. "I've been tired lately. It's nothing."

"Alyssa."

"Maybe if you got home before ten some nights."

Ryan shakes his head. "Tell me the truth."

"There is no truth. I'm just not in the mood."

He moves back. "I don't believe you."

The air leaves my lungs. "How would you like me to prove it?"

Ryan moves to the kitchen table. "You're not in the mood, fine, but don't lie to me about why."

"I'm not lying."

Ryan glares at me. "Why don't you take the spare room tonight?"

I take a deep breath and try my best everything-is-okay nod. There's nothing I can say to convince him this is normal. I can't even convince myself.

But still, I can't leave things like this. "Maybe if we spent more time together."

Ryan shakes his head. "We'll talk about this another time." There's some anger to it, but it's not directed at me. Not entirely.

He recedes into the bedroom, clicking the door locked. I move into the spare room. It's about the same really. A bed, a dresser, a gorgeous view of the ocean.

I can't let this go any further. I have to figure out what the hell I'm doing, and spending time with Luke or Ryan will only make that more difficult.

So that's it. No more boys until I've made up my mind.

CHAPTER TWENTY-SEVEN

I'm a nervous wreck on the drive to the production office. This is my first day back in the saddle, and I need to bring it. I need to kill it.

When I arrive, I'm ferried into a small dressing room. It's nice, clean, with a couch and a soft, yellow vanity mirror. My makeup artist arrives a few minutes later. She's a nice girl, about my age, with tattoos and a bad-ass asymmetrical haircut. I trust her not to make me into a porcelain Barbie doll.

An assistant does a Starbucks run, but I'm too nervous to eat much of my breakfast. This is the first time I've volunteered to step in front of a camera in forever, and everyone else knows the material so much better than I do.

Deep breath. Nerves mean lack of preparation. I need to practice more, to run my lines a dozen more times.

An assistant calls me to the set. I wait as our director, a middle-aged man in a straw fedora, orders around the crew and perfects the placement of the lights. He's one of those directors who needs to feel important. They're always the worst.

When he deems the set ready, we take our places for the first scene. It's easy. Marie Jane and her sister, Patricia, fight over living together. Marie Jane wants things her way and she's completely unwilling to see from another person's perspective.

The assistant director counts us down. Three, two, one, and he slams the slate. The camera is on me. It's my line first. But I'm frozen. I call scene, ask to take it from the top, but it doesn't help. I can't look away from the lights. They are so bright and so hot.

"Hon," the director says, "I respect the process. Take the time you need to start the scene, but do it in under thirty seconds."

I nod of course, and he resets the scene. This time, I jump in as soon as he calls "action"—yeah, we really do that.

"You're overreacting," I say to Naomi, not at all in character, and I butcher the rest of my lines.

The director nods, better, not really trying to hide his annoyance. Jesus, it's the first scene. I know I'm rusty, but I deserve a little warm-up time before I'm deemed a failure.

Deep breath. I always used to freak out too easily, and it always made things worse. Nerves work for a nervous character, but Marie Jane is confident. She's not self-aware enough to be nervous. She's not weak enough to be nervous. She doesn't care enough about what people think of her.

I pretend as if I am back in high school with my best friend from drama class, practicing for the school play. I pretend as if it is just me and the words and a person who really does want me to succeed.

I do a little better, but it's still not great. After a few more tries, I warm up, and Marie Jane claws her way out of my packed mind. I nail it, and we're on to the next line and the next shot. It still takes me a while to perfect my delivery, but I am faster and closer.

This is so much harder than I remembered.

The scene takes two hours. It's just Marie Jane and Patricia arguing. No improvisation, no deviation from the script. Nothing physical. Nothing scantily clad. Nothing tough.

A year ago, this would have been a cakewalk. I knew Cindy Bleachers backwards and forwards and I knew exactly how I needed to play my lines—I had to be a sexy, horny, confident, fucked-up mess.

But this is a new character, a more complicated character, and I am not used to doing much of anything all day.

Still, I manage to fake enough confidence to make it to lunch.

The crew does their magic—moving props, rearranging lights, turning a clean living room into a trashed mess. I practice my next scene in my dressing room, obsessing over my lines until I am sure I have it. I stumble still, but I try to fake confidence. Marie Jane is confident. I need to be confident, too. This scene is longer, bigger. It comes later in the episode, after Marie Jane throws a big bash. I try to stay loose and keep things fun, but I can tell I am the reason why we need to redo takes.

By the end of the day, I am exhausted. My head is swimming. This is so hard. I'm not sure that I can do it.

I need a distraction, something that will rid my mind of this anxiety. Ryan won't be home until late. I could buy two pints of ice cream, stuff my face, and throw up. It would work.

I take a deep breath. There's only one other way to handle this.

I call Luke.

"Hey." His voice is low and deep. It's sweet, but there's a need to it.

"I'm feeling overwhelmed again," I say. "And I'd really rather not talk about it."

"I get the feeling I should object to being used as a distraction."

"Do you?"

"No." He takes a slow breath. "We can talk after. If you want."

"Are you at home?" I press my fingers into the phone. His place isn't the best idea. Ryan could be there.

"I'm at the apartment, but we can meet at the house if you're worried about Ryan."

I check the time. It's almost eight. Late enough that Ryan might be home. That he might arrive in time to see my car in my parking spot and wonder where the hell I am.

"Okay," I say. "Your house. I can be there in twenty minutes."

"Until then."

He hangs up and I clutch my phone tightly. Twenty minutes until I have a release from all this. Twenty minutes until I'm with Luke.

I make my way to my car and drive as quickly as I can. The closer I get to Luke's house, the harder my heart pounds against my chest.

When I arrive, the door is open. I half expect Ryan to answer, to pat himself on the back for his elaborate trap. But it is only Luke, in his jeans and T-shirt, staring out the window. His face lights up when he sees me. It feels so good to see his big, brown eyes bright and full of life. Full of need.

I don't waste any time. I move towards him, wrapping my arms around him, brushing my lips against his. We melt into each other, our arms around each other, our bodies pressed together. It is sweet at first. Then he drags his fingertips across my stomach, and I know I can't keep it sweet. I need to have him. I need to hear him come, his nails digging into my skin, his breath fast and choppy.

He sucks on my lips as he pulls my shirt over my head. My body tingles with electricity as he trails his fingertips over my skin, touching me everywhere.

I grab his ass and press my body into his until I can feel him get hard.

Yes. He's responding to me.

I bring my mouth to his ear. "Mr. Lawrence, I have to ask your permission for something."

I unbuckle his belt.

"Anything," he groans.

"May I make you come?"

He smiles and nods. "Only if I can make you come."

"Oh, you can," I say. "But you may not... Not until I'm finished with you."

He shifts his body towards mine, grabbing my ass.

"Take off your clothes. I want to see you," he groans.

"And why should I?" I ask.

"I wouldn't want to revoke my permission." He unhooks my bra. He watches, mesmerized, as it falls to the ground. By now he's seen me naked a dozen times, but his eyes still get big and wide.

He brings his mouth around my nipple, sucking gently. This isn't part of the deal, but God, it feels so good. My body is a torrent of want.

But he won't stop me from my quest.

I pin him against the wall, pressing my body into his as I unzip his jeans and stroke him over his boxers. I hover my mouth over his ear again. It would normally be so awkward to talk like this, but with Luke, it's easy.

"I'm not stopping until you come in my mouth," I whisper in his ear.

And there it is, that look on his face that screams *I want you so badly*.

I bring my lips to his earlobe and suck gently. Then harder. He groans, so I sink my teeth into his skin until I hear that sound again. Then I move to his neck, biting him harder and harder, his groans getting louder.

"Take off your clothes." I echo his words back to him.

I slide my jeans and panties to my knees and kick them off my feet. He follows suit, pulling his shirt over his head, stepping out of his jeans. Then it's only the thinnest layer of cotton between his cock and me.

I work my way down his body, kissing his collarbone, shoulders, chest. I run my fingers down his stomach, tracing the outlines of his muscles, brushing my fingertips against the soft hairs below his bellybutton.

He shudders. "Alyssa..."

So this is how it feels to be in control of his pleasure. Like he's putty in my hands. No wonder he's such an awful tease.

"Do you want me to stop?" I slip my hand into his boxers and wrap it around his cock.

"No, God, no..."

I drop to my knees and pull his boxers to the floor. I brush my lips against his cock, the softest of teases. He groans, surely realizing that I'm going to torture him the way he's tortured me. I stroke him, up and down, harder and harder, brushing my lips against him again.

And, when he's finally shaking with need, I slip my lips around his cock, sucking on his tip, relishing the taste of his skin.

"Jesus, Alyssa..."

I take in more of him, sliding my mouth up and down his cock, over and over again.

"Fuck," he groans, and he teases my nipples with his fingers.

Want spreads through me. He feels so good in my mouth.

I suck harder and harder, running my hand up and down him to match the motions of my mouth. He's getting close, but I'm not done with him yet.

I pull back and kiss his thighs and stomach. I look up at Luke, into those big, brown eyes, full of desire. And I keep kissing him, moving further up his thighs. He squeezes my chest as he groans. I move back to his cock and swirl my tongue around his head. I lick him, up and down, his groans getting louder and louder.

He's close.

I slip my mouth back around him and slide over him. Up and down. Up and down. Up and down. His moans are quiet and low-pitched. His breath is heavy. He looks down at me, his gaze heavy with want, and digs his hands into my hair, guiding my mouth over him.

His eyes roll back into his head as his eyelids flutter closed. He sinks his teeth into his lips, his groans getting louder and louder as I suck harder and harder.

And he comes. I don't stop until he's finished completely. I swallow as my eyes lock with his.

Luke groans. "I'm going to get you back for that."

He sinks to the floor next to me, not shy about pressing his lips against mine, sliding his tongue into my mouth. He pins me to the ground and pulls my knees apart.

But he doesn't touch me yet.

Then his fingers brush against my thighs, and there it is again—electricity, everywhere. He runs his fingertips over me in wavy lines, curving around my thighs, behind my knees, over my hips, up and down my stomach. He drags his fingers around my nipples and across my neck. Then he traces the outline of my lips as he kisses my neck, my collarbone, my chest.

He brings his mouth around my nipple again, sucking on it as his hands trail all the way down my stomach, moving past my bellybutton, until they are so, so close.

"Jesus," I groan, tugging on his hair.

He sinks his teeth into my nipple as, finally, he slides his fingers over my clit. He strokes me with two fingers, back and forth. My body hums with need.

I dig my nails into the skin of his back, and he moves his fingers in longer strokes, teasing my sex as they brush against it. I arch my body into his. I want his fingers inside me. I need his fingers inside me. I am wet and ready and achy with desire.

But still he teases. His fingers return to my clit, softer this time. His strokes get longer and longer until I can't take it anymore. I arch my back to meet his hand. His finger slips inside me and I groan.

"Make me come," I command.

And in response, he brings his mouth to my other nipple, sucking and biting and flicking his tongue across it. He slides his finger deeper in me, then deeper, and deeper, and I get closer and closer.

But still I groan. "More."

Fuck. I gasp. He slips a second finger inside me and slides them in and out. I arch my back to meet every thrust of his fingers. He moves faster. Harder. God, don't stop. I shift my hips faster and faster, trying to match his frantic pace. The pressure inside me grows, harder and harder and harder, until it can't get any harder, and everything releases in a torrent of ecstasy.

I collapse onto the ground, straining to catch my breath. He wraps his body around mine. His grasp is soft and firm at the same time and I can feel his breath on my neck.

We lie like that for what seems like forever.

He brings his lips to my ear. "Do you want to talk?"

I shake my head and pull him closer. Talking might lead to questions, to demands that I figure this out right away, to something besides the two of us pressed up against each other.

CHAPTER TWENTY-EIGHT

The days on set are long and sometimes slow, but I love everything about it. I love having a job. I love talking with the other actors during breaks.

And God, when I'm actually in a scene, when I'm actually Marie Jane, it's the best feeling in the whole damn world.

When I am not in a scene, I get a few hours in my dressing room. The waiting used to bother me, but now I spend every spare second practicing my lines. Every day, I gain a little confidence. I remember my old tricks.

By Friday, I have it. I can tell. The other actors treat me differently, like I'm finally not a liability. A few invite me out for drinks but I decline. I need to get home, to my bedroom, where I can finally breathe.

But I can't bring myself to leave when there's nothing worth going home to. Ryan and I used to go to dinner on Friday nights. To celebrate the end of his week. The end of my five days of solitude. And, even though it was no big deal, it was special. We dressed up, we got out, we stared into each other's eyes.

Ryan didn't provide the most interesting conversation, but I liked listening to him. I liked being the person he talked to, the person he trusted, the person who really put him at ease.

What happened to that? We used to take walks on the beach. We used to play games after dinner. Hell, we used to have dinner together. And we'd do things on the weekends. Visit museums, see movies, explore new parts of Los Angeles.

We weren't in love, but we cared about each other. And I liked spending time with him. I really did.

There's a knock on my door. I open it, expecting my makeup artist to once again warn me I need to wipe off the war paint. But it's Laurie, with a big smile on her face.

"Come on," she says. "Let's have a drink."

Laurie's office is a hipster paradise. Notebooks with little animals. A shiny, silver MacBook Air adorned with pastel stickers. A mustache pen holder. She catches me looking around her office and shrugs.

"I don't buy this shit. It's my parents. They know I spend all my time here."

She pulls a bottle of scotch from her desk drawer and pours two glasses. Straight up. "I'm not keeping you from some place you'd rather be, am I?"

"No." This is exactly where I should be.

Laurie sips her drink and makes a disgusted face. "Ugh, this stuff is awful. I think I have some melon liqueur. What do you say—do you like sickeningly sweet things?"

"I like tequila."

"No, no, no. I am not giving anyone tequila. I've gotten in trouble for that before. Unless... I know liqueurs have a lot of calories, and I'm sure you have some kind of special diet."

Because, like any other actress, I need to maintain my weight, or because Laurie, like everyone else with an internet connection, knows I spent three months in an eating disorder clinic?

"Liqueur is fine." I offer my calmest, most I'm-totally-okay expression.

"Are you sure?"

I nod. I'm not supposed to have more than one or two drinks—alcohol is a depressant—but a little melon liqueur won't kill me.

Laurie smiles. She jumps out of her chair and wanders to the production office kitchen. There are snacks everywhere. I try to ignore the plethora of candy and cookies and non-diet soda.

She reaches into a top cabinet, all the way in the back, and pulls out a half-full bottle of melon liqueur. "This stuff is amazing. So amazing." She finds red plastic cups, fills them with ice, and brings everything back to her office.

Laurie sighs, relaxing into her chair. She fills both cups to the very top.

"Aren't you going to drive home?" I ask.

"The network will pay if I call a car service. You too. I'm allowed to make obnoxious demands." She takes a long, thirsty sip of her drink. "You want to order a pizza? Jesus, sorry, I should know better. You had to leave that other show because..."

"It's okay. Part of being a C-lister means everyone knows you're bulimic."

"You're still..." She turns her gaze to the ground like she's embarrassed to ask such a horrible question.

Like I'm a broken vase and she can't bear to look at the mess.

"No, I'm not 'still...' but I do watch what I eat. Healthy food in moderation."

"Moderation? That sounds awful."

"It's not so bad." I press my fingers into my thighs. "I don't like pizza anyway."

"Who the fuck doesn't like pizza?"

"I don't like cheese."

She scrunches her nose like she smells something awful and raises her eyebrows. "Yeah, totally, pizza and cheese are awful. Food is totally overrated. It's the worst."

"You don't have to do that. I'm not upset about the pizza."

She stares at me like she doesn't believe me. "Sure. Pizza sucks. What kind of delicious, appropriate food should we order? A salad? Salads are healthy right, and grilled fish or something?"

"Anything but grilled fish or something."

"Okay, how about, hmm, how about steak?"

I hesitate. Steak is not on the recovery diet menu.

Her eyes fill with concern. "Sorry. I need to stop before I start offering you cocaine. Tell me what you want and we'll order it."

"No." I take my first sip of the green drink. It's super sweet, but there is something unique about the flavor. It's been a while since I've allowed myself any exciting flavors. "Steak is good."

"Are you sure?"

"I'm sure."

Laurie sends her assistant a text with our order and she settles back into her seat. "Are you sure the steak is okay?"

"Sure."

"Because I'm more than willing to put up with obnoxious demands if they mean my lead actor stays healthy."

I shake my head. "I'll let you know if anything is a problem."

"Good." She takes a long sip of her drink. It's like all the muscles in her face relax, like the melon alcohol is the best thing she's ever tasted. "I hate to hit this point, but I can't spare you. Not even for a few days."

"I understand." I sip my sickeningly sweet liqueur. "It won't be a problem."

She sighs. "Thank goodness. We can do away with showrunner Laurie."

"She's the one who gave me enough melon liqueur to put me in a coma?"

"It's not that much." She looks at the half-empty bottle. "Okay, maybe don't drink the whole thing." She turns her attention to me. "Let's not talk about this stupid show. How are you? Have you managed anything close to a life?"

"Close."

"You have a boyfriend, right? He's rich or something."

"Yeah..."

Her eyes light up. "Do tell."

"There's not much to tell. He works all the time."

She throws her hands in the air, shaking her head. "That is the worst gossip I ever heard!"

I smirk. "You're going to have to do better than melon liqueur if you want those kinds of details."

Laurie leans across the desk and lowers her voice to a desperate whisper. "Come on, I don't date. I don't sleep with anyone. I barely see my friends. I need to hear someone's drama."

She's tipsy already. Silly. But still, I get a good feeling about Laurie. Like she wouldn't judge me if she knew the truth.

"It's complicated," I say.

"Okay, let's trade. You tell me one little thing about, what was it, Ryan, and I'll tell you five more embarrassing things."

"I'm pretty sure you'll tell me anyway."

"Perhaps." She smiles and tops off her glass. "But you could still tell me, because we're friends and all."

"You first."

"Please, please, please," Laurie says. "How about some dirt on the rich boyfriend?"

"Ryan is..."

"Yeah?"

"Pretty mediocre in bed."

She squeals. "Now, we're talking."

"I shouldn't go into details."

"Come on, I thrive on details."

"Okay, one detail. He uses way too much tongue when he kisses me."

"No, no, no, I mean a sex detail. Not a kissing detail."

"And he's a little... selfish," I say.

"Selfish how?"

My cheeks flush. This is not the kind of thing I normally talk about. "He doesn't exactly go downtown."

She giggles. "Do you ever fight about it?"

"No. If we fought, it would be over someone else." Shit. I said someone, not something.

Did Laurie catch it or has she slipped from tipsy to drunk?

She smirks. "Freudian slip, huh?"

"What are you talking about?" I try to play it cool. Laurie is the closest thing I've had to a friend in a long time, and I'm not about to ruin her impression of me with the truth.

"Okay, okay, don't tell me. But if you do, I've got your back."

"Thanks."

"I won't sell you out, but you might want to stay tight-lipped. Everyone here is a horrible gossip."

"Including you?"

"Yeah, but not about my friends." She folds her arms. Her eyes narrow. "So, who is the other guy?"

"What other guy?"

"No self-respecting woman would put up with her boyfriend screwing around on her."

"How do you know I don't look the other way? Maybe I'm okay with his affair as long as he brings home the bacon?"

"Oh, like you eat bacon."

But maybe Laurie would understand. It would feel good to talk about this with someone outside the situation. I usually go to Ryan with these kinds of things. I can't exactly tell him I'm all torn up because I don't know if I should leave him for Luke.

"I should tell him I'm going to be late."

"The boyfriend or the... what would he be? Not a mistress. Maybe a mister."

I take a deep breath. It would feel so good to tell someone, to ease some of the weight of this. "He would be Luke."

Her jaw drops, but she tries to act like it's no big deal. "He sounds nice."

"He's much better than nice."

Laurie's face lights up. She's eating up this gossip.

She leans closer, lowering her voice to a stage whisper. "Is it just sex or do you really like him?"

I bite my lip. "I'm afraid I really like him."

"Enough to leave... what's his name, Ryan?"

I bite my lip. If only I had things so planned. "In theory."

"Yeah, but what about in practice?"

"It would be difficult. Ryan has been my best friend since high school."

"You love him?" she asks.

I take a deep breath and hold it for as long as I can. "I did once, but now..."

"You don't know?"

I nod. "I should check my phone. Let him know I'm hanging out with you."

She smiles and shifts back to giving me breathing room. She catches on quickly, not that it's especially complicated.

I dig through my purse until I find my phone. When it finally boots, I am met with a flurry of messages.

Ryan has a lot to say, it seems, and none of it is good. Fuck. What if he figured everything out? What if he knows.

My breath speeds as I read his messages.

Where are you?

What are you doing?

Are you out with some new boyfriend?

I have a few messages from Luke, warnings that Ryan is acting suspicious, that I should call him and do damage control if I don't want him to find out yet.

"Fuck, I have to go," I say.

Laurie looks straight at me. Her expression is intense. "Is everything okay?"

"It's nothing. Ryan is a little suspicious. I would tell him, but..."

"You don't have an endgame yet?"

"Yeah." I squeeze my phone. "It's not like I planned this."

Laurie reaches for her phone. "I'll call you a car." She narrows her eyes. The playfulness is gone. She's dead serious now. "If it ever becomes a big deal, you can crash at my place. Okay?"

"It's not like that," I insist.

She scribbles her cell on her business card and slides it into my purse.

"It's never like that. Until it is."

CHAPTER TWENTY-NINE

I look at a text from Luke. *We were at a work dinner, and I said something stupid. He's drunk and suspicious, but he's only suspicious.*

I can handle it. I reply.

Jesus, Alyssa, I'm so sorry. I really didn't want you to have to deal with this. I really wanted you to have time to figure it out and leave his sorry ass.

I can handle Ryan.

He replies. *Are you sure?*

Ryan has rescued me a hundred times. I owe him one.

I drop my phone back in my purse and ignore a flurry of text message alerts. It's almost eleven. Traffic is dead, and the car breezes through the city streets ten miles above the speed limit. I rest my head on the window and watch as the yellow lights of storefronts and street lamps blur into the blue sky. There is so much light here. It's hard to see the stars, but the moon is a silver crescent in cloudless sea.

Sometimes, it seems like life would be easier someplace smaller and quieter, someplace darker, where the lights turn off at nine, and the stars shine until dawn.

I climb the stairs to their suite on the third floor. There's arguing in one of the offices. It's not loud enough or angry enough to be fighting yet. Hopefully they haven't thrown any punches yet.

I clear my throat and Ryan steps into the waiting room.

He reaches out to me. "About time, sweetheart." His arms tighten around my waist.

He kisses me, shoving his tongue into my mouth. I can smell the alcohol on his breath. Jesus, I've never seen him like this.

I push Ryan away as gently as I can.

"Where were you?"

"Laurie and I were talking."

"You've been avoiding me all week."

"You've been working late all week."

Luke steps out of his office. His eyes find mine. He's worried. He nods to the door as if to suggest we get the hell out of here. But I shake my head.

Ryan scoffs. He looks at Luke with disdain. "Are you ready to tell me what the hell is going on with this asshole?"

I bite my tongue. I'm not going to deny it, but I'm not going to have this conversation while Ryan is drunk.

Ryan takes a step towards me, until he's so close I think he might hit me. He never has, but his eyes are so full of hate.

"Alyssa." Luke moves towards us to break it up.

I shake my head. "It's fine."

Ryan rolls his eyes. He moves back and sits on the desk in the lobby. He pats the sleek wood. His voice is accusatory, mocking even. "Did you two do it here?"

"Don't be ridiculous," I say.

"Did you fuck him on our bed?" He scowls at me. "I thought things had changed. I thought you loved me and you agreed to do things my way, but you don't, do you?"

"Ryan, that's not—"

"You'd be dead without me. You know that?"

I bite my lip. "I know."

"Don't you appreciate everything I do for you?"

I try to move, but I can't feel my hands and feet. I try to reply, but I can't feel my lips.

Ryan stares at me, that same hate in his hazel eyes. "You're such a fucking whore."

Luke moves past Ryan. He grabs my wrist. "Alyssa, let's go."

It's a command, but I don't move.

I hold Ryan's gaze. "I'm not a whore."

"No? Am I mistaken? Because as pathetic as this asshole is," Ryan stares at Luke with contempt, "he wouldn't be this nice without getting something in return."

Luke turns to Ryan. "Fuck you."

"Oh, you want to talk, Romeo?" Ryan slides off the desk. He takes a step towards Luke. "Are you fucking my fiancée?"

"Ryan..." I shrink back.

Luke steps in front of me, in between me and Ryan. "We're leaving."

"Ryan..."

"Is it even anything about him?" Ryan asks. "Or were you just desperate for the self-esteem boost?"

I'm frozen in place.

But Ryan doesn't stop. He takes a step towards Luke. "You're not special, you know. She'll fuck anyone who gives her attention."

"Explains why she ever fucked you," Luke says.

And I see the hate and anger build in both their eyes. I am sure one of them is going to throw a punch, but they just stare.

"Ryan, don't," I say. "It's not worth it."

Ryan shakes his head. "It would be worth it just to give this asshole a black eye."

"In your dreams," Luke says.

I shake my head and take a step towards the door. "I'm not a prize and I'm not going to watch anyone fight over me."

Luke nods. He rubs my shoulders. "Come on. I'll drive you home." He grabs my wrist, firm enough I know he means business, and pulls me towards the hallway.

"Bitch," Ryan mutters.

And I stop resisting Luke's guidance.

I expect Ryan to follow us down the stairs, but he doesn't. I expect to hear his rough voice or feel his hands around my wrist, but I don't. I hear nothing, feel nothing, think nothing.

Luke leads me through the dark parking garage, his hand glued to mine until we reach his car. I climb into the passenger seat and press my nails into my fingers.

"I never should have called you," Luke says. "I could have handled it."

"I've been with Ryan for a long time. I can handle him."

"There's only one way you could have handled him." His eyes are wide with concern. He's not okay with me giving into a drunk, aggressive Ryan's advances.

I'm not okay with it either.

I take a deep breath. "He isn't usually like this."

"An asshole?" Luke's voice is rough. Upset but not angry.

"Yeah."

He slides his key into the ignition but he doesn't turn it. "I don't believe you."

Luke brushes his hand against my cheek. It's soft, and warm, and I'm tempted to tear off my clothes and fuck him right here. If only for the distraction.

"I'm not going to let him hurt you." Luke's eyes are heavy with concern.

I swallow hard in an attempt to ease the dryness in my throat. "He never has."

Luke shakes his head. "The way he looked at you. Alyssa, he would have hit you if I wasn't there."

"He wouldn't."

"How do you know?"

My breath catches in my throat. "Because he wouldn't. Because he never has. Because he doesn't even get mad. Just disappointed."

Luke sinks into his seat, sighing in sheer frustration. "I don't get it. You're such a smart person and he treats you like a pet." He leans over me and buckles my seat belt. "It would be enough that he ignores you, that he works all night and day."

"It's not that bad."

"He logs his hours. I know exactly when he arrives and leaves at the office."

I bite my tongue. It is pretty bad, actually. "You're obviously not interested in an explanation. Only in convincing me I'm wrong."

He sighs, running a hand through his hair and shifting back to the driver's seat. "I want to understand. I want to know how to break the hold he has on you."

"I owe him my life. I can't..." It's dark here, even with the fluorescent lights on the cement ceiling.

"Fuck that. He helped you through a hard time. You don't owe him anything."

I close my eyes and take a deep breath. Maybe this is all a bad dream. Maybe it will go away.

I open my eyes. Luke is still sitting in the driver's seat, his attention turned to me, his eyes filled with concern.

"Why do we always have to talk about Ryan?" I ask.

"This is important. I love you too much to let you—" He inhales sharply, his eyes going wide. "I can't let you stay with someone who treats you like that."

"You love me?"

His cheeks turn red. Jesus, he's cute when he blushes.

"I didn't mean. I just... Yes," he says. "But we'll come back to that."

"I'm not sure if I'm going to be able to concentrate on anything else."

I reach for Luke, but he pulls away. This is the wrong time, the wrong circumstance. This kind of thing is supposed to be romantic.

"Pretend I didn't say it," he says.

"But—"

Luke brushes the hair from my forehead. His eyes are so big, so earnest. He would treat me so well. It would be amazing to be with him.

"Fuck how he treats you, that he's an asshole." He leans closer, until he's only a few inches away. "I want you. All of you. Not just the bits and pieces you can spare when Ryan is busy."

I swallow in an attempt to ease the dryness in my throat. It doesn't help. "What are you saying?"

"Leave him and be with me."

The air leaves my body. "Now?"

"Tomorrow, when he's sober enough to understand."

I shake my head. "That's too soon, Luke. I can't..."

"Why not?"

It's hard to breathe. Almost impossible.

He stares into my eyes. "You must know how you feel. If you love him. If you think you could love me."

I bite my lip. He's looking at me, waiting for a reaction. I nod.

"Then tell me the truth. Do you want to stay with Ryan or do you want to be with me?"

CHAPTER THIRTY

"You," I say. "I want you."

Luke's eyes light up, but there's still something missing. This should be sweet, romantic. This shouldn't be happening in a parking garage in the middle of the night.

He runs his fingers against my cheek. I sigh, melting into it. This feels so good. I should give in completely. I want so badly to give in completely.

He leans closer, brushing his lips against mine. It's soft, sweet, perfect.

"But I don't know if I can do this," I say.

"It's easy. Hell, I'll leave a message on his machine right now."

"Luke..."

His eyes find mine. They're hopeful. He's hopeful. "I know how hard it is to let go."

I nod. This doesn't just feel hard. It feels impossible.

He rubs my shoulders. "You don't have to do it tonight. Take the week."

I swallow hard. "What if I can't do it?"

"Then, that's it." He shifts back to his seat.

"No more of this?"

"No more of anything." His hand finds mine. "But you can do it. You're strong enough."

I press my lips together. Am I really strong enough to survive without Ryan's help? It doesn't seem possible. But still, I nod. "Okay." One week. I can manage one week.

Luke pulls his seat belt overs his chest and clicks it on. "You can't go back to his place."

"Where am I supposed to go?"

He turns to me. "Anywhere. Stay with me. Hell, I'll pay for a hotel room if that's what you need to feel sure."

I take a deep breath. "Laurie... my friend. I'll stay with her." I press my nails into my seat belt. "But I have my own conditions. I want you tonight."

"I'm not up for sex tonight."

I shake my head. "Not sex. Just the two of us, together, no talking about Ryan or what's going to happen next week."

"I can do that."

It's quiet at Luke's house. The place is still so sparse, so clean, so much like a photo in a magazine. It's not a place someone would live.

He presses his hand against mine. "Did you eat dinner?"

I shake my head. I didn't stick around Laurie's office for long enough. "I'm okay though."

"Uh-uh." He checks the time on the microwave. "I don't think takeout is happening. How about I make you something?"

"Do you have food here?"

He shakes his head in mock outrage. "Miss Summers, you are so nosy."

"Thank you."

He squeezes my hand and whisks me into the kitchen. He presses me against the fridge, his lips inches from mine. "I picked some things up. Just in case."

"Like how you always seem to have a condom in your pocket, even when you're out for a jog?"

His lips curl into a smile. "You can never be too prepared."

He takes a step back, releasing me. I back into the counter. The spot where we had sex last time we were here. But that's not happening tonight.

If I don't end things with Ryan, that's never happening again.

Luke digs through the fridge. "Do you have any requests?"

I shake my head. "I'm not sure if I can really eat."

A hint of dread creeps onto his face. He doesn't have the stomach for discussions of eating disorders or recovery.

This won't work if he can't stomach my recovery.

He pulls ingredients from the fridge. "You won't be able to resist." He turns the stove on and reaches for a pot. "You can relax if you want."

I shake my head. I don't want to move away from him. Not if there's a chance this is the last night we'll ever spend together.

"You like stir fry?"

I nod.

"You like spicy?"

"A little."

His eyes are bright. There's no more of that heavy concern. He's letting go, enjoying the night.

Does he think it will be the last time?

I take a deep breath and try to push it out of my mind. No matter what happens, I'm going to enjoy tonight.

So I shift onto the counter, and I watch Luke cook. He turns back to me, offering me slices of raw vegetables, asking if I want more olive oil, more ginger, more soy sauce.

He microwaves a bag of instant rice. Brown rice. Does he always eat brown rice or did he assume it was the kind of thing that would put me at ease?

It's good that he was considerate. It doesn't mean he thinks I'm a basket case who can't handle a serving of white rice.

When everything is ready, Luke turns to me. He slides his arms around my waist and presses his lips to mine. It's so easy, like we're boyfriend and girlfriend cooking a meal together. Like this could be our life together.

"You want to eat at the table or with the TV?"

"The TV," I say.

He smiles. "You're an addict, aren't you?"

"I can quit any time I want."

He scoops food onto our plates and leads me into the living room.

He points to the couch. "Your table, madame."

I shake my head. "Let me pick out something to watch first."

There's a shelf of DVDs against the wall. There must be three hundred movies at least. Another twenty TV shows.

He sets the plates on the couch, and turns his attention to me. "I have this great movie, *Mahogany*. I hear a really hot actress gets naked in it."

"Fuck no." I pick up a DVD. *The Maltese Falcon*. Not bad. "Besides, you can't see anything. The lighting is too dark."

"Somehow I have a vision of her naked."

"Pervert." I scan the stack. He has just about every classic film I've ever heard of.

"It was my mom's collection," he offers. "Most of it, at least."

"She had more movies than this?"

"Only a few hundred more than this."

My jaw drops. "Your mother owned, what, it must be five hundred movies?"

Hips lips curl into a smile. "She had a PhD in film studies." He takes a step towards me and slides his hands around my waist. "Some of the movies here are mine."

"Obviously. *Mahogany* is only three years old." I cringe. I just reminded him that his mother has been dead for more than three years.

But Luke only nods.

I dig through the rest of the collection. A lot of it is pretentious. Probably all the films his mother loved.

It must have killed him losing her. Then to almost lose Samantha...

"Do you miss her?" I ask

"Yeah." He holds me a little tighter. "She was the most amazing person. She had something to say about everything she watched and she was always so excited about it. But she had to hide that part of herself from everyone, so she'd fit into my father's idea of what his wife should be like."

"I'm sorry." I meet his gaze. "Does it still hurt?"

He nods. "She was a great mom. She really loved me."

There's pain in his eyes. I want so much to take it away, to promise that I'll leave Ryan immediately, that I'll be Luke's.

But I can't do that. Not unless I'm sure.

I settle on a DVD and hand it to him.

"I can't believe you don't keep this with you in the apartment."

"I'd never get anything done," he says, and he puts in a disc of *Law and Order.*

We settle on the couch, eating as we watch. The food is good, fresh and so much more flavorful than steamed vegetables and grilled fish.

I haven't seen enough of the show to know what season it is. But it feels so good to watch his face light up. He explains the show to me—one detective is a recovering alcoholic, another is a good catholic boy—with such enthusiasm I think he's going to wake up the neighbors. We laugh at the cheesy one-liners and kiss every time a judge answers an objection with a smart-ass comment. *I'll allow it, but watch yourself, McCoy.*

I have never seen him like this, so happy, so relaxed, so willing to completely ignore the subject of where things are going.

We spend the entire night watching. By the time the sun rises, half a dozen killers have faced justice, and only one has escaped with a not guilty verdict. I fall asleep for a while, my head on Luke's lap, and wake to the *thud-thud* of another episode, to

Luke's fingers stroking my hair. It is so soft and sweet and comfortable, I never want to leave.

But I have to if I want to figure this out.

The morning goes far too quickly. I call Laurie and ask if I can stay at her place for a few days. She's excited. Incredibly excited.

I sit with Luke for a long time, savoring cup after cup of coffee. We talk about everything except for the next week. Except for the chance this is the last night we spend together.

CHAPTER THIRTY-ONE

Laurie greets me with an excited hug. "I'm glad you're here."

She leads me inside. Her house, in the middle of a very nice part of Santa Monica, is a three-bedroom. It's messy, but it has everything I need—a couch, a TV, a supply of tequila in the liquor cabinet.

I scan the kitchen. No coffee maker.

So there's almost everything I need.

"So, I'm really hoping you aren't here because the, um, Ryan, hit you or something."

I shake my head. "It's more of a fight."

"Do you want to talk about it?"

"Later." I stretch my arms over my head and yawn. "I didn't sleep much last night."

"Oh yeah?" Her eyes light up.

"Unfortunately not."

"Well, I got you covered."

I follow her to the guest bedroom. It's clean and decorated in shades of purple. It's really purple—the walls, the bedspread, even a rug on the floor.

Laurie catches me staring. "It's my mom's favorite color."

"It's nice."

"It's hideous, but it's yours as long as you want it." She moves to the dresser and pulls out a baggy T-shirt. "I'd enjoy the company, actually."

"I might be an ax murderer."

"At least I'll die before an ax murderer ruins my TV show." She tosses me the T-shirt. "I'm supposed to meet a friend for lunch. Will you be okay alone?"

I nod. "I'll be sleeping through lunch."

"You sure?" There's worry in her voice.

It's something I hear a lot of lately.

"I'm sure." I sit on the purple bedspread. It is comfortable, and I am so damn tired.

"We'll talk tonight." She pushes the dresser closed behind her. "Or we'll watch romantic comedies and eat ice cream. Fuck, I mean fruit or something."

"Fruit is good."

She sighs, wiping her forehead in an exaggerated show of relief. "You want me to show you around before I go?"

"I'll figure it out."

She sits on the bed next to me and offers a hug. "I'm glad you're here." She squeezes me tightly, then releases me and moves to the door. "Now I'll let you sleep."

"Thanks."

She nods and closes the door behind her.

I lie back on the bed. I should go to my phone and text Ryan, tell him where I am at least.

But this bed is so comfortable and I'm so tired.

"Alyssa's phone." There's a long pause. "She's asleep. Can I take a message?"

I push myself out of bed and move to the door. Laurie shifts, her eyes turning towards me.

She covers the phone and whispers. "Ryan."

"Let me talk to him."

"Excuse me," she says into the phone. She looks for the mute button then turns to me. "Is that a good idea?"

I nod. "I don't want to keep him in the dark." At least, not any more in the dark than he needs to be.

Laurie presses the phone to her shoulder. She studies me for a minute, deems me okay, and hands me the phone.

I scramble to unmute it, then hold it to my ear. "I'm okay. If that's what you're wondering."

"Do you want to tell me what's going on here?"

Deep breath. I try to keep my voice as calm and even as possible. "I'm staying with a coworker. At her place in Santa Monica."

"That isn't what I mean." His voice is rougher than usual. More desperate.

"I need a little space right now."

"What the hell does that mean?" He sighs. "You can't go cold on me, Alyssa. Not after everything we've been through."

Laurie is staring at me like the phone is a grenade that could blow at any minute. I nod and try to shoo her away, but she doesn't move.

"I need to figure this out on my own," I say.

Ryan breathes into the phone. "There's really something going on with him, isn't there?"

I press my eyes closed. "Yes."

A great tension in my body releases. That's not nearly everything, but it feels like so much.

Ryan sighs. "Alyssa..." It's not angry. It's sad. He takes a slow breath. He starts to say something but stops.

I take a deep breath. This is going to be okay. Somehow, this is going to be okay.

"I won't be able to live with myself if something happens to you," he says. It's sincere. Honest.

I want to bring up the last six months or so, how much Ryan prefers work to everything else, how little I seem to mean to him. But it's not the time. Not yet.

"Nothing will happen to me," I say.

"Tell me what's between you and Luke."

"Let's talk about this in a few days." My voice is a low whisper. "After we both have time to think about it."

"Fine."

"I'm going to go."

"I love you." He says it like he means it, like he cares about me as much as he cares about his stupid job.

The words bounce around my ears. They aren't going to consume me or engulf me, but maybe things are safer that way.

"I'll talk to you soon." I hang up the phone and press it to my chest.

Laurie's eyes are glued to me. "Are you okay?"

I nod. "How about the romantic comedies and ice cream?"

"Do you eat ice cream?"

I laugh, easing some of the tension in my shoulders. "No."

"Don't worry. I have fruit."

CHAPTER THIRTY-TWO

Before I know it, I'm back on set, with time for nothing but memorizing my lines and giving one hundred percent to every scene.

That's not quite right. I have long breaks. Hours to think about what I'm doing. I want to honor Luke's timeline. I want to end things with Ryan.

But I can't. I stare at my phone. I compose text after text. *Ryan, let's talk. How about Wednesday, after work? We can meet at the bar by the office.* But I look at my phone, my finger hovering over the send button, and all I see is the sweet seventeen-year-old Ryan who would have done anything for me.

So I turn my attention to the next scene. I rehearse over and over. I pretend as if I'm not off book. Anything except thinking about this.

I spend Wednesday night locked in Laurie's spare room, staring at my cell phone.

I rehearse a dozen speeches. Ryan has an idea of what's going on. It's not like I'm going to have to spell out all the details. It's not like he'll want to know how Luke fucks me.

Unless he does.

He could ask. Why wouldn't he ask?

I pull up his contact. This can be easy. A five-minute conversation. *Ryan, it's over.* That could be it. Short and sweet. He'd get the point.

Or he'd ask a million questions, demand an explanation. Even if he's an asshole, he deserves an explanation. Something more than *I fucked him because he's hot.*

I fall asleep in my clothes, my phone pressed against my chest.

I wake up to a text message from Luke.

How is everything?

He sent it last night, late last night. He's probably tearing his hair out waiting. He acts so patient, but he can't really feel like that.

I reply. *Work is exhausting.* It's a lame dodge, but it should give him some idea of how little I want to discuss this.

He replies quickly. *I don't want to rush you, but it is Thursday now.*

Eight A.M. Thursday. I reply.

He responds. *Fair enough.*

I still have another whole day until Friday night. A day and a half even. I respond.

I take it you didn't do it. he replies.

I bite my lip. *Soon.*

There's nothing for a while. I brush my teeth, make my coffee, eat my breakfast.

Finally, Luke responds. *Good luck.*

I need to do it tonight. I can't wait any longer. I only have one more day.

Tonight. After work. I'll see Ryan tonight. In person. I'll go to the apartment. Tonight. I'll do it tonight.

I get lost in the flow of the day. We do a long scene, break for lunch, do two more scenes. I spend so much time standing around, waiting for the director to decide exactly how he wants the lights. I try to compose an appropriate breakup, but none of it feels right.

Ryan will see through it. He'll tear down any excuses, any lies. I have to tell him the truth if he asks how many times I fucked

Luke, if he asks if I prefer Luke, if he wants to know why I've lied to him for so long.

Then we're done for the day, and I'm in my car, my grip tight on the steering wheel. I know the way to Ryan's place. It's burned into my brain.

The streets are quiet tonight. Traffic has already cleared. The sun has already set. Everything is the loveliest shade of midnight blue.

I park in the garage, in a guest spot. I need to do my exercises, to take ten deep breaths.

One. Inhale. Exhale. Two. Inhale. Exhale. Three.

I press the key between my palms. I should take it off the key ring. He'll probably want it back.

Inhale. Exhale. Four.

It's not ten, but it's close enough. I get out of the car and walk slowly down the hallway. The walls are the same shade of beige. The windows let in the same amount of moonlight.

And Ryan's door is the same brown color.

I slide my key into the lock and push the door open.

It's quiet, the way it always was. I spent so much time in this quiet apartment. This can't be the last time I'm here, the last time I sit on the couch or lie on the bed or drink coffee from the machine.

Deep breath. It's only an apartment.

There are no dress shoes by the door. There's no briefcase on the desk. Ryan isn't here.

I sit on the soft leather couch. I can stay. I can wait for him like I have a million times before. There's something nice about being here, something familiar.

But it all feels so wrong.

My chest tightens and I can barely breathe. It's hot here. The air is stale.

All of this is wrong. I need to get out of here.

I push off the couch and walk back to my car.

I'll do it tomorrow. Call him tomorrow.

I'll figure this out tomorrow.

A production assistant taps me on the shoulder. "Laurie wants to talk to you. I okayed it with the director. You're not in the next scene. You should have two hours."

I nod and walk down the hall. Laurie is in my dressing room, giant smile plastered on her tired face. She sits across from Luke. He's all out in a suit and tie, his hair combed back, his eyes bright and brilliant.

"Your lawyer wants to talk to you," she says.

"I can see that."

"Interesting that you need a divorce lawyer when you aren't even married."

Laurie gapes at Luke. She throws me a *you-go-girl* look. Then she pushes off the couch and moves to me. She leans in, whispering in my ear. "Is it okay that he's here?"

"Yeah."

"Are you one hundred percent positive of that?"

I bring my gaze to Luke. He looks so handsome. So perfect. I want so badly to slide onto his lap and press my lips against his.

"Positive."

She examines my expression and nods. I am deemed positive.

Laurie takes a step towards the door. "Naomi's scene should take about two hours. But it could be as quick as ninety minutes. And if your makeup sweats off, you're coming up with your own excuse."

I nod. "I will."

Laurie opens the door. "You coming to my place tonight?"

I bring my gaze to Luke's. He's waiting patiently, and his expression gives nothing away.

"I'll let you know."

She nods okay, and surveys the scene one more time. She must deem it acceptable, because she shuts the door behind her.

Then it's me and Luke in this tiny dressing room.

"Hey," I say.

"Hey yourself."

I move to the couch, to the spot next to him. But he slides away.

"Not right now," he says. There's a sadness to it. Like he isn't expecting this to go well.

"Please."

"Maybe after we talk."

I cringe, digging my nails into my thighs. Talk is such an ugly word.

Luke's eyes are on me. His eyes are on fire, demanding an explanation. "Did you do it?"

I take a slow breath. The couch is soft, too soft. I'm practically sinking into it.

"Alyssa."

"No," I say.

Luke's eyes stay on me. His voice is even. Patient. "Why not?"

I pull my arms across my chest. "I went to his apartment last night to do it. But he wasn't there."

"Was that it?"

I nod. It was most of it.

"Would you have done it if he was there?"

"Yes." Probably.

"Then do it now." He pulls his phone out of his pocket and offers it to me. "Call him now. Tell him it's over."

"I can't tell him over the phone."

"Okay." Luke moves closer. "I'll wait here until you're done for the day, then we can drive to the office together."

The air leaves my body. "That's ridiculous."

"You had a whole week, Alyssa."

"I know." I bite my lip. "I'm going to do it."

"When?"

"Soon."

He shakes his head. His voice is low, soft. "Soon isn't good enough."

"Luke, please..."

He runs a hand through his hair, his gaze shifting to the floor. "I'm so happy when I'm with you. So fucking happy. I told you, Alyssa. You make me feel alive. I've never felt like that before."

My legs shake. "I'll do it soon."

Luke's eyes find mine. "But I want to hurl every time I see Ryan. I daydream about wiping the smug look off his face with my fists. I've never hit anyone, but I want him to hurt. I want him to hurt as badly as I hurt knowing you'd rather be with him."

"I'd rather be with you."

There's a sadness in his eyes, but there's something else too. A resolve. "I'm sorry, but I can't wait any longer."

"But..."

"I know it's hard. Half of me wants to wait for you forever. But I've waited for a woman who didn't love me before, and I learned my lesson."

"Who says I don't love you?"

"Please don't say the words. It will only make this harder."

I meet his gaze. God, those eyes, full of unspeakable pain. Did I really do that to him? Does he really care about me that much? Or is it something else, someone else, some penance for past mistakes?

"So that's it? You're, you're..." I can barely think it, much less say it.

I feel a pang in my chest. This can't really be happening. Not here, in my dressing room, in between scenes. Not now, not on a Friday. Not when I have nothing to distract me all weekend. Not now. Please. Not now. Just a few more weeks. A few more days. A few more hours even.

I look at the floor. A stupid blue carpet, hard and uncomfortable. I press my nail into my thumb until it leaves a mark. It is so quiet and it feels like a million years have passed.

I look back at Luke. "Are you breaking up with me?"

His eyes find mine. He doesn't waver. "Yes."

"But I lo—"

"Don't say it."

I press my fingers together. "What if I need you?"

"I'll still be your friend, but that's all it can be."

My throat cracks. I suppress a sob. Luke puts his arms around me and I bury my head in his chest.

I squeeze Luke tighter. This can't be the last time I hold him. This can't be the last time I kiss him. This can't be the last time I see him.

His grasp slips. His arms pull away from me. His eyes connect with mine, so dark and full of pain.

"You can do it right now. You can call him right now," Luke says.

Again, I shake my head. I wish I could. I really, really wish I could.

"Yeah, that's what I figured. Well, good luck. I hope he's worth it." Luke offers his hand to shake.

I take it, my grip weak, my palm sweaty.

He pulls his hand back and runs it through his hair. "I'm really going to miss you."

He takes a long look at me, and then he turns and reaches for the door. And just like that the door closes behind him, and he is gone, and I am empty.

And for the first time in weeks, I am desperate to fill myself with anything.

I stand across from Naomi, blinding light shining in my eyes. The director insisted on the placement of the light, apathetic to the fact it makes it impossible to concentrate. It's my line, but I can't recall what I am supposed to say. Some fight between Marie Jane and her sister. Some attack on Marie Jane. Something to play big and loud, with the sort of faux outrage Marie Jane loves.

But when I open my mouth, a sob escapes. I try to roll with it. I try to play it off as one of Marie Jane's fake crying fits. I try to play it off as a fake crying fit turning into a real crying fit. Naomi marches through her lines, even as my sobs get louder and louder. Tears run down my cheeks, falling off my chin and landing on my chest. We finish our lines.

The director calls the scene. "Really interesting energy. Maybe we can try something a little more fun," he says.

"Yeah, sure," I say to no one in particular. "Give me a minute?"

The director nods. Used to dealing with temperamental actors, no doubt. I run to the nearest bathroom, passing Laurie in the hallway. I wipe off my tears, wiping away half of my makeup with them. I try to smile. Not even close. I aim for anything but the miserable expression on my face. Closer, but not close enough.

I splash cool water on my face. I try to breathe. I can't feel this yet. I can't admit it yet. I need to finish the day. I have to wait until I am safe, in the spare room, alone. No one can know how much this hurts.

The door opens. I clear my throat and splash more water on my face. I look up into the mirror and see Laurie standing next to me. Fuck, my eyes are red. My makeup is a mess. I'm a mess.

"You okay?" she asks.

"Yeah, just allergies," I say.

"I knew I should have told Mr. Hot Lawyer to leave."

"It's not his fault."

She shakes her head. "You don't have to explain it right now, but you do have to get back out there. We have two scenes until we wrap. After that, I'll drive you home and we'll drink ourselves stupid."

"I'm fine," I say.

"You're a terrible liar. But I won't make you talk about it."

"Thanks."

Laurie pats me on the shoulder. "Unfortunately, I am your boss, and I have to make you get out there and turn on that Marie Jane charm."

I nod. "I can do that. Just give me a minute."

"You want coffee or something?"

"Okay."

"How do you take it?"

"Almond milk and honey."

She smiles. "I'll make sure Michelle has a fresh cup for you on set."

She stretches her arms out to offer a hug, and I take it. It's a strange feeling. I'm not used to having a friend.

"We can talk later if you want."

"Yeah maybe," I say.

"But I need you back there in five minutes."

I nod okay. Laurie walks out of the bathroom, back to set, and I shove the hurt as deep as it will go. I don't have to feel this. I don't have to feel anything if I don't want to.

By the time I walk back to set, I am a blank slate, ready to lose myself in my lines and my character. Ready to lose myself forever.

CHAPTER THIRTY-THREE

After work, I drive to Ryan's apartment. Our apartment. I park in my space. Next to his car. He's home. He's still waiting for an explanation.

There are half a dozen texts on my phone. All from Laurie.

Where did you run off to?

Is everything okay?"

Call me or I'm going to totally freak out.

I press my fingers into the screen. There are too many people involved in this. But she is concerned.

I call her to tell her I'm at Ryan's. She seems worried, but she offers to ease up if I agree to a hike tomorrow. We iron out the details, and I hang up.

Now there's nothing in the way of this conversation.

I get out of my car, walk down the beige hallway, and stop at Ryan's door. It's the same brown color it was last night.

I slide my key in the door and press it open.

Ryan is sitting at the kitchen table at his laptop. He's working, of course.

"Alyssa." He gets up and moves to the door. His hazel eyes bore into me, but he doesn't say anything.

"Hi."

"What are you doing here?"

I suck in a deep breath. "Can we talk?"

He relaxes slightly, but his eyes still bore into me. "Only if you're going to say it."

I take a deep breath. The view outside the window is the same. The stars scattered over the night sky. "I slept with Luke."

"Was that all it was?" he asks.

I shake my head. "It's over between us."

Ryan takes another step towards me. "And what is it?" His voice is rough. "I'm willing to forgive you for this, but not if you're going to lie to me again. Do you understand?"

My stomach is in knots. There's no easy way to explain this. "It's over."

Ryan narrows his eyes. "Alyssa. You need to tell me the whole story."

I nod.

"Did he dump you?"

"Not exactly."

"Yes or no?"

"No," I say. "I chose you."

"Why?"

"I need you."

"Do you love me?"

It's not a fair question. Our relationship has never been romantic. It's never been about silly ideals like love.

"If you're going to leave me, do it," I say. "Don't drag this out. I can't take it."

"Give me one reason why I shouldn't."

"Because I need you."

Ryan sighs, shaking his head. He motions for me to come into the living room.

I do.

Ryan turns all his attention to me. "Do you love him?" It's steady, even, like he's asking if I like oranges.

All that hurt bubbles up to my chest. It doesn't matter if I love him. Love won't do me any good at this point.

I bring my gaze to Ryan's. "It's over. I'm never going to be with him again."

I'm never going to see the joy in his eyes, or hear his laugh, or feel his fingertips. I'm never going to listen to him go on about *Law and Order* or mock the honey I put in my coffee. I'm never going to lay my head on his chest, or fall asleep on his couch, or wake up in his arms.

"Do you love me?" His voice is a low demand.

"I can't survive without you."

He moves to the couch and folds his arms, staring out the window at the calm water of the marina. I sit next to him, moving closer, expecting him to stop me. But he doesn't stop me.

"Why did you do it?" he asks, his gaze still on the window.

"I was angry."

"That's it? You were angry?"

I take a deep breath. I can't lie here. "I needed someone to talk to, and he listened."

"That's all it was?" He scoffs, disgusted.

"I was lonely and he asked nicely."

Ryan's face screws up in that same disgust. "You're a whore."

I recoil. He's mad. He has every right to be mad. But still, the way he says it... the hatred in his voice.

He turns his eyes to me. I have to look away, to the view outside. I can't stomach the vitriol in his eyes.

"How many times did you fuck him?"

"I didn't keep track."

"If you had to guess."

"A dozen."

Ryan paces around the room. He stops at the window, peering into the black sky. "Why did you keep doing it?"

My stomach twists. He deserves an explanation. I have to give it to him. "I liked him. I liked spending time with him and kissing him and fucking him. I liked the attention. I liked that he cared about me. I liked that he wanted what was best for me."

His brow furrows. "I don't want what's best for you?"

"You're always busy."

"So it's my fault you fucked him?" He raises his voice until it's almost a scream.

Mine is a whisper. "Of course not."

Ryan moves back to the table, back to his laptop. "Can you give me one reason why I shouldn't kick you out of this apartment?"

"Because you promised you'd always take care of me."

He folds his hands over his lap and narrows his gaze. "If you want to continue this relationship, it's going to be on my terms."

I open my mouth to correct him. This relationship has always been on Ryan's terms. But all I say is, "Okay."

He launches into an explanation of what this means. I need to tell him where I am at all times, to come home as soon as I'm done with work, to avoid embarrassing him at any more important meetings.

When he's finished, he goes back to his laptop. I climb into bed, my bed, alone, and I spend the night desperately trying to convince myself I was right to let Luke walk away.

CHAPTER THIRTY-FOUR

The view is so beautiful it makes me sick. The entire city of Los Angeles lies on our left and an endless expanse of ocean is on our right. The sky is so clear, I can see for miles. How far away is the horizon? Ten miles? Twenty? A hundred? How far would be far enough to be away from all this?

"You going to tell me what's happened with the hot lawyer and the rich boyfriend?"

"I'm trying to work things out with Ryan."

Laurie scrunchesher face. "That could be good, right? You were with him a while. And you... love him?" It's a question that demands an answer.

I nod. It's close enough. I love him. I loved him. Whatever.

"Not quite the response I hoped for." She stops at the bend to take a picture with her phone.

She motions to me—get into the photo—but I stay put.

"So you and Ryan... working it out physically?"

I dig my nails into my thighs. "No."

"He's the one who's selfish, right?"

"Yes."

Laurie slips her phone back in her pocket and turns to me. "Listen, Alyssa. I respect you're in some kind of awful hungover mood, but I'm going to keep asking questions until your answers convince me you're okay."

"I'm fine." I take a long drink from my water bottle.

Laurie stares at me like she doesn't believe me. "You look awful."

"I'm tired."

She folds her arms. "Tired is a lie."

I shrug as if to suggest it's not a lie. "Let's keep walking."

Laurie groans in agony, but she follows me up the next hill. It's hot today—it's always hot in the Santa Monica Mountains—and there is almost no shade on this path, but I am not going to stop. I am not going to stop hiking until I collapse, an exhausted, dehydrated mess.

"You lost your shit at work," she says.

"I got caught up in the scene."

"It wasn't a serious scene." She hustles to match my pace. "I don't care how hot Mr. Hot Divorce Lawyer is, he's a fucking asshole for making you feel like that."

I shake my head. "It was my fault."

"How?"

I stop at the bend and stare at the ocean. It goes for miles and miles. It goes forever. I turn back to Laurie. "I told him I'd break up with Ryan but I didn't."

"Okay." She studies me like I'm some kind of ancient Egyptian artifact. "Why not?"

"I guess I can't let go."

"So what did Mr. Hot Asshole Lawyer do?"

"I'm the asshole, and he ended it," I say.

"What person in their right mind would end things with you?"

"In his right mind," I correct her.

"Oh, shut up."

"Sorry, it's a habit."

We walk up another hill, and this time I stop and look at the disgustingly beautiful view. We're even higher up and I can see even more of Los Angeles.

She clears her throat. "I know it's none of my business..."

"That's stopped you before?"

She laughs. "No, but, well." Laurie presses her back against a low tree. "I got the sense you'd much rather be with the hot asshole than the rich boyfriend."

"He's not an asshole. And it doesn't matter. It's my fate to end up with Ryan."

"You don't say it like it's romantic."

"That's because it's not romantic."

We turn around a mile later. Laurie stops asking about Luke and Ryan, and I try to stop thinking about them.

I try to stop thinking about what it means to end up with Ryan.

It's about dinnertime when Laurie drops me off. I'm vaguely aware of skipping lunch. Breakfast too. I'm vaguely aware of an emptiness in my gut, an emptiness that desperately wants to be filled.

I stand in the lobby of the building, staring at the elevator. There might be something in Ryan's apartment. The chocolate is gone, but there must be something else. Even pasta would do.

Hell, I'll take whatever I can get, whatever I can to push away this feeling.

I close my eyes. Ten deep breaths. But I can't even get one.

Luke said to call if I'm overwhelmed. He said he'd be my friend. Maybe he meant it.

I dig my phone out of my purse and dial. It rings straight to voicemail. It's an automated message, a machine reading off his number.

I can't call Luke, not after yesterday. It's time to go back to Ryan's apartment, back to the life that's waiting for me.

Ending up with Ryan, being his lonely, bored housewife, is my destiny. There's no use in fighting.

I make my way to the elevator and hit the button for Ryan's floor. The car lifts off the ground. It passes floor two, floor three, floor four.

My finger hovers over the button for floor eleven. Luke's floor. Maybe he's home. I'm sure he doesn't want to see me after yesterday, but maybe he'll understand why I need to hear his voice.

I press the button.

His key is still in my purse, buried at the bottom of one of its many flaps. My fingers slide over it, feeling every one of its rusty teeth. He broke up with me. He probably wants his key back. He probably wants me out of his apartment. He broke up with me.

He probably wants me out of his life.

I walk to his apartment. I slide the key into the door and unlock it. It is still barren here, a little messy, but barren. He has the same view as Ryan—the gentle waves of the marina, the sun bleeding red into the sky—and it's as beautiful as the view from the mountain. It's so beautiful it makes me sick.

I move into the kitchen. Maybe there's something to eat. Something sweet. Some tiny hint of pleasure.

The fridge is mostly empty. Some vegetables. Leftover rice. Almond milk. He probably bought it for me.

I check the freezer. It's better, fuller. There are bags of frozen vegetables, frozen dinners, vacuum sealed packages of fish.

And there it is—a pint of ice cream. Green tea ice cream. Green tea ice cream made from almond milk.

He must have meant it for me. For us. When there was an us.

The air from the freezer is so cold. I know I should close the door, but I can't stop staring at the ice cream. He must have bought it for me. For us.

I can't use it like this.

I press the freezer door closed and pace around the room. I can't stand here. I need to do something.

I move to the bathroom and splash my face with cold water. But it doesn't help. It's not enough.

The shower looks so warm, so inviting. It felt so damn good to be in there with him.

I step into the shower and run the water, not bothering to remove my clothes. I sink to my feet, pulling my knees into my chest. My clothes get wet and heavy, sticking to my skin, and I lean my back against the tile.

It's over. I lost. Now there's nothing left to do but fall apart.

CHAPTER THIRTY-FIVE

The front door opens slowly. I can just hear it over the sound of the shower. Fuck. I'm still here. I should go, but I can't bring myself to move out of my position.

Footsteps move a little closer. It must be Luke.

My purse and shoes are in the living room. He knows I'm here.

The bathroom door opens and Luke steps inside. I hug my knees a little tighter and bury my head between them.

"I was hoping you'd at least be naked," he says. He walks over to me and turns the faucet until the water stops.

I don't look up.

"Come on, Alyssa, that was funny."

"You can do better."

He kneels on the tile floor. "You want to tell me what you're doing here?"

I squeeze my legs a little tighter.

Luke tries to take my hand, but it's too wet for him to get a grip. He steps into the tub, his jeans soaking up water, and tries again. But still I don't help him.

He sits next to me with the slightest plop. I feel his arms around me, his hands pressing into my back, but still he can't get a grip. I lean a little closer, resting my head against his chest. I release my vise grip on my legs and slide my arm around his waist. I know I shouldn't do this. But he's here, and all I want is to be here with him.

Luke doesn't resist me. He allows me to sink deeper into his chest, even sliding his arm around me. We stay like that for a minute, and slowly I come out of my daze.

I let Luke go without thinking.

"I suppose this isn't the time to talk you out of your clothes," he says. "But I'm guessing you don't want to wear those out."

He offers his hand again, and this time I take it. He steps out of the bathtub, and I follow him. He walks to the bedroom, leaving wet footprints on the floor.

It's dark here. Past sunset.

Luke pulls my T-shirt over my head. There's nothing seductive about it. It's only caring. His hands skim my hips and he pushes my shorts to my feet.

He turns and rummages through his drawers. He offers me his T-shirt.

I shake my head. His eyes stay on mine, even as I unhook my bra and step out of my underwear.

He offers the T-shirt again. I shake my head again.

"You're welcome to stay but only if you stay dressed." He pushes the T-shirt into my hands.

"We could..."

He looks at the floor. "Please don't make me ask you to leave."

Luke turns and strips out of his wet clothes. His T-shirt, his jeans, his boxers. He pulls on a new pair of boxers and turns to me. I'm still not wearing his shirt.

He shakes his head. "At least now I know for sure that you're trying to kill me."

I nod and his lips curl into a smile.

His eyes stay on mine. "Put it on."

Better than being asked to leave. I pull it over my head and he relaxes. He lifts me and places me on the bed. Then he lies next to me.

He's only a few inches away. I can feel his breath, hear his heartbeat.

"I'm sorry," I whisper. "I've been selfish."

He curls his arm around my waist and pulls me closer. "You're only trying to survive." His voice is so soft and sweet.

I want to hug him, kiss him, tell him I'm in love with him. But I can't. I've already done so much to hurt him. I have to let him move on.

We lay like that for a while. He holds me and strokes my hair, but he doesn't whisper anything. I guess neither of us know if this will be okay.

Luke presses his lips against mine. Just once. Just a peck, quick enough it could be between friends. He slides out of bed, leaving me in his room alone. There's a sound in the kitchen—the sink running. I turn to the window. The stars and moon are shining, brilliant against the dark black sky. But it all feels so empty.

Luke steps back into the room and hands me a glass of water.

I try to take his hand, but he stops me.

"I want to help you, but I can't play your boyfriend," he says.

I nod. It's more than fair.

He sits with me until I finish my drink. Then he picks my clothes off the floor. "You want me to put these in the dryer?"

"Everything but my sports bra."

He opens a hidden closet, tosses the clothes in the dryer, and sets it for an hour. That's one more hour with him. Maybe my last hour with him.

I turn to him, searching for something in his eyes. Some hint he'd still have me. "Did you mean what you said about being friends?"

He nods. "I doubt Ryan will tolerate that."

I bite my lip. He's right. It was one of Ryan's many conditions. "If he would?"

Luke runs a hand through his hair. It's usually sexy. Well, it's still sexy, but it's also anguished.

His eyes find mine. "He won't."

"What if I left him?"

His gaze turns to the ground. "I'm pretty sure we went over that yesterday."

I pull my knees into my chest. "What if I changed my mind?"

Luke brings his eyes back to mine. "Alyssa, please. Don't do this to yourself."

"What if I break up with him?" I ask.

His voice is steady. "Then we can talk."

He moves to the kitchen and fiddles with his electric kettle. I sit on the couch, hugging a pillow, watching him make tea. He doesn't believe I'll leave Ryan.

I guess I already failed to deliver on my promise.

We spend the hour on the couch, drinking our tea as slowly as humanly possible. I rest my head on his shoulder. He strokes my hair.

It's so soft and so sweet, I could swear we're madly in love, that Luke is the guy I'm supposed to marry, that this is something that will last.

But the dryer buzzes and I change into my clothes.

Luke rubs my shoulders. "You don't have to go."

I shake my head. "I do."

He pulls me into a hug, one last hug, and whispers in my ear. "Please get some help. You deserve it."

I nod okay, I collect my shoes and bag, and I leave.

Relief floods my body when Ryan isn't home. I am a tired, dehydrated mess. I am miserable, more miserable than I have ever been, but I am relieved, because he isn't home, and I don't have to deal with the tension my lies created.

I don't love Ryan. It's never been more obvious that I don't love Ryan. It's never been more obvious that I don't like what's between us.

Luke needs his chance at happiness.

Yes, I love him. I want him. I need him. But that isn't enough.

Luke gave me as much as he could. He gave me all of himself. He gave me plenty of chances, and I failed to grab them. I can't take any more of his time or his love or his attention. I can't take any more from him.

Ryan gets home late. He's wearing his suit. He must have been at the office. He doesn't ask about my day or my hike or how I'm feeling after yesterday. He just sees my puffy red eyes and bloated cheeks and leaves two Ativan on the counter.

"I hate seeing you like this," he says.

"I don't want them."

"Please, sweetheart. You'll feel better."

But I don't believe him.

CHAPTER THIRTY-SIX

Everything between us is tense and awkward. I try to give Ryan what he wants. I wake up early to eat breakfast with him. I come straight home after work. I try so damn hard to feel something other than the dull ache that permeates by body.

But I don't.

Then Ryan springs the great news. He's throwing himself a birthday party next week. Luke will be there.

I try to weasel my way out of it, but Ryan will have none of it. It's his birthday, and he's not going to let my indiscretions get in the way of his plan. He's not going to let my infidelity mess up any more of his life.

The only thing I look forward to is my acting lesson Saturday morning, but when it arrives, I am out of my league. My coach lectures me for skipping lessons. Sure, I'm on set now, too busy to come during the week, but she has a great Saturday afternoon advanced class. It would be good for the other students to work with me, she says, and what's my excuse for skipping practice the last year? She doesn't take my eating disorder treatment as an excuse. Acting would only be good for me.

"Okay, my dear," she says, "enough tormenting you. Here's a monologue. It's great stuff. Right up your alley." She hands me a stark white piece of paper, double-sided with an incredibly long monologue. "Remember, you only have sixty minutes. This is not a lot of time to rehearse. You need to follow your instincts. Acting is making choices."

It's her motto. Acting is making choices. She says it every chance she gets. She says it as if she's mocking my indecision.

I read it three times before I start memorizing my lines. It's about a girl moving on with her life, her ex-boyfriend holding her back. Does she still love him or does she hate him? Is she in denial or is she running away from her feelings? I need to make the choice I can play. Happy is boring. But if she's still in love with her ex, if she's in denial, falling apart because she can't move on. That's something I can play.

I get to work on memorizing my lines. I repeat the first line four or five times, until I have it down pat, then I work on the second, the third, the fourth. I run through the monologue, just trying to recite the lines. Once I say it perfectly a few times, I try to explore the nuances.

My coach returns. "Okay, my dear, let's go," she says.

I hand her the paper and take my place on stage. I start with my previous life. I'm walking in from a meeting with the ex-boyfriend, and I'm tired and a little tipsy. I try to stay in character, finding the anguish and anger and misery in my words. The stage lights are glaring in my eyes, but I manage to slip back into character, and I don't come up for air until I finish.

I know what she will say. She will say I need to have my actor brain working. She always says that.

"How do you think you did?" she asks.

"Okay."

"What would make it better than okay?" she asks.

"I wasn't sure how she felt."

"For an hour, you did great, but you're right. You weren't sure what she felt and I wasn't sure what she felt either."

I nod.

"But you were confident and you had a lot of great moments. 'He's mine.' That was brilliant. That was honest. But when you said his name. What was it?"

"Zack," I say.

"Did you personalize Zack?"

"I tried."

"I know you're engaged, and it can be your fiancé if you want, but it doesn't have to be. It needs to be someone you care about a lot. You don't have to love him. You can hate him, but you need to have loved him once. You need someone who still stirs you up inside, because this character, she's stirred up."

"Yeah," I say.

"So put someone in mind. Your fiancé, an ex-boyfriend, a boss you hate. Get someone."

"Okay," I say.

"Tell me, this person, do you still love him?"

"Yes," I say.

"Now, imagine this. Imagine you were with him, and he left you, and he suddenly came back into your life. He's playing with your feelings. How does that make you feel?"

I catch myself frowning.

"See," my coach says. "I understand how you feel here. I understand that you're torn up, so think about him. He's perfect."

"Okay," I say.

"Now, let's go through the monologue a bit. Your character talks about her plans for the future. Did you have something in mind?"

I shake my head.

"Think of this guy again. What future did you see with him? Did you see wedding bells? Did you see lots of hot sex? Did you see this exact thing—this painful breakup? How is the future you saw different than the present?"

There was never a future, and the present is a big fucked-up mess.

"Remember," she says. "Playable choices. A big difference between what you envisioned and the present is something you can play. Everything being great—that's boring. So, let's try it again, and this time, really think about the future you wanted with him. Maybe it's the future you still want."

"Okay."

"Okay, take another fifteen minutes," she says.

I try to run through my lines again, but all I can think about is Luke. I could see a future with him, waking up next to him, falling asleep on the couch during his TV marathons.

We could have something.

Even if he would be happier without me.

Or maybe I am thinking like Ryan, taking away his decision. He said he wanted me, that he loved me, that I made him feel alive.

I should take him at his word.

My acting coach comes back, and I run through the lines, my mind half-focused on Luke.

"Did that feel better?" she asks.

No, it felt worse. I don't want to get into all these details about my life, but I nod yes, much better.

"What do you think your character was feeling?" she asks.

"She thinks she made a mistake," I say.

"And?"

"And she's afraid there's nothing she can do about it."

"That's good," she says. "It's complicated. But you can't let your character's fear become your fear. She can be afraid to make a choice. You can't. You understand?"

I nod. I understand, and I ask for something about guns or murder or anything less painful than love.

I take a long shower, trying to scrub the thoughts from my mind. I blow dry my hair and pin it up. I apply waterproof eyeliner and mascara, just in case I can't handle this stupid party.

Why am I bothering to get dolled up? It's just another night of Ryan showing me off for the pathetic, divorced men he represents.

Maybe I can still get out of this. Maybe I can claim I am sick, or I can get sick, from purging or drinking too much or taking one too many Ativan. I can claim Ryan gave me too much.

But Ryan is careful, and he would never make such a rookie mistake.

I change into the cocktail dress I bought for the occasion. It's a low-cut, girly thing in the softest shade of pink. I zip the dress and check my reflection. I am a vision of elegance, a vision of beauty and grace, exactly the kind of girl a rich lawyer should marry.

So I'll never love Ryan the way I love Luke. I can still give him what he wants–I can still be the perfect trophy wife—a sweet, demure, young thing with nothing but smiles and compliments.

It's an easy role to play.

I read *The Awakening* until Ryan picks me up. It's about a woman who has a sexual awakening, then drowns herself in the ocean. Right now, that sounds much better than going to this awful party.

"You look gorgeous," he says, the wheels in his head turning with all kinds of ideas about who he can make jealous.

We both know he wants to make Luke jealous.

We're both such immature, pathetic creatures.

CHAPTER THIRTY-SEVEN

The party is at a restaurant on the water. A charming, intimate place where soft, white candles illuminate softer, white tablecloths. It's a small thing, thirty people maybe, all of them laughing and drinking and popping appetizers into their mouths.

Ryan introduces me to a client and I slip into my role. I smile and bat my eyelashes and cling to Ryan's side.

I excuse myself and order a tequila on the rocks. I don't mean to drink it so quickly, but I find myself with a fresh glass. Ryan drags me back to the social scene, introducing me to his friends from law school, his hand tightening around my waist. I try to find the comfort in it. I close my eyes and focus on the sensation of his touch, but it feels empty.

By the time I finish my second glass, it is all routine. I shut down my thoughts and turn on the charm. Who is this guy? Who cares? A friend, a client, a legal secretary—it doesn't matter. None of them want to know anything about me. Lucky guy, they say, she's beautiful.

They don't even decide it for themselves. They hear that I am an actress, that I am on TV, and they assume I am beautiful. They only know that I am the kind of girl who is supposed to be beautiful. The kind of girl who is beautiful and nothing else.

But I am used to this drill by now. I am beautiful. Ryan is smart. I am beautiful. Ryan is determined. I am beautiful. Ryan is lucky.

And then, just when I am sure I've met every stupid asshole here, I see Luke, in a sleek, black suit. He's making conversation with some old guy, probably a client. He looks exactly how I feel—positively miserable.

If he's this miserable without me, maybe he'll be less miserable with me.

I maintain my composure, smiling through more introductions, laughing at more bad jokes, ignoring the glances at my figure. I know what they are thinking—if she's anorexic or something, if she's an actress, why isn't she thin?

They do always say that men prefer curvy women. As if I give a fuck what any of these assholes prefer. As if I give a fuck about anyone besides Luke.

I glance back at the bar. Luke is on his next drink, embracing the whole "it's my firm's party and I'll cry if I want to" mentality. Not that I can blame him. I'd kill to shed this stupid, happy expression I've plastered on my face.

Ryan never gets it. He thinks because I'm an actor, I can act happy to deal with this phony bullshit. I've tried to tell him that acting isn't pretending or lying. Acting is the opposite. It's finding truth in a scene and inhabiting a moment.

It's not putting on a smile and a low-cut dress to show off to your fiancé's idiotic friends.

And, just when I think I cannot stomach another fake smile and fake conversation, I look at Luke and all the hurt in his big, brown eyes. I try to maintain my composure, but I can't manage this for long.

Ryan stares daggers at Luke. He grabs my wrist and pulls me aside. He slips two little white pills into my hand—another dose of Ativan.

"I know it hurts, but it was just a fling," he says. "You'll get over it without causing a scene at my party."

In the bathroom, I wash away any signs of my misery. Cold water to dull the redness on my face. Toilet paper to wash away my running makeup. A fresh coat of eyeliner and mascara.

The Ativan feels so light in my hand. It will calm me down. It will shut down every feeling in my body, until I am a comfortable numb. Ryan wants me to be good, to be quiet, to avoid making a scene.

I crush the pills. The paste sticks to my wet fingers, but I wash my hands, over and over again, until every bit of residue is gone.

I don't need another way to numb myself. It used to be food. I tried so hard to be good, to stick to my diet, to maintain my perfect actress frame. I tried so hard, but I was weak, and I was empty.

There was no room in my mind for anything but fantasies of my next binge. Sure, for the hours I spent binging and purging, I didn't feel any hurt, or anger, or rejection. I didn't feel anything but self-loathing.

I used to think Ryan rescued me. He got me into treatment. He forced me to follow a plan. He watched over me. He took care of me. He loved me.

But the last year felt like a prison sentence.

I don't want this horrible numb anymore.

I want to feel things again.

Like I do with Luke.

Or, like I did.

I used to think Ryan saved my life.

But maybe he destroyed it.

Luke is still at the party, looking as miserable as I feel. I try to come up with an excuse for my behavior, anything I can tell him to earn his forgiveness, but I have nothing. I have nothing to offer him. I have nothing to offer myself.

I watch Ryan make the rounds, laughing and schmoozing and finishing glass after glass. Maybe I should have taken the Ativan. Maybe all I need is a few hours of drug-induced calm to convince me I can handle a life with Ryan.

But that isn't what I want.

I watch Luke take a seat in the corner of the restaurant, sipping another tequila. I want so badly to see his face light up, to do something to wipe away the misery I caused.

Deep breath. I make my way towards Luke. He tries to look away, but his eyes stay on mine. I can't find the right words to explain all this. I can't find the right words to make this up to him.

So all I say is, "I'm sorry. I'm so, so sorry." I move closer to him, until I can feel the warmth of his body.

"Alyssa, don't..." he says, but he doesn't stop me from pulling him into a hug.

I take a deep breath. I need to keep my voice steady. To keep my breath steady. I can't cry or scream. I can't show how much this hurts.

And then I feel Ryan's hands on my waist, a tight grip that can only mean *she's mine*. He takes my left hand as if to show off my engagement ring. His stupid move works, and Luke's eyes dart to my adorned ring finger. Then his eyes connect with mine. I'm not sure what passes between us. It hurts to have him look at me like that, like I'm the one who did this, like I'm the one who broke his heart. It's not angry or accusatory. It's sad.

"You're bringing down the mood," Ryan says.

"I'll leave," I say. "It's not like I want to be here."

"Why not?"

I bite my lip. He knows the answer. He must want me to admit it again, to break down and grovel for his forgiveness.

"I don't feel well," I say.

Ryan's eyes narrow. "You're not going to undermine me again."

"Please. I'll make a point of acting sick. No one will know." My voice sounds so desperate, so pathetic.

Luke's eyes find mine. He's worried about me. But I try my best to maintain my composure.

Ryan stays firm. His eyes pass from me to Luke. "Alyssa is done with you. Leave her alone so she can go back to the party."

"Ryan, he didn't—"

Luke holds his position. "You can't boss me around. We're partners."

He looks at me as if to underscore his implication. Ryan and I may be engaged, but we are absolutely not partners.

"Then go. But do it quietly. This is for the firm," Ryan says. He turns to me. "Don't make excuses. I can't listen to any more of your lies."

"Please," I say. "I don't want to be here."

"Then explain it to me. Tell me it's not because you can't handle being around the asshole you were cheating with."

"Why are you doing this?" I ask.

"Explain it, Alyssa."

"Ryan, please," I say. "Just let me go home."

"Let her go," Luke says.

"Mind your own business," Ryan says. He grabs my arm, trying to pull me away. But the room is packed and there's no way for us to move without making a scene.

"I don't want to be here," I say.

His hand tightens around my wrist. He moves closer, his hazel eyes boring into me. "I don't care if he hurt you. I don't care if seeing him makes you want to cry and scream and lock yourself in your room. I'm not going to watch you wallow in misery over another man. I'm not going to let you fuck up my life because you can't handle your mistakes. You're not leaving."

"I am."

Ryan glances at me. "There are consequences for being a whore."

Luke moves away, shaking his head as if to say, *really, are you going to put up with that?*

I shake my head. I'm not. Not anymore.

"I'm not a whore," I say.

"You fucked another man. What do you call that?"

"I'm not a whore."

"What do you call it, Alyssa?"

"I'm sorry I cheated on you. And I'm sorry I hid it from you. I really wish I'd told you the truth. But I'm not sorry I slept with him. I'm not sorry that I love him."

"He's not going to take you back."

"Fine. I'd rather die alone than spend another day with you."

Suddenly I'm aware of eyes on us. Half the party is watching this conversation. All of Ryan's friends are watching this conversation.

"Keep your voice down," he says.

"So it's okay for you to scream about how I'm a whore as long as your friends don't overhear?"

"You're mad, fine. Are you going to fuck another one of my colleagues just to prove a point?"

"I fucked him because I wanted him, not to prove some point. And I kept fucking him because he was good. No, because he was great." I can only imagine the smug look on Luke's face. "And I spent all that time with him because I love him. I love him more than I've ever loved you."

"You'll be dead in six months without me."

"Better than six months with you." I pull my engagement ring off my finger and shove it into his palm.

"Alyssa, stop," he says. "We can talk about this."

"No, we can't. We've haven't talked in months. You've been too busy running your stupid fucking firm." I turn to the crowd, avoiding meeting any particular person's gaze. There are too many people. I can't see Luke.

"Alyssa," Ryan says. "You can't do this to me. You can't embarrass me like this."

I feel his hand on my wrist. I shake him off and push past the crowd.

I spot Luke on my way out the door. He's looking at me with some kind of inscrutable expression.

Maybe there's still a chance.

CHAPTER THIRTY-EIGHT

The gentle waves of the marina lap against the docks. I stand on the boardwalk, under the soft, yellow glow of a streetlight, and I lean over the railing. The water is so dark and black and calm.

It's over. Those months stuck in Ryan's apartment, convincing myself I still needed him, convincing myself he might change.

I watch the stars and moon bounce off the water. I close my eyes and open them again, to make sure I am not in a dream.

I'm still here. It's still dark. The same cool air is brushing against my skin.

I am free and I am effervescent.

I can see now how foolish I've been, staying with Ryan because I was afraid to fall apart. Sure, Ryan kept me from falling into my old habits, but he didn't make me happy.

Not the way Luke did. Not the way Luke could.

Even if he's done with me, I have the feelings he roused inside me. I know what it's like to feel alive again. I know what it's like to want again. I know what it's like to love.

There are footsteps behind me, but I don't turn to face them. I need to savor the possibility that it's Luke for as long as I can.

Then he gets closer, and closer, until I can hear his breath. I turn around and my body floods with relief. It's Luke and there's a smile on his face. A tiny smile but it's something.

"This party is a real bust."

"What about that crazy woman who caused a big scene breaking up with her fiancé?"

He looks at my hand again, his focus on my bare ring finger.

"So that was a forever breakup?" He moves a little closer to me. His fingers graze my arm. This is a good sign, right?

I nod. "Forever."

I look at the water. Luke must have heard what I said to Ryan, but he deserves to hear it again.

Luke slides his hands up my shoulders. "So all that 'I love him' stuff—was that for his benefit or mine?"

I move towards Luke until I can feel the warmth of his body. His eyes are glued to mine and they're filled with a desperate need.

I take a deep breath. I can do this. "I love you."

His body relaxes.

"I'm sorry it took me so long to figure it out," I say. "I was scared to fall in love with you, and I never thought I'd be okay without Ryan. But the thing is, I wasn't okay. Not really."

Luke's eyes are wide with excitement. He runs his hands over my back, slow and sweet. "And now?"

"There's still a way to go, but I want to be okay. I want to be healthy. I want to be with you."

There's something so sweet about his expression. He wants this too. He must want this too.

"I wasn't living before I met you," I say. "I was in some horrible prison I created for myself. Then you came along to rouse me from my daze and force me to feel again. And it hurt to feel so much, to feel happy and jealous and miserable all at once. It hurt to want you so much."

He presses his hands flat against my back, bringing me closer.

I hold his gaze. "I love you. I love you, and I want to do everything in my power to make you feel alive, to make you happy."

His lips curl into a smile. "I love you too."

He leans towards me, his body pressed against mine, his lips pressed against mine. I feel it again, the electricity, the fireworks, the joy of being alive.

Jesus, I missed him.

We kiss for a long time. I swear I melt into him, that I'll never be able to pry myself away from his arms. His lips are so soft and so sweet. His grip is so firm, so protective.

It's just us now. Nothing else in the way.

We break for air, and Luke hovers his mouth over my ear.

"I missed you so much."

I grin. "You read my mind."

He laughs and brings his eyes back to mine. "Miss Summers, I know you have something much more illicit on your mind."

My cheeks flush. "That could be arranged."

He kisses me again, and every speck of doubt leaves my body.

Luke stands in front of the windows, naked, light surrounding his amazing body in a soft glow.

I suppose that's one way to roll out of bed.

He looks at me with a smile, stretching his arms above his head so I get a long, hard look at his body. I start at his thick, black hair and work my way down. Big, bright eyes. Soft lips. The curve of his neck as it meets his broad shoulders. His arms, so strong and safe and comforting.

God, it's like he gets hotter every time I see him.

I brush my teeth and wash my face while Luke fixes tea in the kitchen. I actually missed stealing sips of his tea, and I don't complain about my lack of coffee. He hands me a cup—Earl Grey, with honey and almond milk—and I sip it slowly, finally allowing myself to think up all kinds of alternate uses for the honey.

"It's really not fair for you to come out here naked," he says.

"And you're not wearing any clothes because...?" I slide my fingers across his shoulders, running them down his back and sides. God, his body feels good. And it's mine. It's all mine.

"Because I want to drive you mad with lust."

"It's working."

"I know. I'm very attractive," he says.

"And humble, too."

"My humility is one of my many amazing qualities."

"Uh-huh."

"But see, my dear Alyssa, the plan only works if I can somehow avoid having my way with you."

"You're what, thirty-five, forty?"

"Excuse you. I'm twenty-six," he smiles.

"Then you should have some self-control."

"You're making it very difficult." His eyes scan my body and he smiles. "Standing here, naked, with that look on your face that says you want to fuck me."

"I guess you're at an impasse. Either you can keep driving me crazy, or you can release both of us from this frenzy of lust."

"I can't just give in. You'll think I'm easy," he says.

"I guess I should get dressed then. I have a lot to do today."

"No, no, no. You aren't going anywhere today."

"And how are we going to spend the entire day in your apartment?"

"I have a few ideas," he says. He slides his arms around me and presses his lips into mine.

I have to say, I like the way he thinks.

Author's Note

Thank you so much for reading Rouse Me. If you enjoyed the novel, please leave a review. Honest reviews help authors and readers alike.

Follow Luke and Alyssa's journey in Stir Me (Book 2) and Fill Me (Book 3).

Join my mailing list for updates, deleted scenes, sneak peeks, and all sorts of other goodies.

Rouse Me Series
Rouse Me (Book 1)
Stir Me (Book 2)
Fill Me (Book 3)

Acknowledgements

My dearest Kevin, you are definitely the honey in *my* tea. I am eternally grateful for your patience listening to all my crazy pitches, blurb revisions, and minor freak outs. I know we are going to have an amazing life together. To my father, thank you for always encouraging my reading and writing, and for taking me to the bookstore when I was supposed to be grounded. To my mother, I know you don't always understand the path I have chosen, but thank you for believing in me.

Sara and Shannon, you are the reason why this book is not riddled with typos. Stacie, Amanda, Elly, and Susie— you are the best beta readers a girl could ask for. Stay honest and brutal. Yoly, you make one hell of a cover.

And to all my writing friends—Eitan, Kevin, Angela, Matt, Jane, Melanie—I wouldn't be half the writer or person I am today without you.

Excerpt from Stir Me

Laurie greets me with her usual goofy smile. She's in friendly mode today, not lioness how dare you mess with my Alyssa mode.

"Is it time for the daily booty call already?" She smirks and motions for me to step inside. "Alyssa is in the backyard."

The backyard, and God is it a backyard—it's huge and immaculately landscaped—is awash in the soft, orange glow of sunset.

And there's Alyssa, sitting on the couch, hoodie wrapped around her bare legs. She's reading her Kindle, of course. She's probably reading something English majors ignore in favor of Cliff Notes.

"Some lawyer here to see you," Laurie says.

"I hope you're not in trouble," Alyssa mimics, rolling her eyes like it's the hundredth time Laurie has made that joke.

Laurie folds her arms over her chest. "You know I write comedy for a living."

"It eludes explanation." Alyssa looks up at me—a quick glance to register my presence—then back down to her book. Her lips curl into a smile. "I have a chapter to finish."

That smile could melt glaciers. I would kill for that smile and the spark it brings to her clear blue eyes.

She sets her Kindle aside.

She's mine now. All her attention is mine.

Her eyes pass over my body, then come back to mine. She bites her lip. God, I love that look—that look that screams I'm thinking about touching you right now, and I like the thought of it. No one has ever looked at me the way Alyssa does. I had other girlfriends before, slept with other women, but none of them stared at me with that kind of lust.

"Oh get a room," Laurie says. She steps back towards the door. "No, really, do you want a room, because I'll make like a tree and get the hell out of here."

Alyssa shakes her head—Laurie really does make the worst jokes—and steps off the couch. "We'll be quiet."

"As much as I appreciate the free porn show, even if it's more of a free porn podcast what with the lack of video, I'll go grab a bite." Laurie steps into the living room and yells back to us. "I'll be back in an hour. But give me five minutes to put on something presentable." She shuts the sliding glass door behind her.

"We should get dinner first," I say.

"You're funny." She takes another step towards me.

"Maybe I want a matcha latte before Peets closes."

"There's a Peets by your house."

"What if I like this one better?"

She shakes her head. "Your protests are pathetic." Her eyes are glued to mine. She takes another step towards me, until she's close enough to touch.

God, she smells so good, like oranges and honey. Like Alyssa. Her fingers skim my waist just under my T-shirt.

I try to stick to my plan. I have to tease her, to get her wanting me so badly she thinks she might burst. I can't give in so easily. "I'm very convincing."

She shakes her head. "You're awful. Completely lacking belief." She presses her body against mine. "I could teach you a little about acting. You could use it." Her grin is ear to ear.

I almost want to stay like this just to keep that grin on her face.

She closes her eyes and presses her lips to mine. She's so soft and so hungry, and she moans the second my fingertips brush against her skin.

She's making this impossible.

"You only want me for my body," I say. A flimsy objection, but my blood is quickly rushing out of my brain.

"I can't help it. You're painfully hot." She takes another look at me as if to confirm. She nods. "Very painfully." She smiles, her teeth sinking into her bottom lip. Some irresistible mix of joy and lust.

"So it's my fault you're objectifying me?"

"Of course. If you had a better personality, I'd care about that too."

I'm going to have to get her back for this teasing. I'm going to have to torture her until she's begging.

She kisses me again, her nails digging into my skin. I love those fucking nails, like a blinking sign screaming I want you. Her lips part and her tongue slides into my mouth.

She pulls me towards the couch.

"I shouldn't reward your insensitivity." I slide my hand over the curve of her waist.

"But you will." Her eyes flutter closed. She kisses me, her back arching, her body straining against mine.

I bring my hands to her chest, cupping her breasts over her dress. She groans softly, almost a beg. She's already desperate. She already wants this so badly.

I trace the neckline of her dress slowly, back and forth. She groans louder, and I slip my fingers into her bra.

She breaks our kiss, nearly panting. "Luke." She reaches for my jeans. "You better not... You better..."

"I better what?" I slide the strap of her dress off her shoulder. Then the other.

She's wearing a hot pink bra. It's so her, and it looks so damn good against her skin. Still, she'll look much better without it.

"You know what," she says.

I push the straps off her shoulders, pulling the cups off her breasts. Damn. Heat courses through my body. I need to be inside her, and soon.

I rub my nipples over her. "Maybe you should enlighten me."

She presses her body against mine again, her crotch grinding against me. God, she feels so good, but I have to wait until she's begging.

I pull my shirt over my head and she relaxes, no doubt sure my protests are just for show.

"You're awful." She lifts her ass and slides out of her dress.

I stare as she peels off her bra and kicks off her panties. Those hips, God, those hips, the smooth skin on her stomach, and her chest...

She's perfect, and she's looking at me like she wants to consume me. It's magic. I'm so lucky that this gorgeous, perfect woman wants me.

Any blood left in my brain rushes downward. I slide out of my shorts and shift onto the couch, on top of her. She rocks her hips into mine, groaning as she rubs against me. I watch the delightful contortions in her face, my ears wide open to the soft moans escaping her lips. She wants me. She wants me so much. And I want her, all of her, all at once.

She's in agony, groaning and shaking and digging those nails into my back again.

I've tortured her enough.

Alyssa talks me into takeout at my place. We sit on the floor, our plates on the low coffee table in the living room, a seemingly endless bottle of tequila between us.

She eats slowly, paying careful attention to every bite. I'm more obvious than I mean to be about watching her, and she looks at me with a weariness usually reserved for conversations about Ryan.

She bites her thumb, her eyes heavy with irritation. "I'm not going to binge just because you aren't watching me."

"I know, but I worry." I hold her gaze and move a little closer.

She shifts away from the table. "You're going to have to get used to it eventually."

"I know."

She stabs another bite of her dinner and takes a long bite. She chews, slowly. Swallows, slowly. She turns her eyes to the table and clears her throat. "Have you heard from Samantha?"

Samantha, my ex-fiancéfiancée, is one of my least favorite topics of conversation. We met at law school. I got her a job at my father's firm. She had an affair with him, fell madly in love with him, tried to leave me for him. When he rejected her, I begged her to take me back, promised things would be like they were in the beginning. She gave in, but I didn't hold up my end of the bargain. I ignored her at every turn, even when she sank into a terrible depression.

Then she tried to kill herself.

Now, we're friends. I call every week or two. Visit her at her parents' place in Santa Barbara every once in a while. I owe her that much.

"Do you really want to talk about her?" I ask.

Alyssa shakes her head. "No, but it's better than wondering." She looks at the floor. God, she looks so worried.

"You're not jealous..."

"Cause you're never jealous?" She folds her arms.

"Never," I say. "I've never been jealous in my life."

"Uh-huh."

"Okay, that's not true. I do get jealous of Jack McCoy from time to time." I move closer to her. "Have you seen his closing?"

"I've seen his eyebrows."

"Oh yeah?" I laugh.

She looks me in the eyes. "They're amazing. So full and lush. I'd kill for those eyebrows."

"They're huge."

"They're gorgeous."

"But he's so old."

"Age is just a number. He's distinguished. He's got the most beautiful, wrinkled face. It's so full of character."

I slide my hands around her waist. "Now I'm getting jealous of him all over again."

"Shock of the century." Her voice is light, happy.

She brushes a hair out of my eyes and presses her lips to mine. It's such a sweet release. I almost feel like we could dodge this topic forever.

"I haven't heard from her in a few weeks," I say. "I'm sure she's the same. Lonely but okay."

She rests her head against my chest, sighing. "I'm more worried about the loneliness."

I brush my fingers against my chin, tilting her head so our eyes connect. "You know I'd never..."

"I know, but..." Her gaze drifts to the pool in the backyard.

The first place we kissed, though from the look on her face I really hope she's not reliving the utter exhilaration of our lips meeting. If she is, she must be thinking of what an ass I was to pursue her so aggressively, what with the small matter of her being engaged to my business partner.

I reach for her hand. God, it feels so good just to hold her hand. I feel safe, like nothing could hurt either of us. "I want a life with you, Ally. I don't have a life with her anymore. A weekend a month maybe."

"Two most months."

"Still. I don't want her. I don't want anyone but you."

"Really?" A little spark returns to her eyes.

"Of course. I want you so badly it kills me. I'd drive to Las Vegas and marry you tonight if I thought you'd have me."

Her pink lips curve into a smile. "And you'd text Ryan a play by play."

"He needs to know all the details of our newlywed sex."

"You're insane."

"You should see what I sent him when you were getting dressed."

"I know what it said—I'm an awful tease and I'm constantly torturing your poor, innocent fiancée."

She smirks, and it's like the lights in the room finally turned on.

"Would you prefer if I didn't torture you?" I ask. "Say if I never sucked on your nipples?"

"Luke!" Her cheeks turn red. Beet red.

"So you don't like that?"

"Of course I... You're awful. You know that?"

I move towards her until I feel the warmth of her body. She unfolds her arms, her eyes still on mine, and wraps them around my neck. I kiss her, hard. My hands slide up her sides and she arches into me, a soft moan escaping from her mouth to mine.

"Alyssa..."

"I like the sounds of that 'Alyssa.'" Her hands slide down to my shoulders and she pushes me onto the carpet. She shifts her body onto mine, straddling me.

"We're going to have this conversation eventually."

"Later is eventually." She lowers her body onto mine, her legs squeezing mine, her chest pressing against mine. She kisses me hard. All I want is to be inside her again, until she's screaming my name and digging her nails hard into my back.

"After we talk," I say.

She rolls off me and flops on the carpet. "Okay. Talk."

"It's a good talk."

"Likely story."

"I love you."

"Okay, it's starting off good," she says.

"I really do want a life with you. I want your face to be the first thing I see every morning, and the last thing I see every night."

I prop myself on my elbows so I'm closer to her. She's so beautiful, but that isn't what matters. It's that she's Alyssa, my

Alyssa. Those blue eyes, that soft skin, the light hair—that's my Alyssa.

"I want all of it," I say. "I want to eat breakfast with you, and text you on my breaks, and eat dinner with you every night."

"Awfully fixated on meals there."

"It's not about your... problem."

She gives me that look. That really? look. "My eating disorder?"

I nod. "It doesn't have anything to do with... your eating disorder recovery." I brush a hair from her forehead. "I see a future for us. I see us building our lives together, buying a house, picking out furniture, arguing over how to decorate the bathroom."

"Hot pink of course."

"Hot pink is perfect." I run my fingertips over her arm. "I want to travel with you, to run around Europe watching you sip espresso in Italy, outraged over why I can't find a decent cup of tea in the entire country. I want to watch you agonize over what outfit to wear."

"I don't agonize."

"Geez, Alyssa. I'm trying to be romantic."

"I know, but you shouldn't misrepresent me in your fantasies."

"I've seen you agonize," I say. "On occasion."

She looks up at me and looks away. She's nervous. "What are you saying?"

"I don't want you to hear this as an accusation, but you act like we're still sneaking around."

"No."

"We hang out here or at Laurie's. You refuse to go out for dinner. And it's not about food. You refuse to go out for coffee with me, and I know you'll drink coffee anytime, anywhere."

"I like hanging out here."

"I know you're not ashamed to be with me..."

"It's not you." She bites her fingernail. "It's Ryan... because I... well, you were there when I was cheating on him."

"Can't we get past that?" I ask. "Don't get me wrong. I love spending time with you here, but I need more than that. We both do."

She bites her fingernail, her eyes once again turning to the pool. "Like what?"

I wait until she meets my gaze. "You could move in here."

"Into your ex's house?"

"We can get a new house."

"Luke..."

"Okay, I get it. It's only been a few months. I shouldn't move so fast. But I feel like we're on hold. Do you..." Fuck, what if she says no? She could break my heart. "Where do you see this relationship going?"

She looks away, at the dark blue sky outside the windows. "Somewhere great." She looks back to me. "But not yet."

"When?"

"Sometime in the future."

"When in the future?"

"A year, maybe."

That's an eternity.

She turns back to me, her eyes clear and bright. "I love you, Luke, and I want to be with you. But I didn't do this relationship thing well before. I made Ryan my whole world. I relied on him so much, I didn't think I could survive without him. I can't do that again."

"I won't let you."

She runs her hand through my hair. "I'm still here. Just not all the time."

"But I want you all the time."

Her hands are on the back of my head. She pulls me closer, until we're almost kissing. "I'm not going anywhere."

"Not unless I fuck it up."

"Not unless you fuck it up," she says. She laughs, and she kisses me again. Her hands dig into my hair.

I try to shut all this out, to feel nothing but her lips and her body under mine. Alyssa is with me now. I have her now. She's intelligent, articulate, thoughtful, and she's mine.

She's perfect, and she's mine.

But it's not enough. I need more of her, all of her, all the parts she wants to keep hidden.

Copyright